A NOVEL

MOON PEOPLE

THE JOURNALS
OF LORDIAH

DIXON TROYER

MOON PEOPLE

THE JOURNALS
OF LORDIAH

Ordering Information & Quantity Sales: Special discounts are available on quantity purchases by corporations, associations, and others. For details, contact the publisher. Orders by U.S. & International trade bookstores and wholesalers at info@abundantpress.com. Printed in the United States of America- Library of Congress-in-Publication Data. Please note: This book was put together very quickly for a conference, so if you find errors, like spelling or grammar, please send us an email.

Title: Moon People
Sub-title: The Journals of Lordiah
Author: Dixon Troyer
1. The main category of the book — Novel, UFO
First Edition, First Printing 7-29-2020
First Edition, Second Printing 10-1-2020
ISBN: 978-1-948287-15-9

To Get FREE Access Additional Bonuses
Visit:

MoonPeopleBook.com

Acknowledgements

I would like to thank the people that helped get me here. I first would like to thank my mom, who understood me and encouraged my free spirit. It's a bummer she passed before she was able to read this book. She would have loved it.

Many thanks to Art Bell, and George Noory for their wonderful radio shows, giving me the fodder and inspiration.

Thank you, my good friend David Michael Gilbertson, for our conversations and you telling me "Stop editing and just publish it now."

Thank you Jo-e Sutton for your feedback, Sami Gilmore for her notes on my first draft, and Anna Sullivan for introducing me to the Conejo Valley Writer's Group, who moved my writing to a whole new level.   -Dixon

CONTENTS

PART 1: MOON PEOPLE

PART 2: EARTH

PART 3: RETURN OF THE HEOFONLY BEINGS

PART 4: BACK TO THE FUTURE

Part 1:
MOON PEOPLE

CHAPTER 1:

THE

FULL MOON

Earth - 20 years ago

This story began on a warm August evening as a slight breeze cooled off the day and dusk set in. On a black velvet backdrop, the heavens were littered with stars, and the bright full moon illuminated the night.

Walking hand in hand, Lee Brooks and his energetic daughter Luna strolled along Casino Pier.

"Slow down, Princess, you're wearing me out." She ignored him and skipped ahead, pulling on his arm.

The sounds and lights of the New Jersey amusement park were in full swing in the background. *"Papa, I want to ride the big roller coaster next."*

"Let's stop at this bench and finish our dinner first," Lee handed her a basket with a half-eaten hotdog in it.

"Please, Papa, please?"

He pointed at the bench. *"Let's sit and eat first. Then we'll go back, okay?"*

Luna plopped down on the bench and shoved a huge bite into her mouth.

Lee laughed, shook his head and sat down beside her. She was quiet now as she chewed the massive mouthful.

"Princess, I know it's your birthday, and you're a very brave five-year-old, but you may not be old enough for some of those rides."

Overlooking the ocean, they dined on the rest of their hotdogs. Lee gazed at the elegance of the full moon.

Luna blurts, *"Papa, you're staring at the moon again!"*

Lee smiled. *"I know. Isn't it beautiful? You're supposed to make a wish on a full."*

She devoured the last bite. Luna looked up. *"OK,"* as she smiled at her dad. *"I made my wish."*

Lee wiped the mustard from her smiling face. *"Besides you being named after a goddess, 'Luna' also means 'Moon'. The moon is wondrous and mysterious just like you. Which is why it's your namesake."*

Luna jumped up and grabbed her father's hand. *"I know Papa; you've told me a billion, billion times. Come on, let's go back to the rides!"*

He is pulled to his feet by the eager child. Once standing, he removed a camera from his pocket. *"OK, OK, but can I get a picture of us first? I want to remember tonight with my little princess forever."*

He imposed upon a young couple walking by to capture the moment. The resulting snapshot revealed one beaming birthday girl with her loving father and Luna's brilliant namesake glowing in the upper right side of the photo.

CHAPTER 2:
THE MAN IN
THE MOON

Earth – Present Time

It was just past midnight, and a full moon beamed brightly in the desert sky. A lonely withered tumbleweed rolled across the ground until it hooked itself at the base of an eleven-foot chain-linked fence topped with several rows of concertina wire. The night was silent except for intermittent howls from coyotes in the distance.

Inside the fenced area, a warehouse structure resided. It was quiet, dark, and appeared vacant.

Unseen on the roof stood Lordiah, a handsome Caucasian man dressed in slim fit jeans rolled up at the bottom, blue high-top sneakers, and a conservative collared shirt.

His hand danced across his phone as he punched in a code. A large hidden door slid open in front of him. Within seconds a dark triangular craft emerged and rose straight up and out the opened rooftop.

"Stop," he said into his phone. The spacecraft stopped and hovered as the doors below it closed.

The silence of night remained; not a sound emitted from this dark floating spacecraft.

"Hatch, please." A drawbridge lowered from the bottom of the craft. He put his phone in his pocket and walked in.

"Close the door." The drawbridge rose and locked tight. He walked up to the front of the craft and sat down in the pilot seat and strapped himself into the chair.

"Thank you, Lordiah," a computer voice said. *"Where is our destination today?"*

"To the moon please," he replied.

The ship rose above the roof and hovered. Two black wings unfolded and locked into position. The floating craft turned its nose towards the bright white glow of the full moon. In a flash, the dark shape accelerated out of view.

A few hours later, the craft hovered over a crater on the dark side of the moon. It slowed and lowered itself. Two enormous doors slid open and exposed a sizable illuminated landing dock.

The black ship maneuvered inside the docking doors and parked. The doors closed, restoring the moon's surface to its typical pockmarked appearance.

Lordiah exited the ship. He frowned having expected for someone to meet him here.

"OK," he mumbled to himself. *"I thought this was an emergency."*

Lordiah looked familiar. Over the years, he had used many aliases, the last one being Lee Brooks, the same man at the pier with his daughter, Luna, twenty something years ago. By his present appearance, he hadn't aged a day since that evening at the pier.

On the metallic wall he punched in the code on an eleven-digit pad. An invisible door opened out of the wall and he walked in.

Inside the guts of the moon were metallic hallways, rooms, controls, engines, sleeping quarters, and humanoid life forms walking into and out of the doorways and openings.

"Hello Lordiah, welcome back," a woman said while she walked by. He smiled and nodded to her.

Lordiah navigated through a spaghetti bowl of intersecting corridors. From his determined gait, it was obvious that he knew exactly where he was heading.

The sound of boots clanged from the metal floors and echoed down the hallway. A human male with a long red scar down his right cheek limped towards him. Alongside him was a bounding nine-foot-two-inch hairy, apish creature.

The huge hairy creature rushed towards Lordiah.

"Oh, crap," Lordiah said as he froze.

The apish creature grabbed Lordiah and lifted him several feet off the ground.

After several seconds, Lordiah slowly patted the creature on the back. "Hello, Henry. Good to see you too. Can you please put me down now?"

Henry smiled and lowered him. He smoothed out Lordiah's shirt that crept up during the hug. Major Thomas, the human male, stepped forward and reached his hand out. "Welcome back, sir."

"Thanks, Major Thomas. Is everything programmed, ready, and aligned?"

"Yes, sir," he nodded.

"Henry, Major Thomas, let's go save the world again."

Henry put his arm lovingly around Lordiah's shoulder while the three of them walked back down the hallway. Reaching a dead end, Major Thomas placed his palm against the metal wall. Two metal doors slid open with a whoosh.

Inside was a large open area filled with active workstations. Diligently working at each post was a technician, all dressed the same. Monitors, buttons, control panels all pointed towards a large concave hexagonal window that looked out at the Earth.

"Two asteroids are traveling on a collision course towards Earth at the velocity of 29 kilometers per second," Major Thomas explained.

Lordiah pointed at the table in the center of the room. *"Is the info loaded?"*

Major Thomas responded curtly, *"Yes, sir."*

Lordiah grabbed a remote off of the table and pressed a sequence of buttons. Appearing several inches above the tabletop, a 3-dimensional hologram of the sun, Earth, and moon emerged. Also, in the hologram, two massive asteroids were hurtling on a direct path towards Earth. The room grew silent, watching Lordiah as he studied the hologram. Several more seconds passed as they watch the asteroids crash into the Earth.

Major Thomas stepped up, pointing at the smoking areas. *"If the asteroids follow their course, Chicago will be flattened, with a death toll estimated at 3.8 million. The second asteroid will hit Delhi, India, causing another 6.5 million causalities."*

"Well, that's not good." Lordiah circled the table, lips tightening as he pondered and studied the hologram. He pulled out his phone and a small notebook from his back pocket. All bystanders in the control room watched and waited patiently while he made his calculations. *"Major Thomas, do you have the holo programmed with the countermeasures?"*

Major Thomas nodded. *"Yes, sir, and with asteroids of this size and caliber, I calculated several full blasts from the proton sound wave cannons eleven seconds apart."*

Lordiah contemplated for a second. *"Let's reset the holo and take another view."*

Major Thomas grabbed the remote. *"I already have, sir."*

Once again, the sun appeared in the center of the table with the Earth and moon revolving around it. Two large asteroids arrived. Major Thomas stopped the hologram.

With his laser pointer, he indicated on the asteroids:

"My calculations are to send the blasts at this projection because it's the shortest range of the orbit."

Lordiah nodded in agreement. *"With the heavier pulses from these blast angles, we can use the cannons from the dark side of the moon too. They'll be impossible to detect from Earth when fired. Proceed please."*

Major Thomas turned the hologram back on. An illustrated ray of white waves was emitted from the backside of the holographic moon. The first ray hit. This set the two asteroids spinning slightly. Eleven seconds later another set of waves hit, breaking up the asteroids into millions of pieces and spinning them off course.

"Nice work, Major T," Henry called out in his gravelly voice as he put his arms around Major Thomas.

Lordiah studied the hologram one last time. *"When are we scheduled to fire the cannons?"*

On the table the sun, earth, and moon vanished, and a new hologram transformed into a digital clock timer. *"2 hours and 27 minutes, sir,"* Major Thomas said.

CHAPTER 3:
THE
BLAZING HEIST

Earth – Present Day

Inside a messy studio apartment, a cluttered pink desk rested against the wall. A police scanner sat on the desk surrounded by stained coffee cups, several half empty Chinese food containers, a notebook covered in scribbles, and an iPad.

Luna, now 25 years old, was seated with her feet propped on the desk as she picked at her General Tso's Chicken in its to-go carton. Her hair was colored light green from a poor dye job with dark roots visible. She sported numerous tattoos on her arms, visible from her sleeveless t-shirt.

A lot has happened to Luna the past twenty years. She lived the perfect life until her fifth birthday on Casino Pier. That evening, her father tucked her into bed and kissed her goodnight like he always did. When she woke up the next morning, he had disappeared without a trace. That was the last time she saw him. To this day she never knew why he had abandoned her.

Luna was an only child with no other family. She became a ward of the state, an instant orphan.

"Three Unit Thirty-five respond to a 911 fire call. Residential home on fire. Fire department has been dispatched," blurted out the police scanner.

Luna perked up. Dropping the Chinese food container on the cluttered desk, she grabbed a pen, ready to write.

"Location is 2-1-0-8 Greenwich Court Drive. Cross street Lakeview and Virginia Street." Luna jotted down the address. She grabbed her iPad and typed.

"Gertrude, stop being an old bi-atch and load." Luna muttered at her iPad while her chewed down fingernails clacked down on the computer.

"Fuck yeah!" Grabbing her iPad, she jumped up and bounded to the door.

"Come *on Rob,*" she called across the room to a slovenly shirtless guy in his mid-forties sprawled on the couch, slurping a beer and flipping channels. *"We have a hot one. Time to go to work!"*

"What's up?" Rob asked hazily.

Luna smiled. *"A house in a pleasant Brentwood neighborhood!"*

For Luna, it wasn't hard for her to scheme up clever and unorthodox ways to survive. Her current money-making scam was rather clever. She stalked the police scanner for a house fire. Then she and her boyfriend Rob would put on a full yellow fireman's suit, enter the burning home like firemen and rob the place.

Luna justified it easily enough, *"It's not a crime,"* she told herself. *"The loot will burn anyways, and the owner still gets their insurance money."*

Minutes later, Rob and Luna were weaving in and out of traffic in an old worn-down Toyota Corolla. Rob piloted while Luna navigated. *"Dude, I have a good feeling about this one, I just do."*

Two fire trucks trailed behind them with their lights flashing. Rob pulled over and let the trucks go by. Luna smiled. *"There's our escort, babe."*

The fire trucks turned the corner into a manicured Brentwood cul-de-sac populated by sprawling ranch homes. Flames devoured the front of a home at the far end of the circle. The immediate neighborhood was already clogged with emergency vehicles when the two fire trucks joined the chaos.

"Yahtzee! Nice house," Luna told Rob as she high-fived him.

"Pull over for a sec and let's figure this out," she instructed as she studied the map on her iPad. *"There's an alley in the back."*

Rob ground the car into gear, turned it around and drove to the back alley.

CHAPTER 4:
THE
UNSUNG HEROS

Inside the Moon – Present Time

The digital hologram clock ticked down to the final minute. *"It's time. Let's get into position everyone and hammer this out,"* Lordiah instructed the team. Major Thomas and Henry walked over to separate stations.

"Major Thomas, let's change the viewing on the HG table to the primary viewing screen please."

On the keyboard in front of him, he quickly typed in a code. *"Done, sir."*

Lordiah nodded and smiled. *"Let's see what's happening."* He placed his hand against the screen in the center. It turned on and the asteroids appeared.

"Henry, turn the key to start the sequence."

Henry's large hairy hand dwarfed the key. He turned it counterclockwise on the panel until it clicked. *"Applied!"*

"Major Thomas, punch in the sequence," Lordiah commanded. When he did, a green light covered the screen, the word *"ARMED"* blinked in the center.

The hologram clock counted down over the speaker, *"eleven, ten, nine..."* Lordiah squinted as he concentrated on the large screens, then grabbed the handles in front of him with both hands. On the screen, two red target sites appeared, one on each asteroid. *"Four, three, two."* Lordiah placed a finger on each trigger. He squeezed the right one.

The room felt a blasting pulse jerk the moon as a cannon fired out of the back, dark side of the moon. Lordiah squeezed his left hand and fired another wave.

Everyone's eyes locked on the monitors as the meteors traveled towards the Earth.

Silently, the first proton sound wave hit its target, rocking the large asteroids and gradually spinning them. The team's eyes were still glued to the screens in anticipation for the second blast wave.

The second wave blast hit. The asteroids jumped and spun at an accelerated speed.

"Here we go. And in three, two." Lordiah counted backward, *"one."* The two asteroids exploded into thousands of pieces.

"Yeah, that's how we do it!" Henry gravelly voice cheered.

Lordiah smiled. *"Thank you everyone. It looks like business as usual on Earth. Superb job, team."*

CHAPTER 5:
THE
HOT TRUTH

Earth – Present Time

Grabbing their firefighter suits from the trunk, Luna and Rob hurried to put them on. The protective jacket and pants were heavy, so they helped each other dress.

"*Bend down,*" Luna said before she placed the full-face oxygen mask on his head and clipped it to his suit. He returned the favor. She handed him the final piece, the fireman's helmet.

"*Okay, you handsome hunk,*" she said into her walkie talkie, "*you ready to put this fire out?*" She smiled at him, giving him a thumbs up. Rob nodded.

Luna turned her air valve on, then activated Rob's.

She looked down at her air gauge. "*Dude, my air tanks are half empty. What the fuck?*"

Rob just shrugged. "*I was busy, babe.*"

Luna exhaled and shook her head. "*Yeah, thanks. We have to split up now. Go upstairs and grab whatever. I'll scope the downstairs.*"

"*Sounds like a plan to me, babe.*" Rob pulled out a crowbar and popped the latch off the rear gate in one movement. Luna pointed to a door, and they dashed across the lawn toward it.

Seamlessly, they slipped through the back door and into a kitchen untouched by the flames. Luna crept past the kitchen and peeked around the corner while Rob hung back. Not going far, she spied two firemen inside the front of the house with their backs turned to the imposters, hosing down the living room. The firefighters took no notice of her.

She pressed her walkie talkie. *"Hey, the house is smoky, but it looks like they have it contained. There're two fire dudes inside, but their backs are to us. Come on in."*

Luna pointed to the stairs. He nodded and dashed up them disappearing. She proceeded forward down a hallway to the other part of the house away from the flames.

She scanned each room while walking. The first on the right was a bathroom. She moved to the next doorway. The following was a bedroom. Nothing stood out worth stealing, so she kept walking. At the end of the hallway on the right, she spied a home office. *"Yeah bitches,"* Luna smiled. She entered, closed the door behind her, and locked it.

"Okay my buried fucking treasure, come out, come out, wherever you are."

The office featured a large oak desk at its center. On one wall, a world map covered its entirety. Another wall had three paintings. One was a copy of *"The Persistence of Memory"* by Dali, another, Van Gogh's *"The Starry Night"* and the third was Leonardo da Vinci's *"Vitruvian Man."* Not what Luna was looking for, but she couldn't seem to look away from the paintings. She ran her fingers across the *"Vitruvian Man"* painting. She stepped back and squinted, studying the art.

She shook her head and then continued looking around. She pushed the paintings aside and looked behind them but found nothing. On the back wall was a bookcase overflowing with books.

"Something has to be in here," She mumbled.

Luna dug around on the shelves tossing books onto the ground.

Then something caught her eye. She froze. Her brow furrowed, and her mouth dropped.

On the top right corner of the desk was a single photograph in a black wooden frame. She gently reached down and grabbed the photograph. She took her helmet off and removed the mask to get a better look.

"What the..." Luna mumbled. She squeezed the frame tighter in both hands and looked around the room. Her eyes dashed left, then right, then back down at the photo.

Frozen again, she stared. It was a photo of her with her dad. The same photo that was taken on the night of her fifth birthday, the last night she saw him. She finally exhaled.

The door handle jiggled on the lock door. She jumped, and ducked down, then crawled under the desk. She curled up into the tightest little ball and held her breath.

They tested the lock a few more times on the other side of the door. Then it stopped. A man's voice resonated through the door, *"Copy that, I'll be right there."*

It was quiet again. Luna let out a breath of relief. She pushed the chair away and started to crawl out. She stopped. She made a fist and knocked on the left side panel under the desk. *"Strange...Now why is there a hidden compartment built into this desk?"* She unzipped her jacket and pulled off the knife clipped to her pants and opened it. She tracked her fingers across the surface and found a seam. Prying the knife into the crack, she worked its way in and pried off a panel.

Inside the compartment was a row of green leather-bound books, eleven in total. Reaching in, she grabbed the one nearest to her. On the front cover, there was a golden symbol etched into the leather: it was a four-pointed star inside of a circle, with all four points breaking the circle's edge, and wavy-looking symbols inside the circle between each point. Below the symbol was the number 1.

She ran her fingers over the insignia. Her brow furrowed again, perplexed. She dropped the book and grabbed another. The same symbol was present, but with a number 11 below it. She opened the book. It was all handwritten, like someone's diary with pages and pages of entries and drawings. She chewed on her lower lip and stared, then ran her finger over the insignia again.

She reached into the hidden space and grabbed the rest of the books and put them in her bag.

She clutched her radio and pressed the call button. *"Rob, we need to bail."*

He responded, *"Why, what's up? I haven't gotten shit."* Luna picked up the desk chair and heaved it out the office window, shattering it. *"Rob, get the fuck out. Now!"*

Luna, lugging the bag full of books, crawled out the window and sprinted to the car.

CHAPTER 6:
THE LONG DISTANCE CALL

Inside the Moon – Present Time

"Major Thomas, Henry, please follow up to see if there was any asteroid fall out hitting the Earth. I'll be heading back there tomorrow when it's dark," Lordiah instructed.

Henry approached him with his arms open wide. *"Henry, I love you and all, but please, no hugs. Don't take this personal Buddy, but it takes forever to get your smell off."* Henry frowned and held out his very large, hairy hand to shake. Lordiah gave him a quick high-five.

"Funny thing, the Earthlings have no comprehension that Bigfoot helped save the day. And all they want to do is hunt you!"

Henry smiled. *"Glad to be of service."* Henry moved towards Lordiah for a hug again. Lordiah stepped back waving his finger.

Lordiah held his hand up to silence the room. *"Hey, did you hear that?"* The room was silent now. The static hiss happened again.

"*I've been hearing that for the past few days,*" Henry replied. It repeated a third time. "*Major Thomas, have you isolated that?*" Lordiah asked.

Major Thomas shook his head. "*I have tried, but remember our equipment is thousands of years old.*"

The sounds had stopped. He bit his lower lip as he listened, then approached one of the communication stations. He exhaled as he pulled out a keyboard and typed. Several screens came to life.

"*Interesting. Major Thomas, put the surface gravity at full. I'm going out. Come on Henry, I may need your Sasquatch strength!*"

Several dozen shiny spacesuits hung on a hook in a locker room. Lordiah pulled on a pair of silver boots, silver gloves, and placed a small breathing apparatus over his nose and mouth. Henry pulled on a pair of very large silver boots, large gloves and also a breathing apparatus fitted for his large hairy head.

By the exit, Lordiah grabbed a talkie and clipped it to the pocket on his jeans. "*Henry, can you grab a toolbox?*"

A double metallic door opened to the outside. They both departed, walking out onto the moon surface. Dust kicked up, and they tracked two new sets of footprints on the moon as they walked.

"*That one over there,*" Lordiah pointed. They walked until they stopped beside a large satellite dish amongst several smaller ones.

"*We're here Major Thomas.*" Lordiah looked the satellite up and down while he circled it. "*Let me know if anything happens.*" Stepping back, he raised his hand and pointed.

"*Henry, come grab this dish and see if you can spin it counter-clockwise until the nose is pointing at that star right there.*"

Henry nodded. Digging in for purchase with his sizable frame, he moved the dish.

"*Atta boy. Anything, Major Thomas?*" Lordiah asked.

"*Negative, sir.*"

Lordiah signaled Henry. *"Move the dish a little more in the same direction."*

"Stop, sir!" Major Thomas bellowed over the talkie. *"Move the dish back a few centimeters. We got a hit."*

Lordiah jumped in and helped Henry move the dish back.

"Major Thomas, anything?" There was silence from the talkie. *"Major Thomas?"*

Several more seconds passed before Major Thomas responded, *"Sir, I think you need to come in here and see for yourself!"*

CHAPTER 7:
WTF?

Earth – Present Time

Luna laid the photo down on the desk and closed her eyes for a few seconds as her right foot tapped the ground nervously. She stood, grabbed her chair, and walked it over to a closet.

The closet was crammed full of jackets, boxes and other junk. She stood on the chair while she dug out an old worn shoebox buried on the top shelf back corner.

When Luna landed in Los Angeles, all she had was the clothes on her body, another pair of pants, a few shirts and the box she just grabbed. It hadn't been opened once since she arrived.

She pushed the police scanner towards the back of the cluttered desk and swept the empty fast-food containers onto the floor not caring about the white rice that spilled onto the carpet. She placed the shoebox down and dug through the contents until she found what she was looking for and pulled it out. It was a photo. She placed it down next to the framed one she took from the house just burglarized. They were the same photo: 5-year-old Luna and her father at the amusement park. She wiped a tear that welled from her eye.

Luna grabbed her fireman's bag and dumped the eleven green books onto the desk. Clutching the book closest to her, she stared at the front cover. An exhale sighed out and her head shook. Almost scared to touch, she nervously ran her fingers over the engraved symbol.

Inside, instead of words, she saw that the pages composed of hand-written symbols and hieroglyphs drawn in several columns. Her eyebrows furrowed.

She placed the book down and reached into the shoebox and pulled out an old, tattered birthday card. She hesitated, then opened it. Inside the hand-written message said:

> To My Dear Sweet Luna,
> Happy 5th Birthday. You make my world complete and you'll always be my little angel.
>
> Love,
> Papa

A tear rolled down her cheek. Drawn in the bottom right corner next to *"Papa"* was the same symbol on the front cover of the books.

"This is bullshit," she muttered, slamming the book shut with the card inside. Luna jumped up, grabbed the car keys and stormed out of the apartment.

CHAPTER 8:
THE KING CALLETH

The Moon – Present Time

The control room doors slid open and Lordiah, trailed by Henry, entered. There was a noticeable change in the room's energy. Everyone in the room was standing, hands folded behind their backs at attention, facing the monitor.

Lordiah stopped and looked around the room. *"What's going on?"*

Major Thomas turned to face him while the others stood still. He motioned for Lordiah to come closer and signaled toward the screen.

On the monitor was a man on a throne wearing a king's crown. Lordiah dropped to one knee and bowed his head in deference.

"Hello Lordiah," the man with the crown said.

"Hello, my King, so nice to see you."

"Please, stand son. How long has it been?"

With a warm smile, Lordiah looked up. *"Father, I know it's been a little under a year for you, but it's been 4,061 years here on Earth since we last spoke. It's nice to hear your voice again."*

King Osilu is the ruler on their home planet, Heofon, where Lordiah and the moon staff journeyed from.

"According to my calculations, taking into account the time continuum difference I estimate it's been eleven months for you since we last spoke?" Lordiah answered.

Osilu nodded. *"Lordiah, come a little closer so I can get a better look at you."* Lordiah moved closer to the screen. An enormous smile beamed across the king's face. *"Eleven months, that's correct. And I thought I had a lot to tell you. You have over four thousand years to catch me up on."*

Lordiah was Osilu's firstborn, the son of his only true love. But he was born out of wedlock, a bastard son born from one of the servant girls.

"I see you have been doing your experiments." Osilu pointed towards Henry.

"Yes, father, that's Henry. He has become quite a celebrity here on the planet."

"I can't wait to hear all about it. But business first in case we lose radio contact. We received your shipment of gold. We are very grateful! It arrived on some strange craft stamped Mars Polar Lander?"

Lordiah smiled, *"The scientific population here on Earth is exploring other planets with unmanned crafts. I sort of stole two of their crafts after they launched and redirected them to you with a shipment of gold on them. I'm glad the Polar Lander arrived in your hands safe, but I sent two shipments. Mars Deep Space 2? Did it not arrive?"*

"No, only the one," Olisu replied. *"We'll be on the lookout for the other. I don't want it to fall into the wrong hands."*

Olisu turned to his right and hand gestured to his advisor to go check into the missing cargo shipment. *"Where's your brother Apollyon? Get him so I can talk with you both."*

Osilu noticed hesitation from Lordiah. *"He's still alive, Lordiah?"*

"Yes, your Majesty, he is, I can assure you," Lordiah replied. *"But I don't know where he is at the moment. He's somewhere on the planet surface."*

Osilu looked over his shoulder as a guy behind him held up one of his fingers. *"Lordiah, I only have a minute left. Send us more gold. Oh, and the humanoid workers you genetically grew? You should have cultivated numerous generations by now, correct? There should be millions, possibly billions of them. Send some of them too."*

Lordiah replied almost stuttering, *"Ahh, y-yes Papa, we..."*

Osilu waved his hand and cut him off. *"Great, I knew I could count on you. I need around 380 thousand brought here to help us rebuild. I will also need another 560 thousand more, ready for sale to help pay off the debt that incurred from the war."*

Lordiah opened his mouth and closed. The implication from the king's request sank in. *"Papa, your majesty, we..."* Before Lordiah can finish his sentence, the screen went fuzzy and the transmission from Heofon was gone.

The control room was silent. Major Thomas broke the ice first. *"Lordiah, the King has spoken, what are you planning on doing?"*

Lordiah folded his arms. *"Well, Major Thomas, I was just asked by our king to round up about a million people here on Earth and force them into slavery. Honestly, I have no f-ing idea! Maybe they would have been better off with the damn asteroids hitting them."*

Everyone was silent. Lordiah walked over to the exit door, then stopped and stared forward. He turned, looking at the occupants in the room, then to Major Thomas, *"Sorry. That was inappropriate and undeserved."* Lordiah turned and took a step forward. The two doors opened. He turned back looking over his shoulder, *"I'm heading back down to the surface."*

CHAPTER 9:
ELECTRO MACE

Earth – Present time

3:53 AM read on the clock from her dashboard when Luna parked her car in the back alley. Silence permeated the air except for an occasional cricket chirp. She stared at the yellow tape that crisscrossed across the doors and the shattered window she threw the chair through. The house stood solid with fire damage only to the front of the home.

She chewed her lip, and her face tightened. Taking in a deep breath first, she slipped out of the car and eased the door shut. The black desk chair still laid in the backyard. Luna wheeled it under the shattered window, pushed the yellow fire tape aside and crawled through.

Lordiah yawned as he turned into the cul-de-sac of his Brentwood home. When he noticed the yellow police tape that now fenced off his house, he pulled his car over before entering his driveway. He put his car into park and got out, stood there for a minute and listened. Nonchalantly, he got back into his car, turned around and drove to the back of his house.

Luna was rummaging through the office. With her flashlight in hand she shined it on the desk, in drawers and around the room looking for more photos.

Lordiah observed the battered car parked when he pulled up in the back alley, and that someone had pried the gate open.

He squinted, and his brow furrowed when he gazed across the lawn and observed the broken window to his office and the yellow tape. His lips tightened when he saw the flashlight shining back and forth inside.

Lordiah exhaled and headed back to his car to grab his cell phone.

He should have dialed 911 that moment, but instead, he scrolled through the apps and stopped at *"Electro Mace."* He put his thumb across it and pressed. The face of his phone changed and now said *"ARMED."* Lordiah proceeded toward the back door and slipped in.

Luna browsed the books on the bookshelf. There were hundreds of classics, old novels, scientific journals, and medical books.

In the middle of several scientific textbooks was a leather-bound book that had *"Bible"* written on the spine.

"Well, that seems out of place, doesn't it?" she mumbled. She shined her flashlight in the spot where the Bible was.

"What's this shiny thing you're trying to hide back here?" She grabbed more books and threw them the floor. Behind the bookshelf revealed a safe.

Lordiah tiptoed down the hallway and was now standing outside his office. The door was cracked open. He held his breath and peeked in. Inside he could make out that there was one person with their back turned to him.

He stepped back and adjusted his phone app to low voltage. On the screen, it now said *"STUN"* in parenthesis under the *"ARMED."*

Moving back to the doorway, Lordiah raised his phone. Next, he pushed the volume button on the side and a red laser dot appeared and positioned it on Luna's back.

Without hesitation, Lordiah hit the *"ARMED"* button with his thumb.

Whap! Books flew as Luna sailed across the room landing face down.

He quickly pressed a different icon turning on a flashlight. He shined it on the person laying on the floor.

Luna was stunned. She tried to get up, but her legs are jelly and her vision blurry from the blast. Her green streaked hair covered her face.

Lordiah cautiously approached, keeping the phone pointed at Luna with the red laser dot locked on her chest. *"Don't move and let me see your hands!"*

She struggled to lift her hands. Her vision was still blurry, as it slowly came back. She tried to focus on the man in front of her.

Lordiah kept his distance. *"Who are you? Why are you in my house!"*

Luna, shocked, and speechless for a few seconds, murmured *"Papa?"*

CHAPTER 10:
11-1

Earth – Present Time

A police car turned the corner and rolled down to the end of the cul-de-sac. He stopped, got out and walked towards the house. He stopped on the lawn, pulled out his cell phone and started taking pictures of Lordiah's house. When he finished, he texted them to someone.

A broadcast over his radio called out. He walked back to his car, flicked on his lights and drove away.

CHAPTER 11:
THE
FAMILY REUNION

Earth – Present time

Lordiah shined the flashlight on her face. *"Luna?"* He muttered and disarmed his phone. *"Oh my gosh, is that you?"*

"Stay away from me!" Luna shrieked as she crawled to the opposite corner of the room and curled up. She grabbed her flashlight and shined it on him.

He stopped and held his hands up. *"I'm not going to hurt you. But why did you burn my house?"*

"What? I didn't burn your stupid house. I came here to rob it!" Luna snapped back.

He scanned the room with a glance. *"Why?"*

Anger welled up in her eyes. *"Why do I rob, or why did I rob you? Well, let's see, I do bad things because I have some abandonment issues? Maybe because I didn't have a decent male role model growing up?"*

Lordiah fell silent. Luna continued. *"As for robbing you... Just my bad fuckin' luck, like usual. I didn't know this was your stupid house! I didn't know that my dad was even alive."*

Lordiah looked down at his feet and exhaled. He removed the flashlight from her face. She kept her flashlight pointed on him though. With his back pressed against the wall, he slid down and sat on the floor opposite her.

"Luna, I'm truly sorry. There's a lot to explain, I know. But I must ask you again, did you or did you not start the fire?"

Luna stared at him, deadpan, *"No, I'm a thief, not an arsonist."*

Lordiah got up and walked over to the desk. He glanced underneath.

"Dammit." He uttered when he saw that his secret compartment had been peeled open and emptied.

She looked away and didn't say a word.

"If you didn't start the fire, then someone else did. That wasn't an accident. We need to leave. Right now!"

Luna smirked, *"Really? You disappear, and presto, resurface 20 years later... and you think I should just say OK, and leave with you? Yeah, no, screw you."*

Lordiah took a breath. *"Luna, the people that set the fire are extremely dangerous. Please, I beg you, let's go!"*

Luna didn't move. She stared at him. *"I'm not a child, so don't talk to me like I'm an idiot. How about telling me why you fucking bailed!"*

"Okay, Luna, that's fair, but not now. It's complicated... I never wanted to leave you, honestly. Long story short, I was taken hostage the day after your birthday. I was chained and tortured for 7.4 years. I have something they want really bad. These people are bigger than the law, and any government. I eventually escaped. The best thing is they never knew about you. And I made sure they didn't. If they had gotten their hands on you, I would have given them everything. That's why I stayed away after I escaped. For your safety."

She held her glare. *"What exactly do you have that they want so bad?"*

Lordiah looked up at her and took a breath. *"The Moon."*

CHAPTER 12:
WHAPPED AGAIN!

Earth – Present Time

Outside of Lordiah's home, the policeman returned. 'I'm here,' he texted before he stepped out of his squad car. He looked around, then stepped over the police tape, crossed the yard to the front door, pulled out his flashlight and shined it through the window.

Lordiah raised his hand. *"Someone's here."*

Slowly, he raised his index finger up to his mouth, then tiptoed across the hall, into a bedroom. He was careful when he pulled the curtain aside. Luna followed close behind like a shadow. She pulled the drape further open so she could see too.

A dark sedan pulled up, and a man in a black suit and tie got out. The officer greeted him. They talked for a few seconds and then walked back toward the front door.

"Luna, we need to go," Lordiah whispered to her.

"Why? It's the police. This is your house, isn't it?" Luna challenged him.

"Maybe, maybe not. But the guy in the suit isn't. As I mentioned, these people are dangerous."

She folded her arms and shook her head. *"Go then, but I'm not going anywhere with you."*

"Luna, please, these people don't mess around. I promise, I will tell you everything. Let's not do it here."

"Sorry, Pops, no can do."

Lordiah pulled out his phone.

"You go and make your phone call. I'm just going to go out the same way I came in." Luna turned toward the window.

Whap! Lordiah hit Luna with the unseen pulse again from his phone. She landed face down on the pile of books. This time she was out cold.

"I'm Sorry, Luna." Lordiah grabbed her limp arms and threw her over his shoulder. He stopped at the door and looked over to the wall with the Dali, Van Gogh and Da Vinci paintings. He shook his head and sighed. *"Sorry Leonardo."*

Glass shattered at the front of the house. With little exertion, he jogged through the hallway and out the backdoor.

CHAPTER 13:
FIELD TRIP
TO THE MOON

Her vision was blurry, and her head rang. She blinked several times to get her eyes to focus.

"Huh, what? What the...? Where am I?" Luna's thoughts ached inside her head. Seat belted in tight, she could somewhat make out she was inside a vehicle with Lordiah in the seat to her left driving. She tried to move, but her hands were handcuffed to the armrest.

Luna kicked her feet and thrashed against the shackles. *"What the fuck, pervert!"*

"Luna, please calm down. You're safe." He told her.

"Why the fuck am I handcuffed, you sick fuck? How did I get here?"

"I secured you for your safety. Please, look out the window."

Once again, she yanked at her cuffs.

In a calm voice, Lordiah repeated. *"Please, look out the window."*

Outside were stars, a black wing and to her right below them was Earth.

"I'm bringing you somewhere safe," Lordiah calmly said.

The interior of the vehicle was black, and the inside area was larger than an average car. Below the windshield were several screens, levers, and buttons. Lordiah's hands were on a rectangular steering wheel as he drove. *"What is this thing? Are we..?"*

"Yes, we're flying."

Luna was still a little hazy. She sat there in silence as she observed her surroundings and gathered her thoughts from her foggy mind. *"Wow, this seems so real."* She muttered.

"Sorry I zapped you again," Lordiah said. *"I had no other choice."*

"Please spare me the fucking apologies. Take me home."

"If they find one strand of your hair at my house, they can track you and from the DNA realize that I have a daughter. Let me take you where it's safe. Please?"

"Safe, huh? You kidnapped me. I'm handcuffed like a convict. You're the one I'm scared of."

"Fair enough. I'll uncuff you when we land."

Luna was silent, looking out the window.

"How exciting. Great to have you back Papa. Let's see...you're a criminal, a kidnapper and wanted by the cops. But hey, you have one badass spaceship for a getaway car!"

Lordiah smiled. She's scrappy, a bit raw, but has a good sense of humor. Lordiah chuckled to himself." *That wasn't a real policeman back there,"* he replied to her.

"OK, Austin Powers secret agent man. And what if I say no? Are you going to zap me again?"

"I hope that won't be necessary."

She was silent for another minute. *"So, Mystery Man, if we can't go to my crib, and we can't go back to yours, where are you hijacking me to?"*

Lordiah banked the craft to the left. The moon appeared in the windshield. Lordiah smiled. *"It's best that you observe firsthand."*

CHAPTER 14:
LUNA AND LUNA

The Moon – Present Time

The ship approached a deep crater and hovered above it for several seconds before it descended. Luna saw the doors crack open below. Several similar dusty spacecrafts similar were docked inside the large hanger. Lordiah maneuvered the ship into the docking port with ease. Luna was silent, lips pressed tight as she looked around, observing.

He smiled. *"Welcome to the moon, Luna. And... This isn't your first time either. You were born here."*

Luna exhaled and stared out the window. *"Well... Dude, sorry I doubted you when you said you were taking me to the moon someday."*

The echo of the gates' air-lock activation sounded throughout the hanger as the enormous moon doors shut above them.

"Give it a second for the artificial gravity system to come online, or you will bounce around in here like a rubber ball." He informed her. A chime resonated, and a green light on the panel illuminated.

"Okay, we're good." Lordiah reached towards her. Luna flinched and moved away from him.

He held up a key. *"I'm going to unlock you."* He freed the cuff from her left wrist, then handed her the key.

Lordiah stood and motioned for her to do the same. *"Shall we?"*

Luna stood and slowly followed him out of the ship. He stopped at a large metal door and punched in a code on the middle of it punched. The light flashed green and a chime sounded.

He looked back over his shoulder toward Luna, *"The code is your birth date if you ever need it."*

The door opened. Luna took two steps inside and froze when the door closed behind her.

Lordiah stopped. *"It's okay."*

Luna put her hand up, turning a full circle looking around. *"Dude, I'm not scared, just taking this shit in. It's like I'm in a sci-fi dream."*

Lordiah chuckled. *"Take all the time you want."*

A monotone female computer voice spoke over the intercom. *"Hello Lordiah. Hello Luna, welcome back. Please proceed forward. Major Thomas is waiting for you in the Control Room."*

"Come on, you heard her. Let me show you the brain center of the ship."

Luna's brows furrowed. *"Welcome back?" Ship?"*

Lordiah nodded. *"Yes, ship."*

She trailed several yards behind him as they walked down a long metallic hallway, her eyes wide the entire time. she ran her fingers down the metal wall to touch it. *"F-U-C-K me! I'm in the moon!"*

The Control Room was in full function when they arrived. At a station, several crew people were monitoring the televised news down on Earth from all over the world and taking notes. Henry was at his station watching an episode of Star Trek, with Captain Kirk fighting a giant alien lizard.

The crew stood and formally acknowledged them. Luna wasn't sure what to do, so she half-hearted waved back.

Henry stood and turned to see who entered. *"Holy moly,"* Luna muttered as he stood and she saw the nine foot two, five-hundred-sixty-pound, hairy creature in front of her.

Henry's face broke into a gigantic smile. *"Luna!"* he said, rushing towards her with open arms.

Luna froze in her tracks, unable to move a muscle. Henry picked her up, hugged her and placed wet kisses on her cheeks.

"Hey, Henry, she may not remember you," Lordiah expressed to him as he calmly patted Henry's arm.

"Oh, sorry Luna, I didn't scare you, did I?" Henry asked in his gravelly voice. He tenderly lowered her down.

Luna jumped behind Lordiah and wiped the slobber from her face. *"Luna, meet your Uncle Henry. He used to babysit you when you were an infant. He's happy to see you."*

Henry waved with his fingers and looked at her, glowing with a big smile.

"He's quite the celebrity down on Earth. Bigfoot? Sasquatch? Maybe you heard of him?"

Henry looked down at his naked size 20 feet. *"I don't mean to be,"* Henry said shyly.

She pulled up her shirt and sniffed. Her nose wrinkled and her nostrils flared. Lordiah snickered. *"Henry's been a very faithful and dedicated friend to me for several hundred years now. I would be lost without him. And yes, you smell like him now."*

CHAPTER 15:
IN THE MOON

Inside the Moon – Present Time

It was a constant show stopping presentation for Luna when Lordiah took her on a quick tour of the moonship. And why wouldn't it, she was now one of the few that has walked on the moon, let alone inside it. Toward the end of her exploration, they stopped at what resembled an elevator door with the number thirty-eight branded into it.

"Your living quarters for now. I hope they're suitable. Would you like to punch in the code? You know what it is now."

She raised a brow at Lordiah, then stepped up to the keypad and punched in her birthdate. A smile formed when the door slid open to the private suite. She grinned even wider at the sizable living area, decorated in plush, ornate furniture, rugs, and the air perfumed with the sweet scent of lavender.

"Not that I have ever been to The Four Seasons, but this room looks fit for a queen," she muttered.

A silky purple opulent bedspread covered the bed. She walked over to it and ran her hand across it.

"Sweet."

Several sofas and lounge chairs were in the center of the room. The coffee table in front of the couch had cut fruit, a bowl of olives, and various crackers.

Over to the left was a full stocked bar. She walked over and ran her finger across the black and gray marble tiled bar and several of the bottles on a shelf.

"Very clean too." She moved to the bathroom and peeked in. *"Okay, this can work. Wow, that's a massive shower with... a lot of showerheads and that bathtub... you can throw a mean party in that."*

Lordiah smiled. *"I hope you'll be comfortable here."*

Luna grinned back. *"Yeah, possibly. Man, I wish you would have caught me robbing your house a long time ago."*

"Me too."

Luna's face turned serious. *"Hey, am I a prisoner here?"*

Lordiah squeezed his lips tight together. *"No, of course not, but I would like for you to stay here until I figure things out."*

She plopped down on the couch. *"OK, I'll try it for now. But if I'm staying, I have a gazillion questions."* Luna said. *"Besides the moon being a spaceship, and finding out about a very large and hairy uncle, any more surprises?"*

"Technically, Henry isn't your uncle, only figuratively, so you don't have to worry about any genes of shaggy, smelly kids. But yes, probably a few more."

"Like?"

It's as good a time as any to tell her. Lordiah thought. I'm glad she's opening up.

"OK, for starters, you have a grandfather and uncle that are both kings, so you have a royal bloodline."

"Oh, cool! So, you're a prince?" Luna asked.

Lordiah shook his head. *"Nope, I'm just the bastard son of the king."*

"Oh, bummer. And you said something weird earlier like you've known Henry for hundreds of years? How old are you?" Luna asked.

"Luna, I'm from another world, and we are designed different where I come from. I have been on this planet for seven-thousand-two-hundred-twenty years.

I can speak languages that are so old they don't exist anymore. In my multifold years of life, I have been married hundreds of times and raised over five-hundred children.

I have also watched them all grow old and die."

Luna looked at him. *"With all the questions... I don't know whether or not to hate you still."*

"That's why I wanted to bring you to the moon. I'm hopeful that by being here you would understand quicker and merit your forgiveness. I promise, I'll tell you everything."

CHAPTER 16:
THE
ENDLESS BEGINNING

Inside the Moon – Present time

Luna kicked off her boots and planted her feet next to the food on the table in front of her. *"Okay, I'm all ears. Let's get this party started."*

Lordiah saw the little girl in her he once remembered. He smiled. *"Okay, so let's begin with where I come from so you can learn about your heritage. In this solar system, there is a tenth planet, unknown to most. It orbits well past Pluto, and it's four times the size of Earth. We know this planet as Heofon."*

She looked at him in awe, then shook her head. *"Wow, I figured by now you differed from the other Daddy-o's, especially this moon stuff. But an alien? Nice."*

Lordiah nodded. *"Heofon has a comparable atmosphere to here. We are a race that looks, speaks, and breathe air just like Earthlings. Its temperature is regulated by a boiling inner core and unique atmosphere that captures and traps the heat. But years of pollution and wars have damaged the thermosphere.*

So much that it doesn't retain the heat like it used to, nor does it shield us from the sun's radiation. We were rapidly moving toward an ice age."

A remote sat by her feet. He leaned in and picked it up. *"You may want to move your legs. This is a hologram table."*

She quickly pulled her feet from the table and sat up on the couch. *"It's a what?"*

The hologram table came to life and a three-dimensional metropolitan city appeared above it. The sidewalks were congested with people, and some people floated above on hover boards. Roads were crowded with vehicles; others flew above in the air. Amongst the skyscrapers were several large pyramids that resembled the ones in Egypt, and a large palace compound in the center.

"That's Heofon. That's where I grew up."

Luna was staring at the hologram. She slowly put her hand in it and watch it disappear inside one of the buildings, and quickly pulled it out. She giggled.

Lordiah laughed and continued. *"Our governments are comparable to yours, due to the fact we set up your administrations here on Earth. Like your world, we also have countries with boundaries and different factions. Some are stronger, more affluent, and more powerful than others, run by kings, presidents, or dictators. I'm from the most powerful country. Its ruler, King Osilu, rules over sixty-five percent of the planet."*

A beautiful palace appeared on the hologram, *"This is the realm of the King's Headquarter and court."*

Lordiah pointed, *"That man there is King Osilu, who also happens to be my father. The man on his left is his son and my half-brother Prince Apollyon, along with my half-sister Princess Leilana."*

Luna squinted and frowned. *"Hey, if gramps is a king does that make me... A princess or something?"*

Lordiah shook his head. *"Sorry, I'm the bastard son so I don't get the royal privileges. My mother was a servant girl. As you can probably guess, his queen wasn't very fond of me, but I always had a close bond with my father."*

"So why are you here? On this planet?"

Lordiah froze the hologram on the Royal family enjoying a lavish dinner at the king's table. *"I'm getting to that... our scientists have traveled to Earth dozens of times studying it, mining it, performing experiments. We brought back many elements to study, one of them being gold.*

The most important discovery is that it can fix our decaying atmosphere. Unfortunately, Heofon is absent of this mineral."

The hologram changed to people and animals lying dead by the thousands, famished, covered in sores. *"Citizens starve, freeze to death, and succumb to radiation poisoning."*

The hologram reformed to a mob marching down the street breaking windows and ransacking buildings. *"The public turned violent. Wars broke out, and our kingdom became the key target of violence because we had more to take. Our armies were powerful, but we knew we couldn't escape the inevitable. Something drastic had to be done, and we had the answer. Your gold."*

CHAPTER 17:
A SLICE
OF HEOFON

Planet Heofon – approximately 7,220 Earth years ago.

Portraits, antiques, statues and lavish velvet drapes filled the heavy guarded primary gathering room inside the palace of King Osilu.

Tapping his foot as he waited, a younger Lordiah sat at the large hand-carved table equipped with a hologram system as its centerpiece, accompanied by his assistant Leonardo. A third gentleman, also seated, was General Aries, with his chiseled jaw and dressed in his perfectly pressed royal military uniform.

King Osilu entered, along with his son Prince Apollyon and daughter Princess Leilana. Lordiah, Leonardo and General Aries dropped to one knee and bowed.

"Rise, please. Let's all take a chair. Time is of the essence," the king beckoned.

King Osilu convened at the head of the table. Prince Apollyon sat on the king's left. Osilu motioned. "Lordiah, you sit to my right."

Osilu cleared his throat, then spoke, *"As you are all mindful, our planet is in a very dangerous place with the deterioration of our atmosphere. We have no choice but to take bold actions immediately, or we all die. Lordiah has developed* a cure for our sky. We will assemble a team, led by my son Prince Apollyon. Lordiah will be Head of the Science Team. My daughter Leilana will accompany them. Her occupation being Chief Medical Officer."

"I have three of my own blood deployed on this mission." Osilu choked on his words before continuing. "This shows the seriousness of our situation, and the obligation put upon us to protect our planet."

He took a breath and sighed as he made eye contact with his three offspring one at a time. "Lordiah, please give your summary."

He nodded and picked up a remote from the table. "This is our solar system. The planets we are interested in are Mars and Earth." Above the holograph table, the sun illuminated in the center and planets orbited around it.

Lordiah pressed the remote and Heofon appeared in the outer orbit, zipping around the sun at a much higher speed. "Fortunate for us, our planet travels close to the speed of light when it rotates around the sun. Earth and Mars orbit significantly slower. This generates a time-continuum difference, meaning time moves at a much slower rate on Heofon in comparison to Mars and Earth. This time difference can be used to our advantage. We can mine for years, even centuries on these planets, but merely hours, days, will have transpired on Heofon."

Lordiah continued, "We performed experiments on planet Earth which were our first trials in DNA manipulation, using small reptiles from our planet as subjects." The hologram changed. It now covered the entire table with multiple species of dinosaurs roaming the Earth.

"This success opened the doors for vast studies in DNA manipulation, which I was fortunate to be a part of."

General Aries folded his arms and rocked back in his chair. "With all due respect, what does this jargon have to do with the mission?"

Princess Leilana interrupted, "Be patient General, Lordiah is getting to that."

Lordiah smiled at Leilana, then resumed. *"When another team went back to Earth, several thousand years had passed. Now the monstrous reptiles had overran the planet."*

A ship landed, and eleven scientists got out. Tyrannosaurs attacked them within minutes, violently ripping them apart and swallowing their body parts.

"So, our military unit came in, and in one day wiped them out."

The hologram changed. Spacecrafts were flying around shooting and blasting the dinosaurs. Several nuclear missiles were launched from the ground, clearing out extensive areas of the dinosaur population.

Aries spoke up. *"According to records, several active missiles sights are still active on Earth if we should ever require them."*

"Well, that's good to know," Lordiah replied. *"So, throughout the past 200,450 Earth years, we have mined the planet for ore, Beryllium, and cobalt."* The hologram table changed to a mining plant in operation. Filthy cavemen were working, carrying rocks, pushing carts and hammering. Men with electrical whips were at guard controlling them.

"We created workers altering our own genes. They were barbaric, but free help. Through gene manipulation, we dumbed them down and hyped their strength to do all the labor and heavy lifting. They would eat anything you give them and could leave them behind when done with them."

Aries lips tightened, then exhaled as he looked at Lordiah and Apollyon. *"Are we going to do the same on this mission, sir? Grow these freaks?"*

"Why wouldn't we?" King Osilu stepped in. *"Mining isn't an effortless task. You're going to need the help. I'm also going to send 209 prisoners with you to help mine so you can start the minute you land."*

Aries raised his hand. *"209 prisoners? I would like to request more men to manage them, and those beasts you plan on making."*

Lordiah looked over at the King.

"Yes, as you wish. We will get you more men. Please proceed, Lordiah," Osilu stated with an insistent tone.

"We need a mineral known as gold, and tons of it. There is plenty on Mars and Earth. When we process gold into a fine powder, and spray it into our atmosphere..."

The hologram shifted to a frozen planet with airplane-type ships generating chem trails in the Heofon skies. "It will repair our atmosphere."

The last hologram image showed planet Heofon returning to normal and thriving again.

Osilu chimed in, "And the Osilu Kingdom will get the credit for saving the planet."

"Most of our resources are protecting your kingdom's borders," Aries challenged. "How are we getting there? We don't have a ship even close to ready that can take us, and to build one will take years which we don't have."

Lordiah smiled. "Brilliant question, General. We have been working on that for the past year and came up with a solution using a fraction of our planetary resources. And it's almost completed."

Aries leaned forward, with a stern look, "You built a ship without my knowledge?"

Lordiah broke the tension, "General, we are telling you now. It was an experiment and thankfully a success. Would you like to see it?"

CHAPTER 18:
LUNA #1

Planet Heofon – approximately 7,220 Earth years ago.

Five of Heofon's six moons hovered in the daylight grayish sky above. The group collected themselves and moved outside to the immaculate landscaped royal courtyard.

Lordiah pointed up. *"Everyone, that's LUNA, our new ship."*

Everyone gazed up. General Aries shaded his eyes and squinted looking back and forth staring upward. He looked at the others, then at Lordiah. *"Ship? Where? Does anyone see a ship?"*

"I do, and so do you." Lordiah smiled and pointed at the moon in the middle. *"That's L, U, N, A. Living, Unit, Navigational, Asteroid. We hollowed out part of that moon and converted it into a ship."*

Osilu chimed in. *"It's brilliant too. We didn't use any materials or time to build the outer shell for this transport vessel, and it's a million years strong."*

Lordiah nodded. *"We found hollow cavities inside this moon, which amended the expedite of the conversion. We added thrusters, living quarters, and the interior of a basic vessel. With a fraction of the time and materials, we have a ship. One of the strongest and safest ships we have ever built."*

"And without the military involved, they completed the ship in half the time!" Apollyon added.

The general bristled.

Lordiah extended his hand out toward Aries to shake, *"It needs your military touch now, General. Would you like to see it?"*

CHAPTER 19:
THE GENESIS
OF THE MISSION

Planet Heofon, a few weeks later

A parade marched down the streets. The awaiting crowd cheered, and the air crackled with excitement watching the fleet of shuttles lift off their planet and headed towards LUNA.

The commotion and noise of the freight ships being unloaded rang in the busy cargo hangar inside the moon. Lordiah, Osilu, Apollyon, and Leilana arrived in a black triangular craft.

Aries and several of his men marched the 209 chained prisoners from their transport and down a hallway. A sweaty, younger Major Thomas was present, minus the limp and red facial scar, was running around with an electronic clipboard in hand checking inventory as the ships unpacked.

With a nod Osilu acknowledged Aries. The general walked over and saluted the King, Apollyon, Leilana, and Lordiah. *"Should we go over our final preparations before we depart?"*

Lordiah signaled for Major Thomas. *"Join us, please."* The group proceeded to the moonship's control room and gathered around the hologram table.

Lordiah looked at his half-brother. *"With your permission, Prince Apollyon, would you allow me to start the briefing?"* Apollyon swirled his finger and gave him the go-ahead nod.

"With Mars being the closest, we will land there first, set up our energy systems, and start the prisoners mining immediately."

"We should be close to departure time." Lordiah looked up. "Major Thomas?"

Major Thomas glanced down at his clipboard. "The countdown departure is scheduled zero-two hours and thirty-six. Everything is loaded and ready. Is that liftoff time to your liking, King Apollyon?"

Apollyon stood taller when he heard the word king before his name for the first time. He looked over at General Aries. "Are the prisoners secure?"

"Yes, sir. Military is one hundred percent accountable and ready."

"Fine. Show me to my royal quarters. I'll be there if needed."

Apollyon turned and proceeded toward the control room exit followed by his personal staff of eleven. Lordiah walked with him to the door. "Prince Apollyon, I hope you will enjoy your royal quarters. We have all of your requests implemented. Please let me know if you need anything else to aid toward your comfort."

"Thank you," Apollyon replied, then leaned in closer to whisper in Lordiah's ear, "remember, my dear bastard bother, the second this ship leaves I am no longer a prince, but King Apollyon, and you shall address me as that."

Lordiah watched his brother leave, then turned and rejoined his father. King Osilu shook his head.

"That boy has been privileged his entire life. Hopefully, he will gain some maturity and wisdom on this mission."

Lordiah put his arm around his father's shoulder. "I'll look after him Papa, don't worry."

"I know you will. I shouldn't be divulging this, but I sometimes wish you and he could switch places and he was the bastard."

Lordiah chuckled. King Osilu smiled and gave Lordiah a hug. A tear welled up in his eyes. "I couldn't be any prouder of you, son."

"Thanks, Papa." Lordiah drew back. *"OK, if we are going to save the world, I better get going."*

They hugged one more time. King Osilu stepped back, folded his arms and his eyes crinkled at the corners, *"You must succeed at all cost. No exception. I know you won't let me down."*

CHAPTER 20:
THOUSAND YEAR OLD BRANDY

Inside the Moon – Present Time

Happy with how things were going so far, Lordiah got up and walked over to the bar. *"This place was stocked when we left and hasn't been touched. Would you like some brandy? It's several thousand years old."*

Luna replied, *"Well, it would be rude to turn that down. Right? Let's do it."*

He poured a glass and brought it over to her.

"This is almost like the old days when you used to tell me bedtime stories, minus the brandy. Nice added touch though, pops. Please, keep going."

Lordiah sat down across from her and shrugged his shoulders. *"That's it. They landed and lived happily ever after. The end."*

"Haha, yeah, whatever... And really? You named me after a big rock with pockmarks?"

Lordiah laughed. *"I'm happy that you have loosened up."*

"Come on, I'm inside the f-in moon right now or I would totally call you an asshole and bullshit on your story. What happened after you left Heofon?"

"Well, the trip to Mars was fairly uneventful. The only drama was your Uncle Apollyon wanting to let us all know

daily that he was now a king. When we arrived, I got to tell you Luna, that was a moment in history for me, seeing another planet for the first time."

CHAPTER 21:
THE
NOT-SO-RED
PLANET

Mars – Approximately 7,220 years ago

The restless crew cheered when the Heofon astronauts finally observed Mars from the control room windows.
Lordiah captured the moment in his journal:

(Lordiah Journal Entry: 01:43.03 Mars) With our ship being another planetary body, when we docked into Mars orbit, it influenced the gravitational pull and created disorder with the weather here. It rained and spewed violent storms for weeks. When the weather finally cleared, we saw that there were forests, rivers, mountains, and above all, clean air. It was picturesque. There is no sign of life except for plants, and now us.

Leonardo asserted that he be on the first mission scout. He convinced me he was more expendable. He suited up in protective gear along with three guards and seven prisoners. The prisoners were without a protective suit to be used as lab rats to see how being exposed on the surface affected them. We have to wait and hope the best upon their return."

*   *   *

The shuttle landed into a grassy area where a medley of flowers, grasses, and other plants rooted. Outside the shuttle window, the trees at the edge of the open field swayed and the moonship embedded in the sea of blue sky above.

Secure in his protective suit, Leonardo turned on his oxygen and motioned for the three guards to do the same. The prisoners, chained together, waited.

The plank lowered to the surface and the Martian air flowed into the shuttle. Leonardo studied the effect it had on the prisoners. They sat there until one waved and the other stuck his tongue out at them and then laughed.

Leonardo motioned to them, *"Move down the plank and outside."*

They closed the door quickly after the last prisoner exited and watched from the shuttle. Several minutes passed. They stood unaffected.

Leonardo grabbed the microphone. *"Jog a few times around the ship."*

They picked up their pace and started to run around the craft. Then they began to dance and skip.

Leonardo stood up, removed his protective suit and stripped down to his underwear. *"Gents, let's not let them have all of the fun."*

He looked back at the guards staring in the doorway still in their protective gear. He shrugged his shoulders, *"Hey, suit yourself. The best way to test this is naked, right?"* His underwear hit the floor, and he streaked out.

He ran around for several minutes jumping and howling. He finally stopped, widened his stance, opened his arms and inhaled the moist air and damp plant fragrances.

"Ahh, the smell of real, untainted air."

The second party included Apollyon, Aries, Leilana, and Lordiah.

Sitting shoulder to shoulder next to Lordiah, Leilana's leg bounced. She reached over and squeezed Lordiah's hand. He leaned in, kissed her cheek and put his arm around her. Apollyon, sitting across from them, stared at them for a moment, then with a disgusted frown looked the other way. She laid her head on his shoulder. Since leaving Heofon they peeled back the secret and came out in the open about being more than half-siblings.

Upon landing, General Aries took his military team and immediately scouted the area. Lordiah and Leilana didn't wait for them to come back and wandered off on their own to explore. He recorded in his Journal:

(Lordiah Journal Entry: 01:53.20 Mars) We are enamored with everything, the soil, plants, the colors, rivers, and above all, the pure smells.

Over the next few days, cargo ships and shuttles flew back and forth, delivering supplies. My first task is to build a pyramid to generate our power. Leonardo is in charge of all mining operations and Leilana set up her medical station.

General Aries and his troops managed the prisoners. He himself stepped in and helped with the labor by cutting rock, building, and whatever else was needed.

All hands are on deck working, with the exception of King Apollyon, his wife, and their royal staff. Apollyon exploited his power and had a throne brought down and installed under a canopy where he did nothing except sit. After a few hours, he would return to the moonship for a lavish meal and cocktails.

*   *   *

Lordiah got up to stretch his legs. He walked over to a fresh cut rock and ran his hand across the smooth edge. He went back and continued writing.

(Lordiah Journal Entry: 01:53.20 Mars) The construction for the pyramid power plant had commenced. The workers are carving large rock blocks out of the mountain for bricks.

Moving the 11-ton granite blocks was a two-man job when using the anti-gravity dolly.

The gold excavating team, however, isn't partaking in the same success. Leonardo has multiple teams digging and panning. But after weeks of mining, they have returned each night void of any product.

With the exception of Apollyon, everyone lodged in tents on the planet. Apollyon sojourned on the moonship and made his attendance every few days making certain to update us we weren't moving fast enough, and we must find gold soon.

*　*　*

(Lordiah Journal Entry: 01:17:20 Mars) After seventy-four days, the first pyramid was completed. It stood sixty-five meters above the ground.

*　*　*

Filthy from the long day, Lordiah and Aries worked up in the topmost part of the pyramid putting the final touches on the generators and hooking them into the power cell blocks.

"All four sides are positioned correctly so I'm confident we're going to have power in the next few minutes," Lordiah told the general.

"I hope so. For the record, four shuttles are grounded because their fuel cells are completely drained, and the others are dangerously low. If we don't charge them soon, we'll be stuck on this planet."

The murmurs of the crew buzzed as the crowd formed and stood outside the pyramid waiting. Lordiah and Aries climbed down the winding stairs and joined them.

Hearing the chatter of the crowd, Leilana left her make-shift medical tent and marched over to see what was happening.

"This could be a moment of history for each one of us," Lordiah addressed the group. He held up a remote. *"If we prepared this correctly, when I push this button, the electrons from the air will be pulled in and funneled into the top of our pyramid. When they all come together, we have an electrical current."*

One of the prisoners yelled, *"Just push the button asshole. We didn't sign up for any bullshit education course!"*

Aries stepped forward and locked eyes with the man. *"Show some respect."* He kept the glare for a few more seconds, then nodded to Lordiah.

Leilana grabbed Lordiah's filthy hand and smiled proudly at him. He smiled back. *"OK, here we go, cross your fingers."*

A low humming roar began, and the pyramid peak started to glow.

"That's my girl," Lordiah mumbled as his gaze fixed on the sight. The top of the pyramid glowed brighter. Lights around the tent city turned on.

Cheers came from everyone. General Aries turned to Lordiah and shook his hand. *"Well done sir."*

Leilana turned to Lordiah and pulled him into a celebratory embrace and pressed her lips against his.

"I'm so proud of you my sexy man." She planted another long, wet kiss on him.

Aries frowned shaking his head, *"We made history today. Where's our king to share in the moment? On the moonship drinking and having an orgy?"*

Lordiah shrugged his shoulders and didn't answer.

Aries stepped forward to address the workers. *"There's plenty of room in the pyramid for you to sleep inside and escape the chill of the night. We will be able to generate heat starting tonight."*

Leilana claimed a small area inside, surrounded by a canvas wall, and set up her medical clinic in the far back corner of the pyramid.

"You got a good size bump, but you'll be fine," she said while examining a worker's head. She handed him a small box. *"Take one pill a day, but only one. It will help with the headache and the swelling."* The patient thanked her and exited the clinic.

Lordiah, Aries, and Apollyon entered the pyramid. Apollyon stood clean, pressed, and perfectly groomed. Lordiah and Aries' clothes remained filthy.

"Leilana?" Lordiah called out. *"Are you in there?"*

She peeked out from behind the canvas wall, *"Well hello, gentlemen."* She walked over and hugged her brother.

She looked over at Lordiah and Aries. *"And for you two, no hugs. You have some serious dirty-ass-itis. Want my professional medical advice? Water, down by the river. It's called a bath."*

Lordiah laughed, *"That river is freezing, Lei Lei, or I would gladly follow my doctor's orders."*

General Aries spoke up, *"Good news, my Princess. We are building shower stalls as we speak, so hopefully soon."*

"Hey, babes, we're heading to the top. I assembled the plasma-channel, free-electron laser and we're going to test it. Want to join?" Lordiah asked Leilana.

"Sure, if it's cleared by the King and the General, I'd love to."

Apollyon retorted back immediately. *"Yes, my dear sister, please join. Your royalty, you don't need the General's permission."*

"Glad to have you join us, Your Highness. The General stated. Turning to King Apollyon, his jaw tensed "And yes, she does need my permission. It's a potential weapon, which falls under my jurisdiction and responsibility."

General Aries and Apollyon locked eyes. *"Remember, there's a new king, and this jurisdiction garble may change,"* Apollyon remarked.

Lordiah broke the tension.*"You two can figure this out later. Let's go up and test the laser."*

Apollyon replied, walking forward. *"Yeah, lets."*

Sweat dripped from their foreheads and soaked shirt collars when they finally reached the last step of the zig-zagged stairs to the top level of the pyramid. Near the north wall on a platform, a long black cannon with an energy panel was mounted.

Lordiah pulled up a few toggles on the panel. Nothing happened. He looked, then kicked the box mounted to it. A buzzing sound hummed. *"There we go. That's the energy gathering.*" The light went from red to green on the main panel, "*And that means she's powered up and ready.*"

The encased red lights on the barrel glowed bright. Lordiah grabbed the handle grips to the cannon and maneuvered the barrel to point down.

"*Can you see that rock down there? That's our focus.*" He flipped a switch on the handle with his thumb. A red dot appeared on the top left portion of the rock. "*That's our marker.*"

The General smiled, "*Let's see what you got.*"

Lordiah slowly moved his finger onto the trigger, "*It should cut this rock like butter, smooth and precise.*"

He checked his aim and then carefully squeezed the trigger. A thin black beam from the cannon connected exactly where the red dot was. Still firing, Lordiah moved the laser to the right. Like a sword with a quick slash, the top of the rock transformed smooth and flat in seconds.

Lordiah beamed. "*This is on its lowest setting. It can power up twenty times more.*"

General Aries's brows furrowed, his lower lip pressed against his top as he studied the rock below. "*Impressive! And that's the lowest setting?*"

Lordiah flipped the switch and powered the machine down. "*Yes, sir. If you place it on its highest setting, you can unquestionably cut holes into the moonship from here. This will certainly expedite our mining and building.*"

Aries walked a one-eighty around the laser. "*You're not kidding. I'll also need to put a guard on this at all times. How many of these can we make?*"

"*I already have Major Thomas building another one. It should be ready in a few weeks.*"

"*Great,*" Apollyon responded. "*Seems like we are going to be here for a while at the rate you're all going. Now we can start to build my royal quarters down here.*"

Trying to relax his jaw from clenching, General Aries took a breath and replied, "*With all due respect, sir, we should build quarters for the workers first. The nights are getting colder.*"

Apollyon glared at him then fired back, *"They find gold, then we will build them quarters."*

Aries turned away from the group to hide his fury. Lordiah and Leilana looked at each other, and then at Apollyon.

Silence held the group until Apollyon broke it, *"I'm famished. I'm heading back to the ship. Find me something so I can report some good news back home!"*

Apollyon turned and left.

CHAPTER 22:
GOLD!

At first sunlight, Leonardo loaded the plasma laser into the shuttle and transported it to the mining camp.

By midafternoon, he landed the shuttle feet away from the pyramid entrance. He jumped out and started to howl in joy. *"Lady and gentlemen! We found gold!"*

Lordiah dropped everything and ran over. Leonardo danced and held out a vile with several ounces of gold flakes inside, and a bottle with some larger nuggets.

Lordiah grabbed both and held them up to the sunlight. *"You tested it?"*

Leonardo nodded. *"One hundred percent pure, Bossman!"*

Lordiah laughed. He grabbed and hugged him. *"Now all we need is about a hundred tons more, and we're good!"*

Leonardo and Lordiah howled together.

Lordiah put his hands up to his mouth and shouted. *"General Aries, we struck gold!"*

Aries held his hand up and signaled to give him a second while he continued to talk on the hand radio.

When he finished, he walked over to Lordiah and the group. *"That was Major Thomas. We need to head up to the ship. We have a call from the King."*

CHAPTER 23:
THE KING'S MESSAGE

Inside LUNA, Mars orbit – 7,220 years ago

Lordiah and Aries didn't waste any time getting to the moonship. With the exception of Major Thomas, the control room stood vacant when they arrived.

"Major Thomas, can you inform us of the nature of this call?" Lordiah asked.

"Sorry, sir, the king was very specific that he wanted a direct communication with you, the general, and King Apollyon. No one else."

Apollyon stumbled in, half-drunk. *"Looks like we got the ol' gang back together! Splendid."* He brought his finger up in a shooting motion. *"Major Thomas, you may excuse yourself. And while you're out, you can refresh my brandy cabinet."*

Major Thomas got up to exit. *"Yes, sir, I'll look into that. Gentlemen, everything is set. The king should call back any minute."*

Silence remained between them while they waited.

The screen flashed and King Osilu appeared. The background appeared drab. The silk shirt he wore was ripped, and his crown absent.

"Greetings. I hear you made it to Mars safe. Congratulations."

"Father, what's going on? Where are you?" Lordiah muttered.

Osilu rubbed dust out of his eyes. *"I'm in the bunker."*

General Aries stepped forward *"Why, your Highness?"*

Osilu looked stern at the General. *"There was a military coup, General. The very minute you left; your military enforced a well-thought-out takeover. I'm confident that you knew nothing about it. Is my assumption correct?"*

Aries straightened up and stood at attention. *"Yes sir, your lordship. I'm shocked to hear about this heinous act! With your permission, I would like to return immediately. I will straighten this out."*

The king shook his head. *"No General, I need you to stay there and finish your mission. All of you! We hold all the power when you bring back the gold."*

"Father, are you OK?" Apollyon asked.

"Yes, at the moment. The Royal Guard held strong against the military rebels, but we had to evacuate the palace. Your mother and your siblings are safe here in the bunker, but please hurry."

Apollyon walked in front of Lordiah and General Aries to get closer to the screen. *"Father, we are all rolling up our sleeves and getting dirty here, even myself, I assure you. We work night and day. And, we found gold today."*

General Aries looked at Lordiah and frowned at what he just heard. Lordiah shook his head, silently encouraging him to not respond.

Lordiah stepped forward. *"Father, please stay safe. The good news is the time continuum difference. We can be working here for months, and only hours will have passed in your time. Don't worry, we won't let you down."*

An explosion in the distance of the bunker shook the screen. The image of Osilu slowly faded, then silence. The monitor went dark...

CHAPTER 24:
THE EMPEROR
WEARS NEW CLOTHES

Mars – approximately 7,220 years ago

As the morning dew glistened on the nearby brush, General Aries and Lordiah waited for the entire crew to assemble outside the pyramid. Aries was pacing back and forth.

"General, I agree we need all hands-on deck, but please, step back and take a breath for a second. You are emotional and reactionary." Lordiah tells Aries.

The General stared forward gazing in the distance.

"General? Are you listening? Please, let's take a moment before you do anything drastic."

Aries looked square at Lordiah and squinted. *"I need to get back as soon as possible with the cargo. I will do whatever it needs to make that happen. And that's means all hands-on deck."*

"I comply with you, but we need to formulate a strategy. Apollyon will not like the idea of us recruiting his staff. Let me address him first."

"Do it soon. I'm going to lay down the law to everyone right now," Aries said as he walked toward the crowd and climbed up on the rock that Lordiah sheared flat with the laser.

"Men," he gazed over at Leilana and acknowledged, *"Ma'am. Gather, please. Everyone. I have critical news from home."*

The remaining bunch emptied out of the pyramid and gathered around. Everyone was now there except Apollyon and his staff.

"To get straight to the point, the palace was attacked. King Osilu has retreated and we don't know whether he is alive or dead."

Mumbles echoed throughout the crowd. A worker yelled out, *"Who attacked our country?!"*

"It wasn't an attack from outsiders. Before we lost contact with our king, he informed us it was a military coup." Aries answered.

Another worker yelled, *"If it's a military coup, then that means it was your people!"*

General Aries wrinkled his nose and his eyebrows furrowed. *"I too have a wife and three children there. I will assure you I have nothing to do with this heinous act of treason, and if anybody wants to challenge me on this, step up now. But be ready to fight to the death. Anybody?"* He continued to glare at the group.

They remained silent. A worker slowly raised his hand. *"Sir, with all due respect, what's next? What about our families? Are we returning?"*

Across the sky, the royal shuttle flew into view. The assembled group paused and looked up. Aries smirked then rolled his eyes, *"We need to stay put and keep doing what we are hired to do. That is the only way we will be able to go back to our families and save them."*

The shuttle landed just yards from the group. So dangerously close that people had to move out of their way and covered their eyes to protect themselves from the dust and rocks that were being kicked up. Apollyon, Queen Anana, and their entourage of assistants exited. Apollyon stopped and stood with his arms folded behind him.

The general continued, *"They may have overrun the palace, but gold is the solution to save our planet and our families."*

A prisoner yelled from the back, *"What about our pardons? We were promised a pardon if we came here to work. How can we still be pardoned?"*

"We bring back the gold, and you will get your pardons as promised. But that means all hands-on deck, working night and day. The building team will postpone whatever they are doing and become the night mining team."

Moans echoed throughout the crowd.

Apollyon motioned for two of his assistants to get down on all fours. He stepped up on them, standing on their backs with one foot on each.

"Everybody, listen!" Apollyon yelled. "We must all do our part unless you want to be stuck on this barren, Godforsaken planet forever! I personally don't desire that. Now let's get moving!"

The General nodded to several of his guards. A group of armed men moved behind Apollyon.

"Thank you, sir, for your support," the general continued. "As you said, everyone must do their part. New rule. All hands-on deck means all hands! No one excluded."

The general pointed over to Apollyon and his team. "I see eleven fresh new miners right there. Apollyon, we're all equals now, including you."

Lordiah and Leilana looked at each other wide-eyed. "Oh, no. This isn't good," Lordiah said shaking his head.

Apollyon shouted, "Tell your men to step away, or else!"

The General smiled. "Or else what? As far as I know, there is no Osilu kingdom anymore. So, you are now like the rest of us, workers."

Aries nodded. The men pulled Apollyon down from the backs of the men. The general approached.

"You won't be needing these," General Aries said as he removed Apollyon's crown and royal cloak. "Put these in the supply stash."

Aries, addressing Apollyon and his staff. "Men, you are miners now. If you don't do your part, you will be deemed dead weight and will be shot. You will eat, sleep, and work with the rest of us. Women, including you, your Queenship, will assist with duties at the mines, and meals."

Apollyon stepped forward. *"I am your king! I will not take orders from you!"* He reached out to slap the general, but Aries caught his hand. He smiled.

"I've wanted to do this for a long time." He took one step forward and embedded a firm punch. As Aries fist smashed into Apollyon's face, blood gushed out of his nose, as he fell unconscious.

The general turned to the assembled group. *"Enough said. Leonardo, get these men suited and ready for mining. This talk about is adjourned. Let's get to work."*

CHAPTER 25:
BEATING
THE KING

Mars – approximately 7,220 year ago

(Lordiah Journal Entry: 01.24.4 Mars) Several weeks have passed since General Aries forced Apollyon and his staff to work alongside the prisoners. They now coexisted as part of the labor force for the day mining team.

He required Apollyon to earn his keep. If he doesn't, he would deny him food that day.

Apollyon's staff endured the persecution along with him. They are forced to sleep outside under an open-sided tent and banned from the warmth of the pyramid.

*   *   *

Later that evening, the shuttles returned to camp, transporting the day mining teams. Apollyon limped off the transport vehicle, carried by his wife and one of his older servants. He bore a new right eye beaten purple and now swollen shut, a bloodied crooked nose, and several broken ribs.

"What transpired?" Lordiah asked.

The servant responded, *"One of the prisoners beat him up and the guards did nothing to stop it. He kept hitting him, even when he was unconscious."*

Lordiah raced away and returned with Leilana.

"Oh no, my poor brother," she cried, as she knelt down beside him.

Apollyon laid there still incoherent from the beating.

"This isn't good." Leilana reached into her bag and pulled out several disinfectant wipes. She washed the dried blood from his face.

"Help me roll him over," Leilana asked.

She pulled out a syringe and reached over, pulling his pants down enough to give him the shot. *"Apollyon, this will help you with the pain. You need to be still."*

"Hey, what are you two doing?" Aries yelled, marching over. *"I specifically said no special attention."*

Lordiah stood up. *"General, please, he needs medical attention."*

Aries stood and studied Apollyon. *"Well, don't waste any unnecessary medical supplies on him. Just enough to get him back working."*

Leilana stood. She glared at Aries. *"General, he's been almost beaten to death. What are you going to do about this!"*

Aries shrugged his shoulders. *"I can't be everywhere. I will tell the men to back off. I don't want to lose a worker."*

Leilana's jaw dropped and then she sneered, *"You're an ass."*

Aries' glare turned to a sneer. He turned to Lordiah and took a step towards him. *"Lordiah, my advice is to stand your girl down."*

Lordiah grabbed Leilana's hand and pulled her back towards him. He looked her in the eyes and shook his head back and forth.

Aries stared at them. *"You do your jobs, and you and I will be respectable. Do you want to help your brother? Fine, go get your possessions out of the pyramid. Your new sleeping quarters are outside with him. Starting now!"*

CHAPTER 26:

THE FAINT

Mars – Approximately 7,220 years ago

(Lordiah Journal Entry: 02.09.00 Mars) General Aries hard-pressed the labor force to work the entire 24 hours, 41 minutes each day, with a day team and a night team, and zero days off. It's as if he became possessed. The good news, we are finding gold daily.

They force Leilana and me to work every day in the mines in addition to our other duties. It's sweaty, disgusting work. I want to slug the general for making Leilana do hard labor. Her hands are getting calloused and cut up. Mine too, but seeing hers hurt me worse. She perseveres as an equal in the workforce and also works tireless when taking care of the injured workers."

*   *   *

Perspiration poured from their bodies, that darkened their stained work shirts with the sweat of the day work shift. The warmer temperatures during the day had a noticeable effect on the miner's performance. But General Aries didn't care.

Queen Anana got thrown in with the day mining crew, carrying rocks, digging, moving equipment, whatever the general wanted to be done.

They were going on their eleventh hour into the shift. Anana stopped when she staggered, dropping the bucket of rocks.

"Keep moving," the guard yelled at her.

She stood still. Her face turned pale as she looked down at her buckets. She rubbed her eyes.

"I said keep moving!"

Apollyon stopped. The same guard turned toward him. *"What are you looking at? It's not quitting time."*

Anana took a deep breath. She bent down, grabbed the buckets and continued. She walked several more steps before she collapsed to her knees and fainted cold on the ground, the rocks tumbling in a spray around her.

"Anana!" Apollyon screamed, frozen.

Hearing the cry, Lordiah looked over. He dropped his cart and rushed over.

Apollyon looked wide-eyed at Lordiah, then the guard. He finally got the courage to join Lordiah.

"Get back to work!" General Aries barked.

Lordiah held Anana's head and checked her pulse. *"General, please. Something's wrong!"*

"Both of you don't need to be there! Get back to work Apollyon."

Two guards approached Apollyon and pushed him backward.

"General, show a little compassion, it's his wife!" Lordiah snapped.

Anana blinked her eyes open. Lordiah grabbed her hand, *"Are you OK, Anana? You fainted."*

She nodded. He helped her to her feet. She placed her hand on Lordiah's shoulder.

"General, we need to take her to medical," Lordiah pleaded.

Aries paused for a second, then replied, *"We have another hour left on the shift. She can sit it out, but under one condition."*

He walked over to Apollyon and handed him a pick. *"If we are down one worker, you do the work of two, or she has to come back."*

"General, really?" Lordiah frowned, shaking his head.

"You know the rules. Each person must do their share. That includes me too, as you can see I'm here doing my shift. If you're that concerned, you can pull double time for her."

Anana couldn't contain her tears any longer. Lordiah walked her over to a shaded area by one of the shuttles. *"You sit here and rest. I'll cover for you with Apollyon."*

Lordiah furrowed his brows and sneered over at General Aries. He folded his arms and stared back. Lordiah picked up the bucket of rocks that Anana dropped and took over.

CHAPTER 27:
GAME CHANGER

Just before sunset, the skies opened, and their first rainstorms poured since they colonized the planet.

Lordiah rushed inside the pyramid and found Leilana in her corner set up. Hearing what had happened, she quickly grabbed her black leather medical bag. Hand in hand they charged through the downpour inhaling the moist air and damp plants until she joined the ex-royals under their canvas shelter. Leilana wiped the wet from her face, removed her muddy shoes with leaves caked to them as the group made what little room available for them under their tight accommodations.

Leilana made her way over. *"Oh, Anana, what have they done to you?"* She knelt, brushed the hair out of her face, and looked into her eyes.

"Are you okay?"

Anana nodded silently, then started to cry.

"Normally I would make you all leave while I examine her," Leilana told the shivering group, *"but you have nowhere dry to go."*

"Anana, I need to look you over. Are you OK with everyone being here?"

She nodded.

Leilana opened up her medical bag and pulled out a round metal instrument. She first looked into Anana's eyes.

Changing a setting, she placed it into her ear. Apollyon sat close to Anana and held her hand.

"You're hot." Leilana reached down and put her hand on her stomach. *"OK everyone, she's still royalty, so can I please get you all to turn away."*

Leilana pulled up her shirt, took her instrument and listened to her heartbeat. She looked at Apollyon and Anana. *"Your heartbeat is elevated too."* Leilana palpated her stomach with her hands.

She stopped for a second, squeezed her hand and leaned in to whisper into Anana's ear, *"You're pregnant, aren't you sweetheart?"* Anana looked up as more tears flowed out of her eyes.

Leilana stood. *"Sorry, everyone, out of the tent, except Apollyon and Lordiah. We need a few minutes of privacy here."*

The group looked at her. *"Now, please!"* her words shot out. They grabbed whatever they could find to protect themselves from the storm and quickly vacated.

"What's going on, Lei?" Apollyon timidly asked.

"Your wife's pregnant. Don't know if that's good or bad news with everything going on, but congratulations."

"Oh my," Lordiah muttered as he shook his head.

Apollyon smirked, *"My legacy begins. My seed. Do you think it's a boy? It has to be a boy."*

"Apollyon, that's what you're concerned about right now? I don't know if this is a good thing in these conditions."

Apollyon stood, *"We need to do something. This is the heir to the throne."*

Leilana scratched her head and got up, *"Lordiah, I need to get her up to the moonship."*

"General Aries will never allow that!" He exclaimed.

"We need to find a way," Leilana firmly replied.

He took a breath, *"Okay, let me think for a second."*

"How about we just kill the general?" Apollyon bellowed. *"It's long overdue. Then we won't have a problem!"*

Lordiah knelt down by Anana. *"Don't worry. We'll figure out something."*

Lordiah stood and addressed Apollyon and Leilana. *"As angry as I am at General Aries, killing him isn't an option."*

"Then what is? Do you have a better plan?" Apollyon demanded.

"Possibly. I'm scheduled to take a shuttle with the gold up to the moonship in a few hours to inventory and store. I can probably sneak Leilana and Anana on board, but if we get caught, who knows what General Aries will do."

"And then what?" Apollyon retorted. *"Bring her back down here after? If that happens, my wife and child will surely die."*

Leilana stepped in. *"He's right, Lordiah."*

Lordiah stood quietly, thinking. Apollyon interrupted the silence. *"We all depart tonight. My staff too, or he will make them do our workload until he eventually kills them. We can deal with General Asshole when we're safe within the ship."*

CHAPTER 28:
THE GREAT
ESCAPE

The downpour continued as the sun set. Lordiah and Leonardo rushed into the pyramid. They shook the rain from their hair and wiped the water from their dripping faces.

Lordiah walked over to the soldier at a desk in charge of the shuttles and reported in. *"We have a scheduled run to the moonship."* He conveyed.

The soldier grabbed his electric clipboard. *"Yep, I have been waiting for you. After I check you out, I'm done for the night."* He typed onto the clipboard then beeped. *"OK, right this way."* He stood up and walked to the door.

"It's raining out, no need to walk us to the shuttle if you don't want to," Lordiah expressed.

"Strict rules from the General. I wish I didn't have to, trust me, but I want to keep this job!" The soldier covered his head with the clipboard.

The three walked out into the storm. Their path led them past the tent where Apollyon and his group slept. They were quiet, their bodies forming lumps under their blankets and tarps.

The soldier pointed. *"One day they're Royals, the next nothing but slaves. That's why I follow the rules."*

When they arrived at the shuttles, the soldier pulled a remote from his pocket. A door opened underneath, and a plank lowered.

"Alright, sir, she should be charged and ready to fly. Those crates underneath contain this week's gold. Load up and you're good to go." The soldier handed Lordiah the remote.

Leonardo and Lordiah each grabbed a container, boarded and closed the hatch. Leonardo got into the pilot's seat and saluted the soldier from the front windshield.

The soldier stepped back when the shuttle elevated off the ground. He returned the salute, turned and trotted away.

In a flash, the shuttle thrusted towards the moonship and in minutes was out of sight.

Lordiah put both hands on his forehead and exhaled a long breath. *"OK everyone we are clear."*

In the cargo area, the tarps moved and were yanked aside. Apollyon, Anana, Leilana and the crew stood up and cheered, embracing each other.

"That was nerve racking. I thought we were going to get caught," Lordiah told the group.

Leilana scampered up to the co-pilots seat, grabbed Lordiah's ears with each hand and planted a big kiss on him. *"You know, that was a big turn-on."* She winked. *"Wait until I get you alone on the ship tonight!"*

CHAPTER 29:
THEY'RE
GONE!

Mars: Approximately 7,220 years ago

After a long night of showers, the rain finally halted. The air was perfumed with the sweet fragrance of fresh wildflowers and wet bush as the sun began to rise over the Martian mountains painting a beautiful pink and blue sky above.

The general's alarm kicked off, startling him awake. He folded his clasped fingers over his forehead and eyes, wishing he could stay and sleep just a few minutes longer.

Aries got dressed and made his way toward the pyramid exit. He stopped at the door, took a deep breath, and admired the beautiful sunrise.

"*Sir, they're gone!*" The soldier yelled running his way.

"*Who's gone?*" The General asked.

"*Them!*" He pointed. "*They're all gone!*"

The general picked up his pace and trotted over to the tented area.

Aries kicked the lump under the covers. It was hard. He grabbed the blankets and ferociously ripped them back finding logs, rocks, and other bedding.

"Find them, they couldn't have gotten far!" The General commanded.

"Sir, a shuttle is missing too," replied the soldier.

CHAPTER 30:
THE RED
PLANET

Mars: Approximately 7,220 years ago

"Please don't bother us when the General calls. We'll deal with him after a good night's sleep." Lordiah ordered Major Thomas before heading to his quarters to get his first decent sleep in months on a soft bed with clean smelling sheets in a climate-controlled environment.

Sure enough, the general's voice barked out over the telecom moments after he discovered them missing.

"I'm sorry sir, but I have strict orders. I'm not allowed to open any docking stations unless I have authorization from Lordiah or Apollyon," Major Thomas informed him.

"You piece of rat fecal matter. I'm not asking for your permission, I'm ordering you. Open up the doors!" General Aries shouted.

Major Thomas lowered Aries's volume coming from the screen so he wouldn't have to hear the foul insults he is yelling at him. *"Sir, I'm a commissioned Major in the Royal Aeronautics Administration and not a part of the military, so my loyalty stands exclusively with the royal family, not you.*

I am now turning off this frequency. I'm sure King Apollyon and Lordiah will contact you when they're ready."

By late morning, Lordiah and Apollyon strolled their way to the control room.

"Any contact from King Osilu or anyone from Heofon?" Lordiah asked Major Thomas.

"No sir, nothing."

Lordiah opened his arms above his head and stretched, exhaled then turned to Apollyon. *"My recommendation, Sir, is to not throw fuel on the fire. When he finds us gone, the General will be out of his mind. We are safe here for now."*

Apollyon tightened his lips and shook his head. *"What he did is treason and heinous. I will severely punish him for his criminal actions."*

"He will be, but let's be smart about this. We still need gold, and they are finding it. Let's set new boundaries with him and find a way to still work together."

Apollyon nodded.

"Major Thomas, hail down to the General."

Aries popped up on the monitor right away with the mines operating in the background.

"Well, look at you Apollyon, King of the moonship. Do you think that makes you the big man again? Your fellow workers miss you down here. They can't wait until you join the team again!"

Lordiah raised his hand upward to Apollyon and whispered to him, *"Please be calm, my king. Don't be provoked. We need this to be civil."*

Apollyon sneered. *"Then you banter with that peasant for I will explode if he addresses me like that again!"*

Lordiah nodded then focused. *"General we need to settle some issues. Can we please put rationale in the space and discuss?"*

The General held up a fist. *"What you did is mutiny, Lordiah. You stole a shuttle and helped prisoners escape. Return them, then you and I can put rationale in the space."*

"*Prisoner!*" Apollyon shouted. "*I am your king! What you did was a mutiny, not us!*"

Lordiah quickly interrupted. "*General, Anana needed medical attention that wasn't available on the surface. We were left with no choice. Please, can we work this out in a calm tone?*"

"*I am calm!*" the General bit back. "*And here is the plan.*"

The General walked over to the plasma laser and cranked the handle to the far right. The lights on the laser shined twice as bright than before, along with a high pitch buzzing sound. "*Lordiah, you said at full power I could hit the ship from here. Well, I have it set to its highest setting and pointed at you! So, here's the plan, you all surrender and come back, or I test out your theory!*"

"*That's impossible. Can he hit us from there?*" Apollyon shrieked.

Alarm crossed Lordiah's face, "*At full capacity, unfortunately, yes he can.*"

"*He won't do it, it's a bluff!*" Apollyon shouted.

"*You think I'm a person that would bluff? How about this!*" The General pulled the trigger. A black beam fired out of the cannon barrel.

The moon shook. Lordiah and Major Thomas grabbed the rail for balance as Apollyon was knocked to the floor.

Aries laughed as he watched the crew scramble on his screen. The soldiers and workers cheered in the background pointing at the small trail of smoke emitting from LUNA.

Apollyon's face darkened as he watched all of this from their telescreen.

"*Have you lost your mind General Aries?!*" Lordiah cried out.

"*Do I have your undivided attention now?*" He barked.

"*Aries, I demand you to cease! This is absolute treason! You fired upon a royal vessel.*" Apollyon yelled.

He pulled the trigger again. The moonship rocked.

"*Stop! You're going to kill us all, including the 38 innocent crew members on board!*" Lordiah shouted.

"*The innocent crew lives are in your hands. Surrender, and I will stop,*" the General insisted.

Lordiah turned the volume off to the telescreen. *"Major Thomas, put up all protection shields! Can we move this ship to the other side of the planet where he won't be able to shoot at us?"*

"Yes, sir. Protective shields are up, but they are built to deflect asteroids, not to withstand a blast, especially from a plasma laser. It can probably only protect us for only a few more."

"This is completely insane. He's obviously crazy enough to destroy us all!" Lordiah bellowed. *"Major Thomas, can you take us out of orbit? Now?"*

"Sir, all engines are shut down. It will take some time to get them to full power."

"I would rather die than go back down there with him!" Apollyon shouted.

Another blast from the plasma laser shook the moonship, but the protective shield absorbed most of it.

Lordiah looked back at the telescreen. *"Surrender or I destroy you all!"* Barked the General. *"If I don't see a shuttle leaving in five minutes, I'm cutting you in half!"*

Lordiah turned to them. *"Okay, we are all in agreement that the general has lost his mind. If we go back down there or stay here, either way we're dead. Major Thomas, if I go to the engine room, can I manually override the reserve and start the thrusters?"*

"Yes, sir. That will expedite the process. Engines will be engaged only at two-thirds capacity though. I estimate we have an eighty-three percent probability of escaping, depending on how long the protective shields hold."

"Does anyone else have a better idea? If not, I'm heading down to the engine room!" Lordiah shouted before he ran out.

Apollyon and Major Thomas sat several minutes alone on the bridge in silence. Major Thomas broke the quietness. *"It must have been dreadful down there, your highness."*

"You have no concept," Apollyon replied. *"I won't go back. Do you believe we have a chance with Lordiah's strategy?"*

Major Thomas shrugged his shoulders, *"He can still shoot at us. It depends on how fast we can get the engines to full speed."*

"This is disastrous. Here I am the king and this imbecile has us cornered like a caged animal making demands? I wish we could fire back at those scums down there!" Apollyon cried out.

Major Thomas paused a moment. *"Sir, we do..."*

"What do you mean?" Apollyon asks.

"We have plasma warhead missiles on this ship."

"Well, that's our best offense. Hit them back but harder!"

"Sir, with all due respect, with the plasma warhead everything on the planet surface will be wiped out and neutralized." Major Thomas advised.

"Enough of this banter!" Apollyon barked. *"What aren't you comprehending? We are under a violent attack! They fired upon a royal vessel. That is treason! Punishment for treason is death. How many missiles are needed to decimate them?"*

Major Thomas' face softened, speaking somberly, wishing he hadn't said anything, *"One plasma missile would do the job, sir, if you're serious."*

Apollyon sat up proud, folding his arms, *"Then let's launch five. Serious is an understatement."*

Major Thomas stood; his face darkened looking at him. *"Are you sure, your highness? Five will extinguish the entire planet. Should we consult with Lordiah first?"*

Apollyon slammed both his fists down. *"I am your king, not Lordiah. Are you disobeying a direct order from your Ruler?"*

Major Thomas looked down, *"No sir. Sorry, your highness."*

"Good. Launch the missiles. Now!"

"Yes, sir." Major Thomas replied.

He walked over to his station and typed on the monitor. A number pad appeared on his screens. He looked over at Apollyon.

Apollyon looked back, *"Now, Major."*

Major Thomas punched in the sequence.

"Warheads are arming, sir."

The main engines started to hum, and the room vibrated. Lordiah smiled. He double-checked the panel screen.

"Okay, you're started and at fifty-six percent power and climbing fast," Lordiah said to the panel.

He took several steps towards the exit door when a loud clack and slam sound rang out. His brow wrinkled, and he craned his neck to hear better. Walking back, he checked the screen. It now showed seventy-four percent power.

The clank and slam sound resonated again. Alarm crossed his face. He walked around the corner to investigate. He froze. His eyes widened.

"No, no, no, no!" he screamed.

Lordiah sprinted out of the engine room and down the corridors.

The two sliding doors opened and Lordiah ran in, breathing hard, out of breath. Major Thomas was sitting at his station. Apollyon and the crew were watching the main screen as five warheads entered the frame.

"What have you done?" Lordiah shouted, eyes wide. He stared at the screen.

"What needed to be done," Apollyon responded without taking his eyes off of the screen.

"But you're going to kill them all!"

Before he can say anything else, the missiles veer off from one another and strike Mars in five separate locations. A destructive current swim across the surface in a circular pattern from the five large mushroom cloud forming on the planet's surface. The room fell silent.

"Hey, it was them or us. I chose us. Besides, they were criminals, including General Aries," Apollyon retorted.

Lordiah's legs buckled. He sat down on the floor in the center of the room. With both hands in a fist pulling his hair, he stared silently at the screen and watched the cloud grow larger.

The smoke started to clear except for the mushroom clouds that were still rising. The once green planet was now a dull reddish orb hanging in space.

Lordiah's face turned pale. He slowly muttered. *"How could you be so cold? There were over two hundred people down there. Some our friends. They had families."*

The room remained silent. Lordiah just stared at the screen. After a few minutes, Major Thomas spoke, *"What now?"*

"We don't have much of a choice," Lordiah muttered.

"What do you mean?" Apollyon asked.

"Looks like you didn't think this through, did you? We still have a few billion people counting on us to finish our mission, minus two-thirds of our workforce you just slaughtered. He answered. We have only one other option or we will kill two planets... Head to Earth."

Part 2:
EARTH

CHAPTER 31:
MOON PEOPLE:
PLANET EARTH

The Moon: Present time

"I haven't told these stories for hundreds of years." Lordiah grinned, and his eyes started to glisten. *"For a very long time I have been dreaming for this day to happen with you."*

There is silence, and then there is the quiet of being inside the moon. And right now, the room was so silent, it worried Luna that Lordiah would hear how fast her heart was beating.

A tear welled up in her eyes. She looked away and quickly wiped it. *"I've hated you most of my life for disappearing."*

Lordiah pressed his lips together and looked down at his feet, his voice hollowed. *"I understand, and I wish I knew how to fix things."*

With a furtive glance to make sure he wasn't watching; she wiped another tear forming. *"You can keep telling me stories."*

He looked up and exhaled deep. *"I wish I had my journals. I kept such thorough records of my journeys here for thousands of years. So much time has passed and I'm not doing justice telling you these stories without them."*

She bit her lip as if she wanted to say something, but instead changed her mind. She got off the sofa and strolled around behind it. Her eyebrows raised, and she grinned.

"So, let's get this straight. Did you get me on a death star that destroys planets? Great. Are you going to tell me you're Darth Vader next?"

Lordiah looked down and swirled his brandy. *"That's funny. This Death Star only obliterates asteroids now to protect Earth."*

"Well thanks, I feel safer." She walked over to the bed and grabbed one of the pillows. She hugged it to her chest and walked back to the couch. *"I take it no one survived the missile party your bro threw for Mars?"*

"No one and nothing could have endured that. The plasma missiles wiped out everything and turned a beautiful plush paradise into a cold, dry red planet."

Luna dipped her finger into the 4-millennium year old brandy she held, stirred and then licked it. *"Well, that's pretty fucked up. How many people got fried down there?"*

"When we left Heofon, the population on board was 290. After we departed from Mars only fifty-six remained."

"Wow, that's a game changer. What happened next? You just put this ol' moon in drive and cruised across the galaxy to Earth?" She asked.

"Yes, that's exactly what we did. For eleven weeks. I was so angry at Apollyon for what he did, but billions of people from Heofon still counted on us, on me. I knew that to move forward I had to swallow those emotions. When we arrived at Earth, I was so stir crazy from being on the same ship with him I would have done anything to get off..."

CHAPTER 32:
WELCOME
TO EARTH!

"There she is. She's beautiful." Major Thomas pointed to the green and blue planet out the hexagon window of the control room.

(Lordiah Journal Entry: 02.22.23 Earth) For my entire life I have been dreaming of this moment since I studied Earth in school. Gazing out the window at this perfect round sphere with beautiful blue waters, large fertile land masses, and white fluffy clouds is a true emotional incident. The opportunity of setting my feet down on this planet is surreal to me.

Earth was absent of any moons or asteroids in its orbit, so it wasn't problematic for Major Thomas to bring the moonship to a halt in Earth's orbit and park it. Similar to Mars though, we noticed that our arrival triggered major storms and volcanic activity.

* * *

Inside the control room Lordiah paced in front of Major Thomas and his small team flying the moon. *"It's best that we send just me and Leonardo down to scout the planet first,"* he told them. They geared up and headed to the shuttle launch pad.

"There are several large land-masses to choose." Outside the shuttle Lordiah pointed out to Leonardo on the rotating sphere of a hologram of Earth in front of them. *"This area appears lush with plant life and plenty of water nearby. I say we make this our first stopover. What do you think?"*

Leonardo smiled, then stuck an arm into the hologram and giving him a thumbs-up with the other. *"Looks like a noble plan to me boss."*

Lordiah grinned back. *"Then let's load up and head down. I'm sick and tired of being crammed on this ship."*

The hanger door slid opened, and a matte-black shuttle glided out. Both were silent for the next eleven minutes as they stared at the planet they were approaching.

"What happens if this fails, Boss? You know, Earth. Then what?" Leonardo asked.

"This is it. So, we have to make it work."

Leonardo nodded. *"Then we'll do whatever it takes."*

They both got quiet again as they studied the canvas in front of them while they cruised above the terrain. *"Looks picturesque, nice and plush,"* Lordiah responded.

"Yeah, it's beautiful. These mountains, the trees, clouds in this amazing blue sky. If all those waterways are... If they are drinkable, we're in paradise," Leonardo responded.

They landed within a grass clearing surrounded by trees in full bloom and the grounds plush with thousands of assorted plants.

"Leonardo, no running around naked just yet. We need to analyze the air and examine the surroundings for any unforeseen environmental or organic dangers. And..." Lordiah froze, then pointed.

A bird landed on the craft. Lordiah grabbed his journal. *"Okay, there are animals that can take flight with ease."*

Leonardo gripped his shoulder, *"Hey, there's more, look."* A flock with hundreds of birds flew over.

"And over there! That one, and another type of animal, in the trees." Leonardo pointed to a curious monkey getting a closer look at what just landed in their terrain.

"Air is breathable. Almost perfect. Temperature is tolerable, on the warm side." Lordiah conveyed while he studied the screen. *"I get a good feeling about this planet."*

"I concur sir. Let's not waste another moment in here."

The shuttle doors opened and Lordiah and Leonardo cautiously exited the craft. The warm wind parted their hair while they looked around in awe.

Eager, they got to work collecting dirt, water, and plant specimens. Lordiah smelled each specimen before putting the samples into the purse-like packs strapped around his stomachs. Leonardo licked and tasted some of his samples.

"We're being watched." Lordiah motioned with his head. *"Those bi-pedal creatures over to your right?"*

A curious monkey seemed transfixed on them. He slowly started to ease closer.

"He's sort of charming and endearing. Do you think it's dangerous?"

Lordiah bit his lip and observed them. *"It looks like he's just curious but let's be on the cautious side. What I find thought-provoking, they look comparable to our genetic make-up."*

Leonardo reached into his waist purse and pulled out a small recording device. He snapped pictures, slowly easing closer. The monkey sat and watched him.

When Leonardo got several meters away, the monkey stood up.

Leonardo stopped, and knelt down to his height.

The monkey shook his head back and forth and let out a distinctive call, *"oooohooooohaaaaahaaaah."* He pounded on his chest with both fists several times.

Lordiah watched. *"He's trying to communicate with you. Do it back."*

Leonardo nodded. He beat his chest back, imitating the sounds the monkey made.

The monkey beat his chest several more times, then did several back flips and lets out more cries, *"Whooh ah ahh."*

Lordiah laughed.

"I think he likes me," Leonardo chuckled.

The monkey stopped, stood as tall as he could sticking his chest out, and threw something at Leonardo, hitting him squarely in the chest. The object stuck to his shirt, and then rolled off and landed at his feet.

"Aw, he gave you a gift!" Lordiah smiled.

Leonardo studied the brown stain on his shirt. His brows furrowed and then a sour look came across his face. *"Ummm... I think he just threw his excrement on me, sir!"*

Lordiah started laughing. *"Yes, I think he did. Welcome to Earth!"*

CHAPTER 33:
THE ENDLESS
BEGINNING

Earth: 7,220 years ago

(**Lordiah Journal Entry: 02.44.1 Earth**) We didn't spare any time moving onto Earth's surface. We genuinely couldn't. We need to produce as soon as possible.

The area we picked is next to a large flowing waterway that we learned is abundant with consumable food, an unpredicted benefit for us all.

The climate is warmer than what we are used to but acceptable. The terrestrial area is lush with plants and trees, including a wealth of appetizing fruits and vegetation. This place seems very suitable for us.

Having our crew reduced in size, there is no shortage of work to do. Mining and building a pyramid started immediately. Fortunate for us, Major Thomas and Leonardo completed the second proton-electron laser during our trek to Earth. Leonardo is in charge of getting the mine staff up and producing with as many people that we can spare, which isn't many.

The remaining 38 staff, including Major Thomas, are tasked to build the pyramid.

Apollyon reverted back to his arrogant ways and his contribution was zero. Anana grew more pregnant each day. It is best off he isn't around or involved.

My core focus now is to bioengineer and grow a new labor force and rebuild the manpower needed to continue with our mission.

*   *   *

CHAPTER 34:
"E-DEN"

The air was perfumed with a sweet thickness where a kaleidoscope of vegetation flowered and trees bearing fruit blanketed the ground. Lordiah and Leilana were strolling hand in hand, stopping occasionally, sampling an unfamiliar fruit or smelling a blossom while pocketing samples.

"I love being around all the plant life Earth offers," Lordiah told her.

Leilana stopped Lordiah, faced him and grabbed his other hand. She smiled as her eyes beamed. *"This is my favorite area right here. I can't help but drink this all in. It's full of life, the colors, and the best bouquets."* She leaned forward and kissed him gently. *"I think if you are going to grow clone workhands you should put your new lab-den right here where life thrives."*

Lordiah smiled and nodded. He kissed her back. *"I coincide, Lei-Love. This will be the textbook place for it. I already have a title conceived for it too. Since it's our very first 'Earth Den' I would like to label it"* *"E-Den?"*

Leilana laughed, *"You're a strange one, but I love it. E-Den is perfect."*

(Lordiah Journal Entry: 02.81.0 Earth) I'm nervous and tremendously excited about E-Den and this project. I have studied genome and telomere manipulation on Heofon, but I have never created, produced, or cloned anything on a scale this large before. Time is of the essence and we must get back on track, people's lives are counting on us. We have no choice but to start immediately.

Leilana works tirelessly getting things organized. With her medical background, she is the perfect partner to assist me in growing these laborers.

On instructions from the Royal Scientific Board, I am ordered to record every detail I do when cloning and bioengineering a new species. I have already started journaling everything since we left Heofon.

*   *   *

Lordiah closed the journal he had been writing in revealing the green leather cover. He pulled out a thermal laser and hit a switch on the handle. The light in the room brightened as he began to burn onto the front cover his personal symbol; a 4-pointed star inside a circle, with waves between the points. The last touch, he engraved the number one below his insignia.

(Lordiah Journal Entry: 02.50.4 Earth) With the help of Major Thomas, we transported down all the glass incubator grow chambers and set them up in E-Den. They are formulated to cultivate the first batch of laborers. There are a total of 47, now set up and ready to produce.

*   *   *

Lordiah checked the settings on the last incubator. He stepped back, kissed his fingertips and laid them down on top of it. He closed his eyes for a few seconds, then opened them. *"Merits to you three, we are now ready,"* he told Leilana, Major Thomas and Leonardo.

"Sir, can I ask you a question?" Major Thomas asked while moving the last growing chamber under the shaded canvas roof.

"Of course, Major Thomas, you can ask me anything."

116

Major Thomas took a breath, tightened his lips, then continued, *"Whose DNA are you using?"*

Lordiah looked over at Leilana before answering, *"As a custom in science, and all of the other genetic modification experiments, the lead scientist's nucleotides have always been chosen when altering one's deoxyribonucleic acid."*

Leonardo laughed at the expression on Major Thomas's face. *"He's talking about his DNA, brother."*

Lordiah's face softened, *"Correct. So, to reply to your question, this batch will be made exclusively from my genetic information, and they will be in my image."*

Major Thomas nodded and pondered for a second. *"It's your creation, so I think that's suitable. How many are we producing?"*

Leilana stepped in, *"We have forty-seven chambers, so we are going to create forty-seven. We want all males for this first batch since we are making laborers."*

"Oh? That's more than I expected. Why not just one or two as test subjects?"

Lordiah's lips slightly tightened, *"Under standard circumstances, that would be ideal, but after Mars, we don't have that luxury. We must act and hope for the best."*

"I understand. What genetic changes did you make?"

Lordiah's eyes twinkled with pride, *"I really didn't modify a lot. I want to keep their cerebral capabilities, so I'll engineer them to be more intelligent than the Neanderthal and Cro-Magnon slave workforce previously brought to this planet."*

"Could that make them dangerous having intelligence?" Major Thomas asked.

"I will close all of their chromosomes first, then open only a few of them. This should make their personalities more docile, so we can control them."

Leilana's voice crackled with excitement, *"What Lordiah didn't mention, we can probably start working them as early as five years of age."*

Lordiah nodded, *"Since they are manufactured solely to be laborers, I will splice certain genes to stimulate maturity into adulthood faster and get them operational full time at a much younger age than our species. The side effect of this will be a shorter lifespan for them compared to ours, but we will hopefully be done with them by then."*

Leonardo put his arm around Major Thomas, *"MT, are you ready to change poop diapers and babysit a bunch of boys that all look exactly like the boss?"*

"I may not be the best babysitter, but I'll do my part if needed."

Lordiah smiled and laughed. He put his arm around Leilana, *"Yeah, Lei-Love may never want offspring with me after she sees how these turn out!"*

CHAPTER 35:
BUNS IN
THE OVEN

(Lordiah Journal Entry: 02:41:22 Earth) It's been several days since our Day 1 start date for growing the laborers. Leilana's mornings have started with nausea and vomiting. I assumed it was fatigue from the extensive hours and the strenuous work, but I was incorrect. We discovered that she's pregnant. I'm ecstatic!

The spirited banter between us is now 'thank goodness we created playmates for our child'. Leilana and I debate since both are from my genes, are they theoretically siblings?

*　*　*

(Lordiah Journal Entry: 02:42:12 Earth) Apollyon and Anana gave birth to their first child. It was a very tough delivery. According to Leilana it almost killed Anana but eleven hours of labor, she pulled the breached baby boy out. They named him Zetus.

*　*　*

Six months have passed. Lordiah and Leilana opened the incubators one by one and the E-Den babies breathed their first lungful of fresh air. Not all survived the process, but thirty-eight healthy specimens became Earthlings that day.

Lordiah, Leilana and Leonardo were silent, looking down at the babies that died. Lordiah opens his hand and releases the dirt he was holding in his fist. *"We must embrace this. It's just a part of the natural selection process. Nature disposes of the weak,"* Lordiah recited when they buried the last infant near the edge of E-den.

(Lordiah Journal Entry: 02:35:10 Earth) Leilana is getting into the last weeks of her pregnancy. She is growing larger with the child every day.

*   *   *

"I find it so endearing there are so many identical baby Lordiah's." Leilana picked up a baby and held him close to her bosom and rocked him. *"What shall we name these little bumpkins?"*

"I already created a solution for that," Lordiah answered.

"Solution? Is that what you call it? You're so scientific, love! These are babies!" Leilana stated.

"Lei, we have to maintain a clear perspective here and remember their function. Our child will be a separate situation. I'm having a tough time intellectualizing this too, but it's for the best."

"I completely understand." Leilana grabbed his arm and laid her head on his shoulder as they both looked at the baby on her chest. *"But it's rough with them being so cute and looking like a miniature you."*

She leaned forward and put the baby back in his crib. *"So, are you going to name them or just give them a number?"*

Lordiah smiled, *"Both, actually... thirty-eight different nomenclature to infants that look identical could get complicated. Since this is our very first design that phenotypically resembles us, I thought to title them all Adam as their forename from the acronym 'Advance Design Anthropomorphic Male, A, D, A, M. Then a number as a surname, one thru thirty-eight to individualize them."*

Lordiah looked for her reaction. *"Does that work for you?"*

She leaned in and kissed him. *"Truthfully, I barely understood a word you just said, but Adam sounds like a lovely name. It's perfect. But… if we make any girls in the next batch, I get to name them. Deal?"*

Lordiah laughed, *"Deal."*

CHAPTER 36:
MORE BEDTIME
STORIES

Moonship: Present time

"Damn, Dude. Thirty-eight Adams? For real?" Luna interrupted. *"That's a tad conflicting to what the nuns taught us."*

"Yeah... I watched the truth get distorted over and over throughout the years." Lordiah raised his right hand and placed his left over his heart. *"As I am a witness and sit comfortably before you on this lovely couch, thirty-eight Adams existed. Think about it. It would be impractical to believe that only one Adam and one Eve could actually generate Earth's entire population. The next generation would have to be incest with siblings reproducing. And... Biblical history states they only had boys."*

"Amen, dude, for real. I so wish you had proof. Oh, the fun it would be to prove that they lied to us all these years." Luna's lips tightened. *"That is if what you're telling me isn't bullshit."*

Lordiah scooted to the edge of the couch and leaned forward, *"I realize what I'm sharing with you is difficult to perceive, but I have no incentive to lie to you. And... I do have proof, or I did. In my journals. There's a thing in your world called photography.*

Well, we had that too back then. I have photos, or had," Lordiah said, shaking his head. *"Would you like me to stop or keep going?"*

"I just heard a wacky story about clones and that my daddy may have created mankind. I can't help but drink this all in. Best bedtime stories ever! Plus, I think you owe me a few more."

Lordiah smiled. *"As you wish..."*

CHAPTER 37:
ADAM GIVES
A BONE

Earth: Around 7220 years ago

It has now been over a year since the Heofon travelers arrived on Earth. The mining team had struck several rich veins of gold, a pyramid was now completed, and E-Den's once plush décor of a shady garden where a kaleidoscope of flowers, trees, and other plants was now strewn with metal clotheslines draped with over a hundred cloth diapers drying daily.

Together with the help of Leilana, Lordiah kept thorough records of every Adam detail. If there was a rash, a bug bite, or if one of them got constipated, he was right there recording the data.

(Lordiah Journal Entry: 02.04.23 Earth) With all the infants looking identical, it was hard to keep track of which Adam it was, so I implemented a system of writing their ID number on the right shoulder with a black marker.

With the river close, to uphold the ultimate hygiene health of our crop, bathing each Adam was part of our daily routine.

We were going through markers rapidly having to rewrite their numbers every few days. With a finite supply, I decided to permanently label each Adam.

Today, we branded each Adam with a black tattoo of their number on the right shoulder.

*　　*　　*

Lordiah fastened wet diapers to the cloth lines with a baby Adam strapped to his chest, trying not to dribble water drops on him. A whistle broke the silence. He stopped and looked around.

The whistle sounded again. *"Boss, over here. Got something to show you,"* Leonard yelled as he stepped out of the small lab he assembled in E-Den.

Lordiah marched over carrying the baby. He pushed the wood door open to his lab and walked in. Leonardo was at a table shaking a vial in his left hand, then held it up to the light. Behind Leonardo was a bird in a cage, and a live rat in a smaller one. On the table were several animal corpses on a tray with their chest splayed opened for dissection. On the other side of the table were notebooks and loose pages scattered with diagrams and writings on them.

"The river...There's gold in it. Look." Leonardo pitched the vial to him.

He snagged it out of the air and held it up. *"That looks like gold."*

"Yes, sir." Leonardo pointed to the pile of papers on the table. *"I'm drawing up some apparatus designs to help us extract it out of the rivers."*

"That's tremendous. Great discovery Leo." He looked at the corpses flayed out on the dissection tray in front of him. *"How are your animal analyses going?"*

"Speaking of tremendous, I put together a report for you. Don't worry, I took a page from you keeping logs and wrote down every detail in those notebooks over there. But in preview... I'm fascinated that a lot of the species on this planet have similar organs and endocrine functions similar to ours. Intriguing, right?"

Lordiah's brows raised as he leaned forward to get a closer look at the raccoon opened up in front of him. He nodded.

"I'm also extracting DNA of each species I catch, a male and female, making a file on each. I have thirty-eight separate specimens to take back so far when we return to Heofon."

"That's great, Leo." Lordiah's nose wrinkled, and he looked down at the Adam baby strapped to his chest. *"I need to go change this little boy. I'll be back, I want to hear everything."*

(Lordiah Journal Entry: 02.06.21 Earth) Leilana gave birth to our first child. I am the honored father of a healthy, beautiful baby boy. We proudly named our son Ramar, after our father, King Ramar Osilu.

Earth became an instant nursery with the 38 Adams, plus Ramar and Zetus. Leilana and I are spending all of our waking and sleeping hours at E-Den taking care of the project.

Leilana is breast feeding Ramar, so he comes with us to E-Den each day and joins the Adams in their daily activities. To make things difficult, Ramar looks exactly like them. Sometimes, we aren't sure which child is Ramar, so we have to check for a navel. Our son is the only child in the group that has one since he wasn't grown.

Apollyon refused to let Zetus coexist alongside any of the Adams. Ramar was his only other child interaction. He made it very clear that royalty should only associate with their kind. Unfortunately, it is Zetus who suffers by having very little contact with other kids.

There is still no word from Heofon and King Osilu since the last transmission in the bunker. Even though we have been away for 1.91 years, I have calculated that on Heofon only a few hours have passed since our last transmission.

We haven't communicated the Mars debacle to him yet, that General Aries is dead, and several hundred of his citizens.

* * *

The sun was setting, and the blue sky transitioned into pink. Lordiah summoned Leonardo and Leilana to E-Den. When they arrived, he signaled for each of them to pick up a baby Adam and hold before they started their meeting.

Lordiah burped the baby he was holding, then put him back and grabbed another. *"I have been doing some calculations. In 5.6 years, the Adams will be 6.5 years old. We can start using them to perform a majority of the labor in the mines at a modified capacity. In another 4.7 years, they should be running full scope."*

He put the baby down and replaced it with another. *"With this being entered into a time chart, along with the rate we are extracting gold, it would take us three-hundred-forty-four years to get half the amount of gold we need. So, it's obvious that we need to grow more workers, and right now."*

Leilana put her baby down, removed his diaper and started to wipe the mess he made off of him. *"I thought we didn't have the materials or supplies to make more."*

"We don't," Lordiah informed them. *"It's conservatively safe to say we have enough material for only one more batch."*

"I can see your brain wheels spinning, boss. Whatchathinkin?" Leonardo asked as he bounced Adam 29 on his knee.

Lordiah's brows raised and he smiled, *"My thoughts... grow an entire batch of females next. When they hit puberty, the males and females can reproduce naturally."*

Leonardo shook his head. *"Chief, don't we have to match the exact same genome sequence for the ladies as the Adams? Won't the fetus self-abort if not?"*

Lordiah smiled and pointed his finger at him. *"That's a valid postulate, Leonardo, and a correct one. Instead of making a new batch in the lab, and hoping for the exact matching chromosomal duplication, what if we could extract the nucleotides from one of the Adams and use it?"*

"In theory, that sounds simple and easy, but we deal in reality here." Leonardo's brows creased.

"What if we extract a few inches of bone from one of the Adams? With bone, it can store forever, and have millions of DNA strands to work with."

"And we just lock the XX female sex chromosome, like we did with the XY for the Adams?" Leilana asks.

Lordiah pointed at her. *"Precisely!"*

"Seems like making a female will be significantly easier than making males!" Leilana laughed.

Lordiah smiled. "Easier to raise and train them too."

"Right," Leilana said looking away.

Lordiah's lips tightened and he exhaled. "I'm thinking of using Adam 11. He seems to be a great specimen. He's the most active and strongest.

I don't want to remove any digits or structural bone. So, my thoughts, remove one of his lower floating ribs, which will be simple and won't hinder any of his abilities to work after he heals."

"When do you want to start this, boss? Leonardo asked.

"I would like to start now. Agreed?"

Leilana looked at Leonardo and shrugged. "Yeah, sure."

Leonardo grinned. "You know you can count me in!" He turned Adam 29 around on his lap to face him. "Good thing you're not Adam 11, because that's going to hurt."

Lordiah nodded. "Leilana, can you put that one down and go grab Adam 11?"

CHAPTER 38:
THE NEW GIRLS
IN TOWN

Several yards away from the Adam nursery, the incubators opened, and the batch grown from Adam 11's rib turned out forty-seven healthy females.

"Love, I'm so excited for you." Leilana grabbed his hand and held it to her face. *"If this had transpired on Heofon, creating the Adams and these female babies, you would with no doubt be honored with the Royal Society Scientific medal."* She leaned forward and kissed him.

Leonardo nodded. *"I concur with that statement, sir, but I'm not going to kiss you."*

"Well, thank you both," Lordiah bowed to them with a proud smile. *"And I will keep my word, Love, and let you name this female batch."*

"I won't get all fancy pants like you and acronym name them. I want to call the girls Eve," Leilana told them. *"Eve means 'source of life,' which these girls will be all of that, and more. Without these girls, we wouldn't be able to grow and continue Lordiah's creation."*

"Then Eve they shall be. And a numbering system?" Lordiah shrugged and smiled.

"Yes, you win, Love. I have to admit your numbering system seems to work out well for the boys."

(Lordiah Journal Entry: 02.33.03 Earth) Leilana is correct. It is significantly easier to educate and train females than the group of boys. The girls are intellectually quicker to focus and simpler to train.

With the boys being older and stronger, the Adams are now being groomed for their labor-intensive obligations. The Eves coexisted close behind and are being trained for domestic occupations and tending to the always-expanding E-Den garden.

(Lordiah Journal Entry: 02.34.11 Earth) The Adams started working the mines at age six. Now, at age eleven they labor full time and have surpassed the output of our original crew.

The cloned laborers intelligence appeared to be on the same level as Ramar and Zetus. They learned to be fluent in our Heofon language at the equivalent frequency as our children. The boys appeared more subdued and submissive in personality, corroborating that I had programmed their genes correct. They also appeared to develop and reach puberty much faster because I shortened their chromosomal telomeres. The purpose, to expedite the time from infancy to maturity. I am proud to state for the record it was a success!

We have now exponentially increased our gold output by over 200 percent.

CHAPTER 39:
GROUND RULES

The Moon: Present time

Luna gave him a weird look and threw one of the smaller pillows at Lordiah. *"You made those boys full-time slaves by age eleven? That's messed up."*

Lordiah sat up. *"Depends on how you view it. The Eves were even younger."* He threw the pillow back at her. *"Look, they didn't know any other way of life. The Adams and Eves were happy though and enjoyed their lives."*

"Well, I'm glad you didn't grow me," she snickered. *"Were you cool with it all?"*

Lordiah exhaled and looked away. *"We grew them for one specific purpose, Luna, to work. With them, we accomplished so much. We let them rest every seventh day, if that makes you happy."*

"Oh wow, how kind of you." Luna leaned in and grabbed some olives on the table in front of her. She inserted them on her fingertips and started to eat them off one at a time. *"Did they all work the mines, including the gals?"*

"We separated them into several job categories. The majority of the Adams did. A smaller group of boys worked at building the pyramids, housing structures, and... a royal palace demanded by Apollyon. His royal housing being built first, of course."

"Ol' Uncle A Hole. The true wiener tip." She put her hands up. *"What about the chicklets?"*

"The Eves?" Lordiah leaned forward and grabbed an olive and popped it into his mouth. *"Some of the girls worked the mines, but most of them tended the gardens at E-Den and prepared the meals. I put a few of the Eves into the employment and servitude of King Apollyon and family."*

"Poor girls." She grabbed one of the larger pillows, wiped the olive juice from her fingers on it then hugged it to her chest. *"Amazing how you manipulated them to work their asses off. That sure wouldn't work these days."*

Lordiah frowned and eyed the pillow where she cleaned her hands. He looked up, *"True. But we were their everything. Their creator, teachers, providers, medical, you name it. They only wanted to serve and make us happy. Knowing that the Adams and Eves were genetically altered to be stronger than us, we had to structure some very strict ground rules and be the lawgiver at a very early age. They were given simple guidelines, and always enforced through fear and strict punishment, then rewarded them when they followed the rules."*

"The same for raising a dog. Just sayin."

"I'm sorry you feel that way."

Luna giggled, *"Hey, I get it. You had a science project to do. Must have been a hormonal mess when those clones all hit puberty the same day. What kind of strict ground rules did you have to throw down then?"*

CHAPTER 40:
HISTORY'S FIRST
SEX ED CLASS

Earth: Around 7220 years ago – Forty-Seven months Later...

The latter-day sky was an eggshell blue, and the evening temperatures were still warm from the sun baking down all day long. Lordiah summoned Leilana, Major Thomas and a shirtless Leonardo to a rendezvous outside of the Large Pyramid. *"Let's walk for this meeting,"* Lordiah suggested to the group when they arrived.

"Seventeen full planet revolutions around the sun have transpired since the day we set foot on this planet."

They walked around to the back portion of the Pyramid. Lordiah turned his back to the pyramid and leaned against it. He pointed outward. *"Look at that. The genesis of a city is emerging. Having two pyramids now erected, we have more than enough power to run our operations. It is now imperative that we expand to the next stage."*

"I motion that we move out of the small pyramid and into the large one for starters," Leonardo interjects.

Lordiah and Leilana looked at each other. Leonardo looked at them, raised an eyebrow, and frowned. *"What?"*

"Apollyon and his family will take control of the Larger Pyramid. He demands that he, his family and their servants make it his palace."

Leonardo rolled his eyes, *"Noted."*

They continued to stroll along the dirt path until they stopped on the outer edge of E-Den. In the center, a rock and wooden lodge stood which housed the Adams and Eves. It functioned as one large room filled with bunk beds where they lived, cooked, ate and slept.

"The workers are self-sufficient thanks to you three for being great educators."

Lordiah put his arm around Leilana, *"The main purpose of this talk about is our next expansion. I did an inventory of all the gold mined so far. We have almost 47,000 ounces in our stockpile. I estimate 3.8 times more is needed for just the first tier layered into our Heofon skies. We'll need another coating after that."*

"Okay, then what is the plan, boss?" Leonardo asked.

Leilana spoke up, *"It's obvious, isn't it? It's time to expedite things and produce more workers. Since we no longer have the materials to grow them, we need to start the natural reproduction process with the Adams and Eves. They're old enough now. The true test though... Can they reproduce?"*

(Lordiah Journal Entry: 02.08.11 Earth) Can they reproduce? Another scientific project will have to take place more natural. On this day, after their work shift, Leilana, Leonardo and I have gathered all the Adam and Eves for a classroom session. The topic: Sex Education.

This is something that has never been mentioned, discussed, nor present in their environment. Their hormones are unquestionably existent, but they are naïve on what to do with them.

The Adams and Eves were perfect little angels when they strolled into their lodge where we awaited them. They strolled in one at a time, sit down, and smiled content at Leilana and I in the front of the room. Leonardo chose to be in the back, and I quote him 'to watch the show.'

Leilana and Leonardo have elected me to take lead as the instructor for the sex education lessons. Leilana soon moved from the front of the room and sat amongst the Adams and Eves. And to quote her 'to watch the show too.

I never thought in my career that I would have to teach seventy-four teenagers how to have sex.

*   *   *

Behind Lordiah were several hand drawings on large sheets of paper pinned to the wall. Lordiah blushed. *"Hi everyone, thanks for being here."* Lordiah finally looked up at the room full of adolescents that looked exactly like him, even more now they were in their teens. They beamed and smiled looking back at him.

He turned and looked to Leilana for encouragement. She waved and smiled back at him shrugging her shoulders. *"Right."* Lordiah turned to the drawings behind him. *"This is a penis. Each of you Adams have one and use it to excrete excess fluids out of your body known as urination, correct?"*

The students look around at each for confirmation, nodding their heads, and mumbling, *"Yes, sir."*

He points at the other chart, *"and this is a vagina. Each of you Eves have one, and you also use your vagina to excrete excess fluids out of your body. True?"*

The Adams and Eves looked around for an acknowledgement from each other and then they all smiled and nodded in agreement.

"Well, today, I'm going to tell you that there is another purpose for them. And that's to make babies."

They looked at each other confused. Then they gazed back up at Lordiah.

"Yes, you probably don't know what babies are, do you? That's because you haven't seen any. Well, we created you, and now it's your turn to create more like you. But you need each other to do it, and you will use your penis and vaginas to do it."

Leonardo's face had turned red in the back of the room, trying to contain his laughter but was failing. Lordiah looked at Leilana for support but she was doing the same.

Lordiah face turned red now too. He continued, *"So how you make babies is that an Adam and an Eve get together."* Lordiah turned back to the chart of the penis and points, *"Adam will use his penis."* Lordiah moved over to the chart of the vagina and pointed, *"and very nice and gently put it in here."*

The Adams and Eves looked at each other, shocked and expressionless. Leonardo is now laughing so hard he started to snort and had to walk away. Leilana covered her reddened face trying to conceal her amusement. Each Adam and Eve looked at Lordiah, still listening intensely.

Lordiah looked over at Leilana. *"I guess we should get them started now, right?"*

Leilana looked back at Lordiah smiling and shrugging her shoulders.

"Okay, let's have all the Adams stand up and line up against the wall over there, and all the Eves line up on the wall across from them."

The Adams and Eves stood and moved across the room.

"Starting with Adam 1, pick an Eve that you get along with the best. Go ahead, pick whoever you talk with the most."

Adam 1 pointed, *"I speak a lot with Eve 10."*

"That's great. Eve 10 and Adam 1, you both grab hands and go stand by the door," Lordiah instructed them.

"Adam 2, you choose the Eve you speak with the most."

Adam 2 chose Eve 9, then Adam 3 chose next until all the Adams picked a mate. Being that there were more Eves than Adams, Lordiah chose some of the stronger Adams to pair up with more than one Eve.

"So, here's the plan," Lordiah tells them. *"Adams one through ten, go out into the E-Den garden and find a private area away from the others. Once there, you both need to disrobe and do what I just told you. When they come back, Adams Eleven through twenty and their Eve counterparts are next."*

They all looked at him. Lordiah picked up his hands and waved them at him, *"Go on, shoo, get moving."*

The first set of Adam and Eves, holding hands walked out into the brush.

Lordiah shrugged, *"I guess all we can do is wait and see if any magic happens."*

CHAPTER 41:

THE

WEDDING

155 days later...

The workers returned to their E-Den lodge dirty and exhausted after their eleven-hour shift. The sound of the thrusters slowing the aircraft to land were Lordiah's and Leilana's cue. She grabbed her black medical bag and they exited the small pyramid making their way over to them.

"I'm confident that I'm seeing some baby bumps," Lordiah told her. *"Am I accurate?"*

Leilana pulled a round metallic instrument out. She plugged the white cord hanging from it in her ear and placed the instrument on Eve 38's stomach.

"I'm picking up a second heartbeat, so yes, you are correct. Congratulations, you're going to be a grandpa."

Lordiah smiled. *"Procreation Earth is a victory."*

"You're a good teacher, Love. Not only do I see baby bumps but also a lot of mood changes around here."

(Lordiah Journal Entry: 02.40.23 Earth) The Adams and Eves treasured their new activity... Sex! It became an open and constant act.

They were copulating everywhere - in the mines, on the shuttle trips to work, during group dinners, all over the dwelling!

So, I came up with a proposal to resolve their constant display of breeding.

*   *   *

Off the northern side of the pyramid, Lordiah entered Leonardo's laboratory. He moved a few trays of dissected animals and cleared an area on his worktable. He laid a scroll down and rolled it open on the table in front of Leonardo. *"Even the animals in the wild go off to reproduce in private. We need to write some guidelines and make it law."*

Leonardo grabbed a marker and tossed it to him. *"You're the one that taught them to hump, so go easy on the horny youngsters. What's the big deal? That's part of their job description now."*

Lordiah walked over to the window. Outside by the river, he observed an Adam and two Eves having a threesome. *"I would like some moral boundaries set."*

Leonardo looked over his shoulder, out the window, and saw the group sex ensemble. He smiled and laughed. *"So, you're going to go all old fashioned on them now, boss?"*

"No, but it's smart to set up some new systems because each couple will be responsible for raising their offspring."

Outside, Adam stood up, enamored by his erection. He jumped up and down and twisted his hips making his upright penis dance by having it slap against his hips and waist, doing a show for both of the Eves. They pointed at his penis and laughed hysterical.

Lordiah turned red, and opened the window, *"Adam! You stop that right now! I never want to see you do that again."*

Adam stopped his dance and looked confused at Lordiah.

"Go! Get dressed and...Do whatever!"

The Eves got up. Adam, still naked and erect, grabbed each Eve by the hand and walked away.

"Oh, my gosh. I see what's going on here." Leonardo laughed out loud and put his arm around Lordiah, shaking him. *"They are molds of you. You don't want us to see their hard sex tool, because it's the same as seeing yours."*

Lordiah's face reddened even more, and he pushed out of Leonardo's grasp. He moved toward the door. *"You may find it funny, but I don't. I propose we have them marry and create vows for each pair or trio."*

Lordiah opened the door and exited.

Leonardo walked over, watching him walk away. *"If it's any comfort, if you're toting what the Adam's are packing, you have nothing to be embarrassed about."*

(Lordiah Journal Entry: 02.40.32 Earth) And thus, the very first weddings were performed on Earth... We made it a special occasion. I conveyed to the group that it was their reward for being obedient.

Leilana and Leonardo unanimously elected me to perform the 38 simultaneous nuptials. Afterward, we had a grand feast.

Stated below are the latest rules administered for their marriage vows that I wrote this day, on Earth:

Thou shall be loving, faithful, giving warmth
and shelter to each other at all times, til death do you part.

Thou shall be equally loving, faithful,
giving warmth and providing shelter and safety
for each and every child born unto you, til
death do you part.

Thou shall reproduce abundantly to grow
families, but must do so in a private place
where no one can bear witness.

All children born shall be taught the rules written by the creator, and their parents will be held responsible for their children's actions if they disobey.

*   *   *

CHAPTER 42:
THE FIRST NEXT GENERATION

(Lordiah Journal Entry: 02.41.22 Earth) Forty-seven babies were born within the same week. Unfortunate for Leilana, she had to deliver every one of them, working day and night. We labeled the batch "Natural Born Laborers Gen #1".

Child rearing teachings are the next prerequisite. The Adams and Eves were never exposed to parents and are naïve to raising offspring. Leilana and I are the closest thing to parents, but our rearing method for them is similar to tending a flock.

What is fascinating and also curious, there is an equal ratio of males to females. What surprised me more, the children born varied in size, hair color, eyes, and even skin pigmentation. With the variation in phenotypes, it was significantly easier to recognize who was who this generation.

*   *   *

CHAPTER 43:
A FLOURISHING FLOCK

Eleven years later...

Each Adam and Eve family unit birthed several more children within the decade. There were 173 children populating the planet, turning E-Den into a large family community. Most of the families had built their own household dwellings in the naturally formed city.

Still, there was no communication from King Osilu and planet Heofon, but Lordiah kept the mission marching forward and on track.

(Lordiah Journal Entry: 02.41.31 Earth) Each family's parental unit did a respectable job educating their children with the *"Written Creator Words,"* as well as preparing them for their employment.

All of the first and second born from the Adam and Eve units are now working full-time. Most of them followed their parents. If they were mine workers, then their children followed in their footsteps. If their parents were builders, so were they.

With the population growth, more specialized trades were created to attend the food crops. A select few of the first-born batch coexisted as tillers of the land. Several of the second-born where chosen to be the keepers of the animals that we now raise for consumption.

Apollyon and his family still never lift a finger to do any labor or even help in the slightest way. Zetus was raised to do the same.

I make sure that he and his family are taken care of with several laborers on staff for them at all times to keep him at bay and out of the way.

*   *   *

CHAPTER 44:
CAPTIVE AUDIENCE

Moonship – Present Time

Luna got up and poured herself another glass of brandy, filling it up to the brim of her snifter. *"Would you like one?"* she asked Lordiah.

Lordiah nodded, *"Sure, why not. But a third of what you poured yourself, please."*

"I love the smell of this room. Lavender, right? That's my favorite flower," Luna said bringing him his brandy.

"Yes, Lavender. Good nose," he nodded.

She set her brandy slowly down on the table trying not to spill, and walked into the bathroom, leaving the door open. She raised her voice so Lordiah could hear her, *"Well, I have to say you have aged very well after all these years."* She walked out tying her pants. *"If I didn't know you were my papa, I would say you're pretty hot. Hotter, if you put a few tats on you, though,"* Luna chuckled. Lordiah smiled and looked away.

"How come you don't age? Is this the way it is on your planet? Or is it in the genes? In my genes?"

"We naturally live eight to ten times longer than the humans do here on Earth. As mentioned, I designed it that way.

As for the longevity that I now obtain, there's another story behind that."

Luna picked up her brandy and plopped back down on the couch, *"Cool. Please continue. I'm your captive audience, literally."*

CHAPTER 45:
THE POWER
OF GOLD

Earth: Around 7220 years ago

The sky was velvet black peppered with stars, and the glow of the moonship illuminated E-Den. In an old tattered robe, Leonardo was working alone in his lab doing inventory of the gold they excavated for the week. As Lordiah and Leilana pushed open the door it creaked.

"You wanted to see us?" Lordiah asked Leonardo.

"Yes, I do, boss and your timing is perfecto."

Leonardo licked the tip of his index finger and placed it in a plastic bag filled with gold flakes. He held his finger out. *"You ever notice a white residue dust that comes off the gold?"*

Lordiah was staring at a dissected fifty-six-pound cat with its chest splayed open laid out on the table.

"Sir?"

Leilana nudged Lordiah.

"Um, yeah, white dust, yes I have."

"I need you to track with me here boss." Leonardo took out a dry rag, *"I was doing some cleaning a few weeks ago.*

I gathered some water to wipe up. I grabbed salt water instead of fresh because it was closer."

He grabbed the towel and started to scrape off white residual substance caked on it. *"Several days ago, I wet this rag with the salty water and wiped up the gold dust with it. When it dried this white crusty residue was left behind."*

He presented a small glass container and poured out another pile of a white powder near the residue he just scraped from the dry rag. *"This here is gold powder that I swept up without any water."*

After pausing a few seconds, he turned to the shelf behind him, picked up a metal hammer and sharply hit the white powder he just poured. Nothing transpired. He hit it several more times until the pile became flat.

"Quite anti-climactic I would say, correct-o? Now watch this." Leonardo took a few steps closer to the other pile of white powder. *"Remember, this is the same gold dust, but scraped off the rag with the dried salty water."*

He lowered his safety glasses that were resting on his head. *"Probably smart to take a step back."* He raised the metal hammer and slammed it onto the pile in front of him. Sparks shot out from all sides of the mallet.

Lordiah stepped closer. His brows furrowed. *"Do that again!"*

Leonardo struck the powder. Sparks sprayed again.

"That's extraordinary." Lordiah replied. *"And that's a combination of evaporated salt water and gold dust?"*

"Yep. Correct-o. Somehow the combo of the two creates a charge. But it gets stranger." Leonardo held up his hand, palm facing towards them. *"Look."*

Lordiah and Leilana stepped closer. *"Okay, what?"*

Leonardo responded excited. *"Exactly! That's what I'm getting at."* He held up both palms and smiles. *"My hands are always cut up and calloused from working the mines, but not today."*

Leilana grabbed his hand and ran her fingers across his palms. She looked at Lordiah. *"They're baby soft too."*

Leonardo's smile grew larger upon his face, *"I was handling the dried rags the other day. My hands were covered in the sparky dust. Today, all of my calluses and cuts are gone, like they never existed."*

Lordiah took Leonardo's hand away from Leilana and procured a closer look. *"This is unexpected."*

Leonardo raised his palms upwards. *"I wanted to experiment with it more, so I took a knife and cut my hands in several spots. It hurt like wild, but all in the name of science. Then I rubbed some of the dust in the fresh cuts, and within the day, woo-la, all the cuts were healed."* Leonardo rubbed his palms together and grinned.

He looked seriously at Lordiah and Leilana, *"What if we concocted a white gold cocktail and injected it into our bloodstream for it to travel throughout the entire body? Imagine what it could do?"*

"You know we are going to have to experiment with it before we ever get to that point. You have plenty of animals in your lab. Test it on them," Lordiah firmly stated.

"I knew you were going to say that, so I already injected myself, an hour ago."

Leilana's mouth dropped, *"You did what?"*

Leonardo smiled and shrugged, *"It's too late, it's done. Saves us all a lot of stupid time and bureaucracy anyway. Now all we have to do is see what happens to me."*

CHAPTER 46:
THE FOUNTAIN
OF YOUTH

(Lordiah Journal Entry: 03.00.35 Earth) Two days have passed since Leonardo inoculated himself. We decided that he should maintain his normal daily routine during this observation period.

Was I mad at him? I should be, but I strangely found myself more intrigued and excited with what the outcome may be than what was proper etiquettes and protocol. I truly hope nothing bad happens to Leo, but I'm also extremely enthusiastic of seeing the after-effect this brings.

Leilana and I checked out a shuttle and flew to the mines where Leonardo was working. From our first observation upon arrival, he was working shirtless, carrying rocks he just blasted with the proton laser. He seems normal, actually better than normal.

*   *   *

"I know you're checking up on me."

"Yes, dear, of course we are. How are things?" Leilana asked.

"Do you mean how am I feeling?" Leonardo responded. *"I have never felt better!"* He smiled, flexed his biceps and bounced his pecs up and down playfully. *"I'm telling you boss man, I'm stronger than I've ever been.*

My strength matches any of the manufactured workers now, if not stronger. I don't fatigue, and whenever I get a cut, I heal."

Lordiah walked around him and looked him up and down.

"You're being creepy boss."

"Sorry, but you're the one who made themselves a test subject." He pulled out a tape measure and gestured Leonardo to hold out his arms. *"Strange, you actually look like you have put on a little muscle mass since we saw you last. Hold out your hand and push as hard as you can against mine."*

Leonardo pushed. Lordiah was shoved several feet before he stumbles backward to the ground.

Lordiah gets up and brushes himself off. *"That was quite impressive. What about your mental health?"*

Leonardo raved, *"I have never felt better."*

Leilana opened up her black leather bag, *"I would like to take your vitals?"*

Leonardo widened his stance and positioned his hands out horizontal. *"Sure. Examine away."*

Leilana pulled out the silver metal disc and placed it on his chest. She slowly moved it in a counterclockwise circle. *"That's interesting."* She moved her hand in a circle again. Her brows wrinkled, *"That can't be right."*

"What is it?" Lordiah asked.

"His heart rate is at 47 beats per minute, and that's after heavy physical activity. Normal should be in the 90's or 100's."

Leonardo beat his chest letting out a loud howl, *"So there you have it! My advice for you is to get on the gold juice too!"*

CHAPTER 47:
BACK TO
THE MOON

Moonship – Present time

"I was the next subject to be injected. It was magical," Lordiah told Luna. *"I felt stronger, quicker, clearer, and every ailment in my body basically healed. It wasn't long until Leilana joined us, then, of course Apollyon. We wanted the same for our kids, so Ramar and Zetus were also injected."*

"And?" Luna asked.

Lordiah got up and walked over to the bar. He grabbed a few coasters then opened a drawer and pulled out a cloth rag. *"None of us ever got sick, nor did we age."*

Luna exhaled, then her lips tightened, *"Earth is full of sickness and people dying. How come you haven't shared your secret with everyone?"*

Lordiah picked up her snifter, put a coaster under it and wiped the spilled olive juice up on the table. *"We tried it on the workers, but it didn't have the same results. In fact, it had an opposite effect. They started losing their hair, became sick, and some even died."*

"And me? What if I want to try it? I'm your child so I'm like you. Do you think it would work on me?" Luna asked.

He went back to the bar, turned on the sink and wet the towel. *"Would you want to live forever?"*

She grabbed a pillow and put it on her lap hugging it, *"If it was like the last 20 years, hell no!"*

"Something to ponder."

"Yeah, suppose so. Okay, so you kept mining for gold, building all of those pyramids with the free slaves you concocted. What were the children like?"

He returned and further wiped up the olive mess, then folded the towel and laid it down by the trays. *"After a generation or two, the offspring grew shrewder, and production dropped."* He sat back down on the couch, *"The second and third generations were lazy. Our Adams and Eves got old and started to die."* Lordiah shook his head and exhaled. *"That was sad seeing the entire first-generation pass."*

"Yeah, I bet. So, what happened? Everyone go on strike? Demand worker's comp?"

"Actually, you aren't that far off," Lordiah responded shaking his head. *"We needed to transform the incentives. We started trading the gold they collected from mining for food, clothing, and eventually charged rent so they had to work and produce. They didn't like it at first but figured out that if they wanted to eat and sleep with a roof over their heads, they better be productive."*

Luna leaned forward and grabbed the remote. *"Hey, are you able to punch a few buttons and show me on your cool three-D TV thingie?"*

He shook his head, *"Sorry, I wish. Your Uncle Apollyon didn't get his way and act out. He erased almost all of the archives."*

"Wow. What a butthole."

Lordiah continued, *"The exchange of gold was the very first money exchange system on Earth. Gold was traded for everything. No gold, no food. We started giving a day wage for the builders, tillers of the land and keepers of the animals. Gold became the money standard, and basically still is to this day."*

"But," Lordiah continued, *"we had other problems to contend with. The offspring were, how do I word this? They were beautiful in every way. Carefree, adventurous, and a lot of the time, clothing optional. The Heofon men saw the daughters of*

the manufactured workers as beautiful and enticing. They acted on their temptations and had relations with the daughters of the manufactured workers. Zetus and Ramar included."

"Ouch. Surprise, surprise. Go bro and cuz. What's wrong with a little fun, if no one gets hurt, right?"

"Luna! It just wasn't right. We were their creators. They looked up to us. Trusted us," Lordiah retorted.

"Easy Papa, just messin' with you," Luna smiled.

"Well, things work out in mysterious ways," Lordiah answered.

CHAPTER 48:

GENESIS 6:2

Earth – Around 7,130 years ago

Adam 29 and Eve 38 married. Adam 29 lived eighty-two years and begat Seeth along with ten more children.

And Seeth married Asurah, and begat Galia.

And Galia performed coitus with Zetus, Apollyon's son, and they begot something that Lordiah and Leilana were trying to figure out how to classify.

Inside the medical ward located at E-Den, Galia screamed for hours as she gave birth to a larger than normal, red-haired baby boy.

"What on Earth?" Lordiah and Leilana mouthed at the same time when they saw this newborn.

This was the first sight of red hair seen on Earth, and Heofon.

Childbirth was rough on Galia due to the enlarged head of her newborn. He was also 8.3 pounds heavier than a normal newborn and his hands and feet were twice the normal size. What baffled Lordiah and Leilana even more than the red hair was that each hand had six fingers and each foot had six toes, with green reptilian scales on the topsides and the soles of his feet.

"This is our first abnormal birth, Love," Lordiah said enthusiastically. *"Born between a Heofonly father and a bioengineered being."*

A few weeks later, another servant girl gave birth to a male child with the same gigantic characteristics, the 6 digits and the green scales. After asking the girl who the father of this red headed creature was, she confessed to Leilana that it was Zetus.

Within the month, several more of these oversized, red headed, scaly babies were birthed. All males, and all of them sired by Zetus.

After the eleventh baby, Lordiah and Leilana knew it was time for them to have a conversation with Zetus.

Even though Leilana was Apollyon's sister and a princess, Apollyon still made them set up an appointment to see him for the following day.

"He's becoming a young man. And they're just servants. He didn't do anything wrong," Apollyon, sitting on his throne stated to Lordiah and Leilana while Zetus sat next to his dad with his arms folded.

"Apollyon, my dear brother, we aren't saying anything is wrong here, but there are eleven of these grossly abnormal babies. We just want to know if there are going to be any more," Leilana paused to carefully choose her words, *"Childbirth is hard on the girls, and several have died before the baby reached full term. We just want to be prepared."*

Apollyon crossed his legs. *"Well, Lordiah, you are not going to be doing any scientific experiments on Prince Zetus, if that's what you are inquiring,"* Apollyon retorted.

Even though I would love to analyze Zetus and research the cause of this genetic phenomenon, I knew this door was now closed forever. Lordiah thought to himself. *"No sir, we just want to see if there are others out there. We don't want to lose any more workers than necessary."*

"*Zetus, you have done nothing wrong. But you will tell me if there are any other slave girls that you have sprayed your royal seed into?*" Apollyon advised his son.

Zetus looked at his father for a few seconds. "*There may be a few others, but I'm not the only one. Ramar has been humping the slave girls too!*"

CHAPTER 49:
DIPPING THE PEN IN
COMPANY INK

(Lordiah Journal Entry: 03.00.44 Earth) When we heard Ramar was copulating with the servant girls, my stomach emptied. I was shocked, upset, but mostly worried. If factual, this means he could produce a monstrous hybrid offspring like Zetus.

He has been out at the mines and not due back for a few days. Not wanting to waste a moment, Leilana and I absconded with a vacant shuttle and flew out to him straightaway.

*　*　*

Outside the mines at a table with a large umbrella shading him, Ramar was organizing next week's mining plans when the black shuttle landed.

Ramar looked up and smiled when the walkway ramp lowered to the ground and it was his mother and father that exited. He popped up and greeted them.

"Hi Mom! Dad. What special occasion brings you to the mines?"

Both Lordiah and Leilana looked at Ramar, and then back at each other.

"What? What happened?" Ramar asked.

Lordiah and Leilana looked at each other again. Both spoke at the same time, cutting each other off. They did it a second time. Finally, Lordiah held his hand up and Leilana let him speak.

"Ramar, we just had a talk about with your cousin Zetus. He informed us that your gametes may have possibly produced a zygote with one of the maid servants. Is this truth?"

Ramar brows wrinkled as he looked at him, then back at his mom.

Leilana exhaled forcibly and rolled her eyes, *"Ramar, what your dad is trying to ask, have you been screwing the staff?"*

It didn't take long for the red faced Ramar to confess to having relations with Kamila, a brunette maidservant that was assigned to their family part time.

"Kamila? She's a sweet girl, Ramar, how could you? Leilana's words shot out. "I want you to leave right now and bring this maidservant to our living quarters. Your father and I will fly back meet you there."

Ramar opened the door and slowly walked in, followed by Kamila. Leilana eyes widened and she squeezed Lordiah's arm hard when Kamila waddled in carrying her oversized belly.

An awkward silence trailed. Kamila uncomfortably looked down at her feet, but her view was blocked by her pregnant stomach.

"Kamila, you're not in trouble, but we must ask you, have you had relations with Ramar?" Leilana asked her.

Kamila nodded.

"Kamila, you're obviously with child, am I correct?"

Kamila nodded her head again, shyly. *"Yes, I, I am, My Creator."*

"Again, you are in no trouble, but we must know, is Ramar the only one that you have had relations with?"

"Mother!" Ramar objects.

Leilana words sharply shot back. *"You can leave if you don't like the question, Ramar. We need to know for certain reasons."*

"Am I going to have one of those red-haired freak babies?" Kamila asked.

"That's why we need to know whom you have had relations with, and it's very important that you tell me the truth for your own health sake and the baby's. Would you like Ramar to leave the room?" Leilana asked her.

Kamila looked over at Ramar, then shook her head. "I have only been with Ramar in that way. I'm sorry."

Leilana gave Kamila a hug, "No need to be sorry, my dear. We will need to monitor you closely. So, from now until birth you'll have to stay here with us."

Leilana turned to Ramar, "And you, my son, unlike your cousin Zetus, you are going to be responsible for your actions no matter what comes out of her!"

CHAPTER 50:

THE

GRAND CHILD

(Lordiah Journal Entry: 03.00.44 Earth) Eleven days have passed since we found out that Ramar, our son impregnated a manufactured offspring. Today Kamila's water broke. Leonardo and I unquestionably want to be present for this childbirth. With the freakish hybrid baby outbreaks (all sired by Zetus) I'm not going to lie, I'm worried and stressed. Leilana even more than me.

*   *   *

"You go wash and clean up the birthing bed in E-Den," Leilana dictated to Ramar. *"And then scrub up. You get to assist me with the birth. Now hurry!"*

Walking over to E-Den, Leonardo spoke in a lower tone to Lordiah, *"So Bossman, what are you going to do if he is, well you know?"*

"It's going to be my first grandchild. I'm going to love him. You should know that with me being a bastard myself."

"Let's be real, my friend," Leonardo gently gripped Lordiah's shoulder, *"when we return to Heofon, you're going to be*

okeydokey bringing back a red headed monster with six fingers that your son fathered by porking one of your creatures?"

"Thanks Leonardo, for stating it so elegantly."

"Well? You know you couldn't bring it back as your grandchild."

Lordiah shook his head. *"Leo, I'm just hoping for a healthy baby right now. If it's not, then we will figure it out."*

When they arrived, Leilana and Ramar were aiding a screaming Kamila that was sprawled out, legs spread open wide on top of the birthing table. Lordiah and Leonardo danced around trying to get a better look at what was coming out, but their view was blocked by Leilana and Ramar.

"Push," Leilana gently said to Kamila as she was stationed between her opened legs. *"You're doing great."*

Between screams, Kamila pushed. Within a few minutes a head inched out. Lordiah and Leilana smiled at each other in silent acknowledgement, thankful that the child had dark hair.

All in the room were confused and relieved at the same time when they saw that the baby boy was normal in every way. Normal in comparison to a Heofonly baby, and also the children born to the manufactured workers, with 5 digits, without freakish red hair, or gigantic characteristics.

Leilana wrapped the baby boy in a cloth blanket and handed him to Ramar. *"Here is your son Ramar. He's beautiful."*

Ramar held his son and studied him carefully. He walked over to Kamila and showed him to her. *"Look what we made. It's mind-blowing, isn't it?"*

Kamila smiled and nodded.

And thus, they named their child Enoch. Ramar and Kamila were the first from Heofon and a manufactured human to marry.

Kamila moved in with Lordiah, Leilana, and Ramar. Enoch grew up to be a sweet normal child and was loved dearly by his grandparents, Lordiah and Leilana. Ramar turned out to be a wonderful father.

Leilana and Lordiah never did figure out why Ramar's child turned out normal, and Zetus's offspring were freakishly abnormal. They were very grateful though.

CHAPTER 51:
SIZE DOES MATTER!

The eleven freakish children sired by Prince Zetus turned out to be a different story. They grew double the rate of the other children. Their heads, hands and feet remained larger than what was considered the norm.

Apollyon turned to Lordiah, Leilana and Leonardo.

"Lordiah, make them your science project, or dispose of them, I don't care. But neither my royal self nor Prince Zetus will be disgraced by them. I never want to see nor hear of this matter again."

Leonardo raised his hand, *"Ummm, I'm cool-o with the science project part."*

Lordiah tightened his lips and shook his head, *"No, Leo, I'm not going to allow you to dissect them. Hopefully we can make them useful somehow."*

(Lordiah Journal Entry: 03.00.53 Earth) When the eleven hybrid giants were at five years, five months of age, they stood to be over six feet two inches tall and weighed close to 245 pounds. They were significantly less intelligent than the other children, and for some reason quick to temper and even tantrum. I decided it was best to construct a special facility for them away from the others. A rock wall was fortified around their compound to lock them in at night.

Now at age eleven, most of them are over nine feet tall, the smallest weighed in at 470 pounds. They have the mental capacity of a four-year-old, and never develop any further.

To be somewhat beneficial and earn their way like everyone else, we trained them to work in the mines. They were decent at doing manual labor if chaperoned but not capable of doing much more.

*   *   *

This story began one evening as dark clouds swirled and a storm brewed in the skies. Thunder started to roar. The giants were already fed and locked in their compound for the night.

Nephil, the largest of the giants, grabbed his ears and was shaking his head back and forth. He curled in a ball on his knees and cried out.

Thunder cracked loud again. Nephil got up and in a rage run full throttle into the rock wall that fenced the giants in. He kept plowing into it over and over, until it weakened, and finally pushed over.

Nephil got up to his feet and looked around. Thunder roared again. Grabbing his ears, he darted back into the compound. In his rage, he grabbed a large wooden support that he knocked loose and started swinging it violently, hitting any structure he could find in his path.

The other giants watched. He stopped for a moment when he noticed his peers staring at him. One by one, they clapped their hands and jumped up and down in excitement until all of them cheered him on. Nephil continued swinging the wooden pole and proceeded to demolish their compound. The cheering from the other giants fueled Nephil. He continued over to the pummeled fence, and the 560-pound Nephil escaped the compound area.

He then meandered over to the common living area of E-Den. Nephil started tearing down walls, ripping out trees, and hurling whatever he could get his hands upon. The workers were no match for his rage and scattered in every direction to get away. His rage turned into laughter. He chased the workers, grabbing them, throwing them, dragging them along until they stopped moving. It turned into a game for Nephil.

The commotion roused the other giants. Emim wandered out of the compound and strolled over to E-Den. He clapped and jumped up and down when he witnessed Nephil grab a worker and tossed him. He joined in on the chase, catching workers and tossing them as far as he could.

Lordiah was in his living quarters when he heard the thrashing and screams. He followed the sounds.

Within seconds upon his arrival, he witnessed the destructive rage for himself. Eleven of the workers laid mangled on the ground or embedded into a wall.

"Nephil, Emim, stop!" Lordiah shouted.

They either didn't hear him or were too involved with their fun, for they continued ripping apart E-Den's living quarters.

With one hand, Nephil flipped over a wooden framed bed. Hidden under it was a young teenage female. She jumped up screaming and ran out the door. Like a dog chasing a cat, Nephil chased after the terrified, crying girl.

"Nephil, easy. What's the matter, fella?" Lordiah calmly said to the giant as he calmly put his hands up.

Nephil stopped and looked at him for a moment. He then let out a howl, beating his chest.

Okay, he stopped chasing the girl. Lordiah thought to himself relieved. *"That a boy. Come on, let's go home. I have a treat for you there."*

Nephil looked at him for a few more seconds, then reached down, grabbed a bed frame, lifted it over his head and hurled it at him. The bed flew towards Lordiah, but he managed to jump out of the way as the bed shattered against the wall behind him.

When Emim saw this, he let out a laugh, grabbed a bed and threw it at Lordiah too, barely missing him.

Worry tightened his cheeks and dented his brow, *"I need to get out of here now or I'm going to get trapped,"* Lordiah muttered to himself.

He backed out of the lodge away from the front door.

Nephil and Emim followed him out.

175

Lordiah looked over to his left, then his right, and noticed no one else was around.

Emim laughed and walked over to a boulder. He picked it up.

"Nephil, Emim, I command you to stop!"

Emim stopped, but Nephil took the boulder from him and pushed him back. He turned and heaved the rock at Lordiah, laughing.

Emim clapped and picked up another large rock, throwing it at Lordiah.

Lordiah leaped out of the way, but this time, he didn't fully clear the boulder's path. It clipped his leg, spinning him a full 360 midair until he crashed hard onto the ground.

Emim jumped up and down in victory.

Blood started to seep through Lordiah's pants below his knee. He tried to get up, but the sharp pain in his leg was too much.

Nephil smiled and picked up another boulder.

Lordiah got to his knees. Sweat started to trickle down his face. He held up both hands. He pleaded, *"Nephil please stop. I'll get you food, lots of it. Please put the stone down."*

Nephil dropped the rock.

"Good boy."

He tried to stand up again. He grimaced in pain and stumbled back down to his knees.

Emim growled, shook his head rabidly back and forth and picked up a boulder. He raised it above his head, aiming it at his target.

Lordiah lifted his hands, *"Emim please, don't."*

Emim let out a growl. His arms cocked the several hundred-pound boulder behind his head.

Oh my gosh, this is it. My poor Leilana, Ramar, will find me dead, Lordiah thought. He covered his head and curled into a ball, shaking, waiting. A tear trickled down his cheek.

WHAP!

Emim's upper torso was abruptly cut in half! His blood and guts rained all over Nephil. The rock he held above his head dropped to the ground with a thud along with his upper trunk.

Just a body from the waist down stood until it finally toppled over backward.

Lordiah looked over his right shoulder and saw Leonardo, perched behind a proton laser cannon.

WHAP! Nephil's large head exploded as Leonardo nailed it with a second blast.

"Boss, you alright?" Leonardo called out.

"Oh, thank goodness," Lordiah choked out, "I thought I was going to die."

"Not on my watch. You're bleeding. Are you hurt?"

He tried to get up again, then gave up. "My leg. I can't walk."

"Gotcha. Stay put. I mean, sorry, you kinda have to. I'll be right back." Leonardo flicked a switch on the proton laser and turned on the anti-gravity. He glided the cannon over to the giant's compound.

Several of the other giants had wandered out of the compound.

"You big dumb idiots, get your ugly asses back inside or I'll split you in half!"

The group of giants turned and slowly started to walk back into the compound.

Dontum, one of the giants in the middle of the group turned toward Leonardo and took a step.

WHAP! Leonardo hit him with a direct charge into his chest. Bone, blood and intestines splattered all over the other giants.

"Get! Just give me a reason. This is fun!"

The other giants quickly ran back into their compound.

Leilana ran to Lordiah. "Are you OK?"

He nodded. "I am now, thanks to Leonardo."

Lordiah glanced up. He saw Apollyon and Zetus standing, watching. Apollyon signaled to Zetus, and they turned and walked away.

"Here, let me help you back to our living quarters," Leilana said as put her arm around Lordiah.

Lordiah shook his head. "No, please. Go and help the others. You can look at me later."

(Lordiah Journal Entry: 03.00.53 Earth) Today, I saw my life flash before me as I thought for sure I was going to die. Stoned to death. I was just waiting for the end. What an eerie and fascinating emotion that was. Eleven of the workers perished today thru a violent death. I wonder what went through their minds before things ended. I was lucky... I only broke my leg.

CHAPTER 52:
SOLUTION TO
A GIANT PROBLEM

(Lordiah Journal Entry: 03.00.53 Earth) Several hundred manufactured workers collected to rebuild the wall to the giant's compound. For added security, Leonardo designed the new fence to hole an electric current. Two proton lasers are also parked and pointed at the compound opening with strict orders to shoot without hesitation if any of the giant's approach.

*   *   *

Leonardo tossed a cooked goat leg over the fence. They waited and watched. It took less than half a minute before they darted out and attacked the limb. The largest giant won and wondered off with the prize.

"Alright, let's test er," he told the workers, smiling as he turned on the fence.

One of the giants wondered over to the new wall. He sniffed it.

The giant's large tongue inched forward to lick the new fence. Sparks flew, and electricity blew him back several yards. He laid there unconscious.

"Oh shit... Well, that worked better than expected."

Later that day, the workers gathered outside the smaller pyramid. Lordiah, with the aid of a makeshift crutch, came out and greeted them.

Adam 29 took a knee up front, bowed his head and spoke for the group, *"Our creator, many of your children have died today. We have always feared the giants, and today our worries came true."*

Lordiah shook his head and responded, *"I hear you. Today was a horrible misfortune. I recognize you rely on us for your wellbeing, and I apologize for any vanished loved ones. Please let your worries terminate. You are moral, righteous people that have always served us well. Go home, make peace with today. We as your creators will protect you."*

The elderly Adam 29 nodded. *"Thank you, our wise Lordiah."* He turned toward the crowd. *"He has spoken. He will protect us. Go home and make peace."*

And the people turned and left. Leilana approached Lordiah to help him walk back into the Pyramid. *"And you, the man with the broken leg. What is this plan you have?"* she asked him.

"I'm not certain yet. Undeniably, we have to do something. But you want to know something strange? I can already put weight on my leg. Our healing abilities. Amazing, isn't it?"

Several hours later Leonardo, Major Thomas, Ramar, and Lordiah hauled in the giants' daily provisions, and threw it over the fence. Like animals, they attacked and devoured it.

"That's disgusting!" Major Thomas responded.

"What do we do now?" Ramar asked.

"We wait until the Dopsepine kicks in," Lordiah replied.

It took less than an hour for the drugs they layered into their food to kick in and the last of the giants to collapse.

"Let's do this!" Lordiah ordered.

Leonardo turned off the fence and opened the gate.

"Are you sure they won't wake up?" Ramar asked.

"I hope not. I put enough medication into their food to knock out an army for weeks.

Leonardo floated the anti-gravity plate over by the giants. *"How do you want to do this boss man?"*

"Just float them over and place them on the drop gate of the shuttle. That way, if they wake up, we can just open the door and they will fall out," Lordiah suggested.

Leonardo smirked, *"Bossman, you're getting naughty evil in your days. I like-o."*

Major Thomas got into the pilot's chair of the shuttle and Lordiah hobbled his way over to the co-pilot seat. Leonardo and Ramar climbed in back with the sleeping giants.

Lordiah yelled back, *"If they awake Ramar, don't hesitate to open that hatch. Is that clear?"*

"I have no problem with that order Papa! Uggggg, these guys smell horrible!" Ramar put his hand over his nose. *"I think I'm going to throw up!"*

"They're nasty farters too, so it may get worse," Leonardo added.

"Let's fly out of here then. Major Thomas. It's about a 470-mile flight."

Ramar kept his word and vomited minutes after takeoff. Forty-seven minutes later the shuttle landed in a jungle area within a rocky mountain range. The giants were still out cold.

"Let's hurry and push them out," Lordiah ordered.

The drop door opened, and several of the giants naturally rolled out. Ramar and Leonardo had to roll the remaining ones down the ramp.

"Uggg." Ramar whipped his hands on his pants. *"Why here, Papa?"*

"I selected this region because there is ample food growing here, and I'm optimistic they will discover the caves in the mountains for shelter. It's also far enough away that I'm confident we will never cross paths again."

"Why don't we just dispose of them Papa?" Ramar asked.

"You mean slaughter them?" Lordiah's brows knotted together. He looked at Ramar, and then the group. *"It's not their fault that they're the way they are. I personally need to*

take responsibility too. And... I refuse to teach my son nor allow that killing is okay. It's an old law, 'Thou shall not kill.' This solution is what's best."

Leonardo put his hand on Ramar's shoulder, *"I would love to keep just one to dissect, but your papa wouldn't allow that either."*

One of the giants started to stir.

"That's our sign to get out of here, please," Major Thomas stated.

The shuttle hovered upward, then shot back in the direction they came from, leaving behind the smelly, red headed giants.

CHAPTER 53:

NOAH

Earth – Later

Several generations passed since Ramar begot his first born, Enoch.

And Enoch grew up strong, married and begot a son naming him Methuselah.

And Methuselah became a leader of his people, and he begot Lamech.

And Lamech grew up and became a fine builder, and he begot Noah.

And Noah, now forty-seven years old, grew up and followed his father's footsteps. He married Naamah, and they begat three sons.

(Lordiah Journal Entry: 03.01.16 Earth) The population on Earth has thrived. There are over a hundred thousand workers now.

Leilana, Ramar, myself and all the Heofon travelers that injected the gold cocktail into our bloodstream have never phenotypically aged a day, while the manufactured workers grew old and died. Ramar sadly watched his wife Kamila and his son Enoch grow old and expire. He also watched his grandchildren age, become fragile and pass.

Ramar, a great, great grandfather, still can't grow a decent moustache nor beard on his youthful face.

Adam 11 and the Eve 38 have passed. They were the last living Adam and Eve. I'm preserving them to bring back to Heofon and showcase my work for my colleagues to study. Leonardo designed a glass chamber and a special preservative fluid to immerse them in. I'm placing them in the vault for safe keeping.

I have the teams mining to their fullest potential. Now that the manufactured workers have a taste for capitalism and being paid for their work, they demanded more.

Crime also became a new issue. Bandit teams have now formed. Prostitution is also on the upswing. I tried to enforce new laws, but we don't have much of a police force in place.

With the increase in crime, I have asked Leonardo to move all the gold up to the moonship at the end of each workday.

There are still countless good, righteous laborers here. I have become quite fond of Noah, my forty-seven-year-old great, great, great grandson. He is a kind, caring man, and a very good worker.

*　*　*

Inside Leonardo's windowless lab, he and Lordiah were doing inventory, which also doubled as a bank vault now. Noah and Ramar were building additional containers to put the gold in for shipping.

Ramar's nose and forehead wrinkled as he pulled his shirt over his nose covering half his face. *"Uncle Leo, how do you stand the smell in here with all of these dead animals? It's so nasty."*

Leonardo took in a deep, slow inhalation as if smelling the greatest thing ever. He then pushed a dissection tray with a racoon with its chest pinned open toward Ramar. *"Oh, young Ramar, science has its prices. You get used to it after a spell."*

Ramar jumped back away from the racoon.

Lordiah shook his head, *"You may not have the need to get used to it, son. I'm proud to say we almost have enough gold to set our course and voyage back home. I calculate only a few months more on this planet. Ramar, are you ready to see your heritage?"*

"Yeah, one hundred percent, thanks to your stories."

Leonardo chimed in, "Lordiah, still no word from King Osilu?"

"Unfortunately, no."

"What if we don't hear from him?" Ramar asked.

"If there's a problem, I'm confident it's something we can readily solve. We have the best bargaining tool in the galaxy, the gold."

"And what about the workers here. What will happen to them?" Ramar inquired.

Lordiah glanced over at Noah who had stopped working and looked over at him. "Everyone will be fine here when we leave. They're smart. And..."

A crackle sound from the walkie interrupted them. Major Thomas' voice filled the room. "Sir, do you copy? I think we have a problem."

Lordiah grabbed the walkie off its wall mount, "Go ahead, Major Thomas."

"Sir, we have a large meteor heading directly towards the moonship," Major Thomas stammered out.

"OK, can we move the ship out of the path?"

"Yes, sir, of course we can, but then the meteor will strike the Earth where the majority of our worker population is."

CHAPTER 54:

NOAH'S FIRST STORM

Lordiah threw the walkie to Leonardo. His words shot out, *"Ramar, grab a shuttle and set the course for the moon. Noah, go with Ramar. It will be good for you to see this. Quickly, let's not spare any time."*

(Lordiah Journal Entry: 03.01.25 Earth) Noah was white knuckled gripping the arm rests and also awe-stricken riding in the shuttle up to the moonship for his first time. Sometimes we just take things for granted. He jumped back each time we approached an automatic door when it opened. At first, he was afraid to enter, practically diving through the opened space.

The Control Room astonished him even more, and he stood there with his hands at his side tight making sure he didn't touch anything.

*　　*　　*

Lordiah stepped up to a station with several monitors. He swiped the middle screen right several times with his hand until he found the display he was looking for.

"Major Thomas, let's have a visual," Lordiah commanded.

The displays in front of him flickered on. The central screen showed a substantial meteor slowly spinning toward the moonship.

Lordiah's brows furrowed as he bit his upper lip, *"Damn, that's a big one."*

Ramar put his arm around Noah and helped him into the nucleus of the ship. Noah jumped once again as the entrance shut behind him. He stepped away from the doors, keeping one eye on them.

"Is it a cluster or just the one?" Lordiah asked.

"Just the one, sir. Propulsion thrusters are fully charged, and ready to transport this ship out of orbit," Major Thomas informed Lordiah.

"Noah, please take a seat and strap in. Major Thomas, are the warheads loaded and ready for launch?"

"Yes sir. Locked on target."

"Everyone, strap in. We're going to maneuver the moonship out of the trajectory." Lordiah pointed at the screen. *"Then we will fire two thermal proton warheads to intercept the meteor. The missiles won't annihilate the rock completely, but our goal is to alter its course away from us and, optimistically, Earth. Any questions?"*

The crew nodded their heads in agreement.

Lordiah's heart raced, and his palms started to sweat. *I hope this works*, he thought to himself.

"Major Thomas, it's been a while, let's put this ship in gear."

CHAPTER 55:

THE
WARNING SIGNS

Earth – The same time

The lights hanging down from the ceiling swayed back and forth as the room shook.

"What the...?" Leonardo mumbled to himself. He stood motionless and listened. Another large reverberation shook the room. A dissection plate with a pelican pinned to it flew across the room and several primate skeletons fell over. He grabbed the table this time to keep his balance as several more dissection plates sailed by. One tray hit him, dumping its contents on his arm and chest.

The room stopped shaking. He regained his stability, wiped some of the gooey contents from his shirt and then quickly proceeded to the only exit door of his lab.

A third earthquake hit. The roof couldn't take the stress any longer and a large crack ripped across the gray stone ceiling and crashed down, just missing Leonardo's pressed body up against the wall. Covered in dust, he scrambled over the rubble and escaped out the half-buried door.

Outside, Leonardo looked around. His eyes crinkled at the corners, and his mouth pressed tight. Several buildings had collapsed. People were walking around dazed, confused.

"Leonardo!" Leilana called out. She marched toward him as she helped an elderly woman walk. Blood trickled down Leilana's face.

"Leilana, you're bleeding! Are you okay?"

"I'm okay. I got cracked on the cranium getting out, but I'm fine. What happened?

"I don't know. Last I heard Lordiah was dealing with an asteroid heading this way."

"Oh no, that doesn't sound good."

"I'm sorry, but it may be worse. It was heading directly toward the moon. Lordiah and Ramar are up there. I'll return and check up on you in a sec. Glad you're safe."

Leonardo turned and looked back at his demolished lab. His heart was pounding in his chest. He took a deep breath then darted back toward his lab. He climbed over the rubble until he reached the front door. Leonardo spotted what he was looking for, the walkie in its holder mounted on one of the walls that was still standing. He maneuvered in and grabbed it.

The Earth shook and rumbled. He slammed into the wall, pushing it over, and falling with it.

"Shit-o!" Leonardo winced and screamed getting up. *"Not cool."* He gathered his balance. Still holding the walkie, he scrambled towards the entrance. He stopped at the door and quickly looked back. He gritted his teeth, took a quick breath then raced back in and grabbed the tray with the dissected pelican, and sprinted out.

Once out, he hurried to the middle of the street.

"LUNA, this is Leonardo from the Earth surface. Come in please!"

CHAPTER 56:
THE ROCK

Moonship – Same time

Lordiah sat belted into his seat. The moonship was creaking and shaking as it pulled away from the Earth.

"Major Thomas, that doesn't sound good!" Lordiah yelled.

"We are on 70 percent thrust, and barely moving. It seems as if the Earth has a grip on us, sir."

The moon engines kept thrusting. The control room vibrations continued as they slowly broke away.

"LUNA, this is Leonardo from the Earth surface, come in please!"

"This is LUNA, we copy you Leonardo," Major Thomas shouted over the noise.

"What's going on? Were we struck by the meteor?"

"Not that we know of. We are viewing the asteroid on our screen now."

Leonardo started to answer but his balance was interrupted by another quake. *"Sir, we just got hit again"*

Lordiah put his right hand up as he looked over to Major Thomas. *"Major Thomas, stop all thrusters!"*

Major Thomas gripped the control handle and pulled it back. The thrusters shut down and the control room stopped vibrating as the moon grew silent and came to a halt.

Lordiah waited a few seconds before his next command. *"Major Thomas, fire the missiles at the target, now!"*

"Yes sir!" Major Thomas quickly typed in a code and pressed the screen in front of him.*" Missiles are launched toward the target, sir."*

The entire control room watched the monitor in anticipation. The missiles appeared on the display traveling toward their target.

Lordiah grabbed Ramar's hand and squeezed, eyes focused on the screen. *"Come on, you can do it."*

Major Thomas started a countdown. *"Five, four, three, two, one!"*

The first missile made contact with the rock. Eleven seconds later the second missile exploded on target. The control room was silent as they waited for the dust to settle.

A minute passed. The debris started to slowly clear from the explosion. *"Papa?"* Ramar muttered.

Lordiah stared at the screen, *"I don't know yet, son."*

Half a minute passed in silence. Finally, enough of the view cleared and they got a clean picture. Forty-seven percent of the meteorite was still intact.

"Major Thomas!" Lordiah shouted, *"What's its trajectory?"*

"I'm sorry sir, I don't know yet."

Noah looked over at Lordiah, *"My creator, are we in danger?"*

Lordiah kept his eyes glued on the screen. *"I don't know yet, Noah."*

Another fifty-six seconds passed.

Major Thomas exhaled. *"We can all relax. The rock is passing by."*

The room let out a collective sigh of relief. Cheers, and hugs moved throughout.

"And Earth?" Lordiah asked.

"Earth is safe too."

Lordiah sat, eyes closed with both hands clasped on top of his head collecting himself.

He exhaled, *"Major Thomas, can we please hail down to Leo?"*

"Comm is open sir."

"Leonardo, are you OK?"

Leonardo's voice filled the room, *"For the moment, yes."*

"Has the shaking ceased?"

"For the moment, yes." Leonardo repeated.

"Is Leilana OK?"

"For the moment, yes."

"OK, so I think I know what happened down there." Lordiah responded. *"And unfortunately, it's probably going to happen every time we move the moonship."*

CHAPTER 57:
THE END
FOR HUMANKIND?

Earth – Hours later

In the distance, lightning licked the sky. Heavy rain poured down when Lordiah, Ramar and Noah returned to Earth. The first thing Lordiah did when he left the transport was sprint to Leilana's medical station in the small pyramid.

He ran in, grabbed her and wrapped his arms around her tight, smothering her with a huge hug. *"Thank goodness you're safe."*

"Love, what's going on? Is it bad?" she asked, still in his embrace.

"Yes, I think it is." He released his hug, then kissed her deeply.

"I have work to do love, and I could really use your help in talking me off the ledge with this on."

Lordiah, with Leilana in tow behind him returned to their living quarters. They walked over to the hologram table. Clutching the keyboard, he tapped a few keys. The Earth appeared, then the moonship circling in its orbit. He pointed to the holographic Earth.

"*So, love, earthquakes and volcanic activity struck over two thirds of the planet when we moved the moonship. The volcanoes that erupted on the ocean floors induced a rise in vaporization of water, that caused a drastic increase in precipitation.*"

"*Oh... Yeah, I definitely felt the quakes.*" She pulled her hair up and showed the swollen cut on her hairline. "*Especially the knot on my head. Scary too. But why?*"

He leaned forward to get a closer look at the wound, then leaned forward and kissed her forehead near it. He shook his head. "*My hypothesis... when the moon disembarked from orbit, it must have attached to the Earth's magnetic core. The moonship has magnetic properties in it, similar and opposite to the Earth's core.*"

"*Love, use your simple terms voice, please.*"

He tapped a few keys. On the hologram floating above the table, the moonship moved away from the Earth. Storms violently brewed, volcano's smoked and spewed, and continents started to break apart.

"*Oh my... If this is true, the north and the south poles are going to shift when we depart destroying most, if not all life on Earth. Or we do the humane thing and not move the moonship, then everyone on Heofon will die.*"

"*We really only have one right choice.*" She put her hands on his. "*Complete the mission no matter what...*"

Lordiah shut off the hologram and stared at the table with a sweaty brow and a blank stare. His guts ached like he had just been disemboweled, the contents drug on the dirt and then slammed back inside him. He shut his eyes for a second, then popped up, ran to the bathroom and vomited.

CHAPTER 58:
NOAH'S PLEA

Earth – About 7,004 years ago

Noah started the day early by preaching and praising Lordiah to the others. He raised his hand up to the sun, *"Lordiah, thou creator ascended up into thy sky, and our great maker saved all with just a command from his voice. Thou must be righteous and follow thy laws forged by our creators."*

It mostly fell on deaf ears, but he persevered with his preaching.

(Lordiah Journal Entry: 03.01.34 Earth) Our departure date is now locked and scheduled one-hundred-eighty-two days from today. It's great and also a surreal nightmare. I architected a new form of life and in the simplicity of departure, we will destroy it all. This is extremely disturbing, but have found no other option.

I'm losing sleep at night and sick to my bowels as my brain slowly churns with all the possibilities for an alternative solution. I have nothing.

*   *   *

The rising sun brightened up the room where Lordiah laid awake. It was another restless night. He quietly put on his clothes so he wouldn't wake Leilana and exited the small pyramid. He wanted to seek out Noah, who was a fifty-six-minute hike away.

When he arrived, Noah, his wife Naamah, and their three sons were already hard at work sawing, making pitch, and laying the foundation for their future home.

"Our creator has arrived," Noah announced to his family when he saw him walking up the path towards them. *"Naamah, fetch some water to wash his feet!"*

Lordiah put a hand up and shook his head, *"Noah, that's OK. I'm fine. I came up here to speak with you in private."*

"Our creator seeks to speak with me in private!" Noah announced to his family.

Noah got down on his knees and bowed his head, *"We are thankful for thy blessings you give us. Let us feed you and bathe your feet first from your journey up thy mountain."*

"That's not necessary, Noah, but thanks."

He stood, *"How can I serve thee?"*

"Why are you building a house up here, so far away from the others?"

"My creator, we will still journey each day and do our part of thy work. Please forgive me if this displeases thee. I thought it best to distance from thy evil and misconduct present in thy populated areas. We have chosen this spot where thou could farm, raise animals and keep my family safe."

Lordiah exhaled and put his hand on his shoulder, *"Noah, as you know I'm from Heofon."* Lordiah pointed to the sky. *"I have to go back to my home."*

Noah got down on his knees again, *"I have always served thee, my creator. If it's something I have done that displeases thee, please punish me."*

"No, it's not that. You are a just man and have always been devoted and honorable."

"Is it because the people have become immoral, and filled with wickedness?"

He reached his hand out to help him up. Lordiah noticed Naamah and his children watching and listening. *"Noah, let's take a walk."*

Noah turned to his family and yelled, *"Our creator wants me to walk with him."*

Down the dirt path they walked from the house. Lordiah was silent, and Noah waited patiently for his wisdom. strolling for several minutes, Lordiah stopped and faced Noah. *"Remember when we were inside the moon?*

Noah looked up at the sky.

"And we moved it?"

Noah nodded.

How can he tell him? He thought. His heart raced. He forced his voice to stay calm from the emotions he was feeling.

"When we moved the moon, it caused the Earth to shake and tremble down here."

"If you say so, then it must be so, my creator."

"When I leave, it will be much worse, many times that." Lordiah looked away. *"The ground will shake harder, fire will erupt out of the soil, and it will cause water waves taller than the pyramids. It will rain for days, flooding the planet. Many will die."*

Noah was silent.

"There's nothing I can do to stop this. But... Come with us. There's room for you, your wife and your children."

He was still silent.

"Noah?"

A tear started to well up in Noah's eyes. *"Lordiah, my creator, I have brothers, sisters, their children. I can't leave them here if they are in danger. I must help them."*

As Lordiah glanced up the pathway toward Noah's family, he watched them toiling with laughter as they worked on their new home. *"Noah, you will perish and there is nothing I can do. I can't stop the quakes, nor the floods that will happen. I'm sorry."*

Noah looked over to his family. He got down on his knees and held his hands together. A tear rolled down his cheek. *"Please, our dear creator, I beg thee, help us."*

As he looked up the path, Lordiah took a deep breath. Naama and one of the boys waved to him. His lips tightened. He placed his hands upon Noah's shoulders. *"Noah... I..."*

His bloodshot eyes looked back at him. It was the tear that dropped on Noah's prayer held hands that made Lordiah almost lose it.

"Don't worry Noah, if you stay, I will figure something out, I promise."

CHAPTER 59:
THE
GREAT DELUGE

Moonship – a few hours later

Hunched at the holograph table, Lordiah studied the situation. Leonardo was sprawled on the couch to his left, fingers dancing as he waited...

"This is literally killing me knowing we will be responsible for their deaths," Lordiah mumbled.

Leonardo shrugged, *"Not to mention your entire DNA project will be destroyed. With the pole shift thingie happening, I'm not sure there is anything we can do."*

"Show me a calculated visual, please."

Leonardo's fingers became animated on the keypad that sat in his lap. The hologram table sprang to life. A large, slowly spinning sphere appeared, and then morphed into planet Earth.

"This is Earth today. Here's the calculated prediction of what happens when the moonship leaves."

Continents started to crack and break off. Some sank while other pieces moved. Steam billowed up, and the water volume in the oceans shrank and evaporated into the atmosphere. He paused the hologram.

"This is just the beginning, bossman. All that water will need to come down eventually."

The hologram started again. The water in the atmosphere poured down, and they watched the land disappear.

"With the volcanic activity being so active for weeks, this will be continual, causing torrential downpour for what I predict to be forty-seven days and forty-seven nights drowning everything."

Studying the display, Lordiah took a breath. *"Leonardo, can you rewind right before the rains?"*

The hologram reversed. The water gathered back up in the sky and the land went back to normal.

"Can we zoom in with E-Den being the center focal point?" Lordiah asked.

"Sure thing." The planet tripled in size, and a red circle was seen glowing in the center. *"That's E-Den."*

"Thanks. Show me the flooding again," Lordiah responded, not taking his eyes off the hologram.

The atmosphere blackened as the clouds got dark, then they opened and the oceans in the sky started to empty. The shorelines shrank. The pyramids and E-Den slowly drowned and disappeared. Mountains started to sink while the water table rose, higher and higher.

"Stop right there!" Lordiah belted as he walked closer. His lips tightened and his brows wrinkled together.

"What if..." Lordiah pointed to the top of a mountain range. *"We build a boat right here? If a boat was on a mount or stilts at this elevation, it could rise with the water and float away. With enough provisions, maybe they could survive and seek land or wait it out until the water recedes. Yeah?"*

"Conceivably. If they survive the quakes." Leonardo tapped the keypad. A boat appeared in the mountainous area where Lordiah pointed earlier. The flooding on the hologram resumed. As it reached the model boat, it was lifted from the mount, and it floated away.

Lordiah pointed, *"From this view I can still see land above the water. If we tell Noah to travel northeast, he should find land."*

Leonardo shrugged his shoulders, *"This is all just calculations and predictions."*

"Well, I think it's the best plan so far. Their other choice is a violent death, so what is there to lose?"

CHAPTER 60:
NOAH'S ARK

Earth – The next day

The morning sun began to peak over the mountain top. Noah and his family were already up and working, cutting lumber, notching logs and piecing together their new home.

Noah was excited upon seeing Lordiah walking up the path. He was even more enthusiastic when he told him his idea about building a boat.

"If this is what thou command, then one of the finest boats we will build," Noah barked to his offspring, *"Children, fetch a chair, and some water. We have found grace in the eyes of thou creator. Naamah, bring forth a bowl to wash his feet! Our creator has spared us."*

(Lordiah Journal Entry: 03.01.52 Earth) It took Leonardo half a day to draw up the master plans for the boat. I must say, I was quite impressed. By early afternoon, we transplanted Noah and his family to the top of the mountain.

*   *   *

"Assemble all of your family and friends that you want to save. You will need their help to build this boat," Lordiah told Noah. *"Gather fruit and game to dry as food for your journey. All that you can find."*

(Lordiah Journal Entry:03.01.52 Earth) Leonardo became the chief engineer for the boat project and Noah was the foreman. He gathered 47 family members and friends, promising them a spot.

We chose Gopher Wood trees because they are large, strong and we have learned the wood is durable. To expedite the progression, Leonardo transported one of the proton lasers to cut down trees, and several anti-gravity dollies to move them. Ramar flew the shuttles to haul back large trees to the build location.

The women cooked up the pitch and applied it to the wood to seal it. The younger workers went hunting for game and gathered fruits and berries. The elderly ones dried and bagged food.

Leilana sterilized blisters and did whatever else was medically necessary.

Not one person working ever questioned why they were erecting a boat on top of the mountain. They trusted Noah.

* * *

The morning had a chill in it, and dampness clung to the air. There were now seventy-four people building endlessly around the clock.

The frame and shell for the three-hundred-eight cubit long rectangular boat was now complete resting on stilts.

Leonardo and Noah took a moment and rolled out the architectural plans on the lower floor of the three-story vessel. *"To make this work, each room should be these exact dimensions, and you must seal every board and crack with the black pitch. No exception. It's going to be wet ride."*

Lordiah arrived behind them. *"Leonardo, can I have a talk about with you for a second?"*

"Yeah boss, what's up?"

"You're doing a great job. This may actually work, and that's mainly because of you. Thank you."

"Thanks boss." Leonardo folded his arms. "Whatcha really come here for?"

Lordiah shook his head and smiled. "Fair enough. Remember when we first landed here? Day one we were introduced to so much interesting and wonderful animal life. It's a shame that most will perish in the flood. Even the ones we bio engineered."

"That is definitely true, it will be a shame," Leonardo agreed.

"I'm thinking... You have done extensive research with the creatures on this planet. What if..." Lordiah stopped for a second.

"What if what, Lordiah?"

"You have DNA samples of each of these animals, correct? What if we send them with Noah on his boat? Teach him and his sons how to re-grow the animal population?"

"Whew... That is if they even survive this flood," Leonardo stated. His fingers started to twitch, and he got a blank look in his eyes. He pressed both hands under his armpits to stop the fingers as if hugging himself.

He looked back at Lordiah. "The beauty of being on this planet away from the politics on Heofon, is we don't have to be rational or have a committee tell us whether we can or cannot do something."

Leonardo started to pace. His fingers still under his armpits. "I would normally say that's a far-fucked idea, but then again, we are building a boat on top of a mountain. I say why the fuck not bossman. That could be another genius idea."

"Is it going to take a lot of work to get ready?" Lordiah asked.

"Nope, not at all," Leonardo answered. "I already have everything categorized and labeled. I planned on taking everything back to Heofon to see if we could regrow the animals there, that is if they would allow it. The bigger question will be if Noah and the gang are smart enough to run the equipment we give them to do it."

CHAPTER 61:
THE FINAL DAYS

Earth – months later

(Lordiah Journal Entry: 03.01.70 Earth) It's so hard for me to write this. Tomorrow is our final day on Earth. Last night I vomited thinking about it. We are going to devastate this place.

We have been on planet Earth for 209 years. By my calculations, with the time continuum only 182 days have passed on Heofon. Still no contact from King Osilu since the coup and the day we lost radio contact. We have no comprehension of what we will find into upon our return.

With only 47 original Heofonly astronauts remaining, the moonship is vacant compared to when we departed. With that, we have decided to take 227 workers back with us. This is productive in threefold:

1. It will save 227 worker's lives from the flood.
2. These manufactured workers can help rebuild our planet.
3. I get to bring live samples of my work back to show my colleagues.

Apollyon is expecting a hero's welcome, which unfortunately he will probably get because we will be saving Heofon from extinction. For the record, not once did he lift a finger to help.

So... tomorrow we leave for home. I know I'm repeating myself, but the horror of what will happen is wreaking havoc on me. I truly don't know how to accept this. Life on Earth will end, and I am the monster causing it. Am I Evil? Is it a crime worthy being tried on my judgement day? Hopefully those on Noah's boat survive but I have my doubts about them too.

*　*　*

CHAPTER 62:
PRELUDE
TO A DISASTER

Earth – The next day

Music blared. Shuttles unloaded while the Heofon crew danced and celebrated on the landing deck. Not Lordiah though, nor Leonardo. They were busy loading a shuttle with the vials of animal DNA for their very last trip to the surface.

With an electric clipboard in his hand, Leonardo carefully typed in his inventory. *"Over two-hundred-eighty-two different animals. Thank you, Leonardo. I have two of each species. Damn, I hope Noah and his stooges don't screw this up."*

Exiting the shuttle, several men unloaded the two glass containers with the floating naked bodies of Adam 11 and Eve 38 with their identification numbers pressed against the glass.

Dressed in full formal royal attire, including capes and crowns, Apollyon, along with Zetus walking at his left side, arrived. Apollyon carried a long-jeweled staff which he planted on the ground with each step.

"That's disgusting!" Apollyon retorted as he pointed his staff toward the containers. *"What are you planning to do with them?"*

"I'm taking them back to Heofon for the science associations to study," Lordiah responded.

"No, actually you're not! My family and I are not riding in the same vessel with those creatures! That's bad luck."

"Apollyon, this project was a huge success. It will be immensely beneficial to have them studied back home."

Apollyon stomped his staff on the floor twice, *"That's King Apollyon, bastard. And I said they aren't going on this ship. Zetus, stay here and make sure they remove them."*

Apollyon pulled his flowing robe over his shoulders, adjusted his crown, turned and walked away.

"You heard your King. Load them up and get them the fuck out of here," Zetus commanded.

The collars on Ramar and Leilana's shirts glistened with sweat as they helped Noah and his people load the boat. They had an assembly line of folks stocking the food they had gathered and dried, as well as a few living animals they could butcher.

When Leonardo arrived, he summoned Noah and his three sons to help him unload his DNA containers.

Lordiah stood next to the ramp. He stared sadly at the Adam and Eve corpses on the ground in front of him. He felt a hand on his shoulder. He turned.

Leonardo was standing there, *"Bossman, our work is done here. Come on, time to go."*

Lordiah looked one last time at the bodies, then nodded. *"Let's go find Noah and say our goodbyes."*

On the upper deck they located him. Lordiah reached in his leather purse strapped around his shoulder. *"Noah, I want you to have these."* He handed him some blank journals and a box full of ink pens.

"Thanks to thee, my creator," he said as he took a knee. *"What doth thou want me to do with these?"*

"I would like for you to document your journey while we are away. Then pass it onto your children. Share this day, and the days to come, so that they pass it down to their children and the story is told forever."

"Yes, of course, my creator. I owe mine life to thee."

Lordiah put his hand on Noah's shoulder. *"It's your responsibility to preserve mankind. You will be challenged, but you must persevere. Be strong."*

"I will do as thou commands. I will not let thee down."

Lordiah helped Noah to his feet and gave him a long, solid hug. *"I'm going to miss you my friend."*

He turned to Leonardo. *"Let's go. They're waiting for us."*

Leonardo stood there in silence.

"What is it Leonardo?"

"I'm not going with you. I'm staying here," Leonardo stated.

"What?" Lordiah responded.

"Boss, look, with me staying, they will have a better chance of surviving. And I can make sure the animals on this planet get repopulated. That's the shit that's important to me. This planet makes me happy. Here, I get to experiment freely. Home, not so much."

Lordiah was silent.

Leonardo continued, *"I've always had ideas, but they constantly squashed them on Heofon. I felt useless. But here, I have freedom to do whatever."*

Lordiah exhaled and looked away, then muttered, *"I, I don't know what to say."* Lordiah shook his head and half chuckled, *"I'm not surprised though. If it wasn't for Leilana and Ramar, I would probably stay with you!"*

"Yep, I know you would."

Lordiah's lips tightened. He drew in a deep breath then exhaled. *"You know the odds of you surviving aren't in your favor."*

"Yep. They suck. But I would rather take my chances here than to go and be held back again."

The two men clasped hands, then pulled each other into a hug. *"You're a good friend, Leo. I'll miss you. Take care of them, okay?"* Lordiah pointed at Noah.

Leonardo nodded and smiled.

Lordiah started to walk back to the shuttle. He stopped and turned back to Leonardo.

"Yes, I'll be happy to keep your precious Adam and Eve doll collection safe for you. That way I know you'll come back someday. Not for me, but for them."

Lordiah nodded, "Thank you."

CHAPTER 63:

WHEN THE
GODS FLED THE EARTH

The Control Center doors swished open. Lordiah entered with his hand held tight between Leilana's.

Major Thomas acknowledged him. *"Sir, all systems are go. Propulsion engines are primed for departure. Ready for your command."*

Lordiah turned and looked at Leilana. Sadness swelled up in his eyes. She reached up and cupped his face gently with her hand. Her lips tightened and she nodded.

Lordiah exhaled and turned to face the center of the room. *"Thank you, Major Thomas."* He looked over at the other Heofonly crew members in the room staring back at him. *"One last thing I would like to do before we depart, and that's to take a moment together and wish good tidings for our colleague and dear friend Leonardo. Let's remember that due to his great discovery of the white gold dust, all of us get to return healthier, stronger and younger. A gift we get to bring home with us and share."*

The crew politely clapped.

"We couldn't have fulfilled this mission without each and every one of you. Are you ready to go home?"

The bridge cheered. A crewman yelled out, *"Ready is an understatement, sir."*

Lordiah took in a deep breath, and then exhaled out slowly. The sad look returned as he chewed on his upper lip. *"Everyone, take a seat, and buckle yourselves in. We have an umbilical cord attached from this planet that we need to sever, and it may get rough."*

The eleven monitors all turned on and Earth below appeared on each screen. Then a loud hum chimed on as the thrusters kicked in. Lordiah scanned the crew to see if they were watching the displays before he finally glanced up himself.

Major Thomas waited until the last person was buckled up. *"In five, four, three, two, and we are moving!"*

The moonship trembled as it shook, enough that it felt as if it could rip apart any minute. Every member on the bridge kept their eyes locked on the viewing screens.

Within seconds, caustic changes began to the planet below. Clouds swirled, chunks of land broke off and drifted apart, and volcanos started to belch smoke.

Leilana reached over and grasped Lordiah's hand. His hand remained limp for a few long seconds then he gripped hers tightly.

The moonship finally broke out of the orbit. The ride smoothed out.

"Turn off the screen. I've seen enough," Lordiah commanded. The screens went back to black.

He unbuckled himself and stood. His legs were a little shaky at first as he walked towards the exit. Leilana followed close behind. When the doors opened, he stopped and turned to Major Thomas. *"It's so sad. Seems like every time we go to a planet, we destroy it."*

Part 3:

THE RETURN OF THE HEOFONLY BEINGS

CHAPTER 64:
THE MUSEUM

Moonship – Present Time

A deep intake of breath cut the silence. Lordiah's head lifted and he stretched his neck from side to side. *"It's getting stuffy in here. My guess is that they turned the air off in this suite."* He got up and went over to a flat touch screen on the wall, swiped right and typed. Within a second, the air kicked on. He returned to the couch and sat back down in the same spot.

"In my life span, I have watched hundreds of my children be born, grow up, grow old, and die." He exhaled; his lips tightened. *"But that day, as we left Earth, I watched it twist and destroy itself, knowing that thousands upon thousands of people died. That was one of the most somber days in my seven thousand four hundred years."*

"Sounds like you didn't have a choice," Luna responded. *"Kinda like the choice you made to leave a five-year-old girl behind."*

He leaned forward. He shook his head as a tear welled up in his eyes. *"That was just as hard, Luna. Please, believe me."*

Luna leaned back away for him. She smirked uncomfortably. *"Just busting your ass, Pops! Yes, sir, it must* have been hard. I have a question... You talk about your children, but what about their mothers? How come you don't mention them?

"I have taken sixty-five wives. I loved them all in their own way, but in all honesty, no one could hold a candle for the love I had for Leilana. She was my everything and will always be."

"What happened to her?" Luna asked.

Lordiah was still for a moment. His eyes saddened. He closed them and bowed his head. "That story is for another day."

Luna got the point and now wasn't the time to push.

He looked down at the fabric on the couch next to him. He slowly stroked a slightly worn spot on it with his fingers. "This space we're in, it's Leilana's suite," Lordiah revealed.

She ran her hand down the velvet couch feeling the softness of the fabric. She breathed in the air. "Oh wow, and you trust me in here?"

"Of course, I do."

She glanced around the room, then got up and walked behind the couch. "Now it all makes sense. That's why it's so perfect and clean. It's a shrine."

They sat in silence for a few minutes until Luna spoke. "Well, if history is correct, the boat you made with your bud, Noah, must've worked out."

He nodded. "Yes, surprisingly they survived."

"Seems that your story and my Bible studies differ, like they packed it full of animals shitting everywhere. Your 'DNA version' is so much more realistic. Kinda brilliant too!"

"I thought so. Noah took my advice and journaled everything in the books I gave him."

Luna shrugged, opening up her hands. "Which became biblical, I'm assuming?"

"Partially." Lordiah got up. "Wait here for a sec."

"Like, I really can't go anywhere, can I? She chuckled.

"Yep, that's right," Lordiah grinned as he left.

Luna glanced around. Curious, she stood up. On the desk, she found a foreign medical device and examined it. It was perfectly shined, and not a speck of dust on it. After a few minutes, she gently placed it back in the exact spot and position she found it, then wandered over to a closet. There she discovered several outfits hanging, each protected by a clear, tight sealed wrap.

"So, this is what a princess wears?" she mumbled to herself. She unzipped one of the bags. She pulled the sleeve up and sniffed it. *"And it carries a faint scent of Lavender."*

She thumbed through them. One outfit was very extravagant, a sparkling silver formal, long flowing gown with gold designs on it. Hanging from the same hanger was a leather purse held by a silver shoulder strap covered in jewels. Next to the dress, a pair of black slacks with a white blouse, and several more dresses. Luna unzipped the bag and removed the long flowing gown and held it to her body.

Carrying several green leather-bound books, Lordiah slipped back into the room. He watched her as she placed Leilana's gown up next to her.

"Leilana didn't care much for formal attire. She liked simplicity and comfort," Lordiah stated.

Startled, Luna dropped the dress. *"I'm sorry for snooping."* She bent down and scooped the dress up, put it back in the bag and returned it to the closet.

"It's okay. Take whatever you want. You look to be about the same size. She would have liked that."

Luna, blushed. *"I'm sorry, it's like a museum, and...* She chose the books in Lordiah's hands to focus on. *"Whatcha got there?"*

"Remember when I said Noah journaled?" He came over and handed them to her. *"These are his books."*

Her eyes got big. *"Wow. For reals?"*

Lordiah nodded. *"And no one has seen them except you and me."*

Luna grabbed the top book and opened it. *"What the fudge, dude."* Each page was full of drawings, shapes, and figures. *"Hey, I think I've seen these books before."*

"Yes, you have. I used to read stories to you out of them before bedtime."

"*I sorta remember. And you telling me they were old, and I couldn't color in them with my crayons.*"

"*Yeah, and you almost did once. You preferred that I read Noah's stories to you over Cinderella and The Little Mermaid. And you learned how to read the ancient language too, reading along with me,*" Lordiah told her.

"*Wow, yeah…*"

Luna closed the book and put it aside. "*Did you ever make it back to your planet and save it?*"

"*Yeah, we did.*"

"*What happened?*"

CHAPTER 65:
GOING TO HEOFON

Moonship – Heofon

(Lordiah Journal Entry: 03.01.61 Heofon) It took eleven months for the moonship to travel back to Heofon. Every day on our journey home, with hundreds of attempts, we have tried to contact home. We still have no communication with Heofon. This is disconcerting for us all. Is it too late? Did our planet destroy itself? Has the Kingdom been taken over?

*   *   *

Leilana was sitting at the radio station in case someone responded. Apollyon barged into the Control Room.

"I'm tired of sitting on this stupid rock doing nothing. I demand we hold a meeting right now! Let's send down some manufactured workers. They can gather information and report back to us."

"Apollyon, seriously? That's stupid. It's a foreign planet with technology they have never seen before. They're like children. They won't understand the place," Leilana snapped back.

"Well, I demand we send down a scout first. I'm not going until I know who's in charge and that it's safe!" he informed her.

"*I completely agree with you,*" Lordiah replied, entering the room. "*We do need to make sure it's safe down there first. Father may be dead, as far as we know.*"

"*Then whom are we sending?*" Apollyon asked.

"*Me,*" Lordiah replied. "*As you have informed me over and over, I'm not royalty. As far as we know, the palace and the royal government is ousted. But... we have gold, which gives us the power to bargain.*"

"*And if they kill you, we will leave and let the planet turn to icicles! That's not up for debate!*" Leilana's words shot out.

Lordiah looked over at Apollyon. Even he knew when to not argue with his sister. "*My goal is to locate our father. Hopefully, he is alive. He will know what to do*"

CHAPTER 66:
WELCOME HOME

Planet Heofon

Strapped in the pilot seat of the black shuttle, Lordiah flew solo down to The Royal City. He wrote:

(Lordiah Journal Entry: 03.01.70 Heofon) Am I scared? Yeah, I am. Very much so... I have no idea what I will encounter when I land. Still no contact. Are we too late? Hopefully not.

*   *   *

A voice crackled over the radio. *"LUNA Shuttle, you are in Heofon Royal airspace. Please land on the coordinates sent to your ship in three-two-one,"* the voice said professionally and firm.

On the screen below the windshield, a map emerged, with a specific graphic landing point.

Lordiah dropped his journal and grabbed the radio receiver. *"Oh, thank goodness. We haven't heard from anyone for quite some time. It's nice to hear a voice from home,"* Lordiah responded. *"This is Lordiah, the Chief Scientist from the LUNA mission, completing a royal assignment for the King. May I please speak with King Osilu."*

"LUNA Shuttle, you are in Heofon Royal airspace. I repeat, please land the shuttle on the coordinates sent to your ship," the voice repeated curtly.

"Sir, may I please speak with my father, King Osilu?"

"LUNA Shuttle, you have your orders. If your vessel waivers off the course, I have orders to shoot you down."

"Copy that," Lordiah replied.

Out of the corner of his eye, Lordiah saw movement. He turned his head to the right and spotted several military shuttles settle into formation beside him.

When Lordiah landed, twenty-nine military vehicles, manned with large guns raced toward him from all sides.

His forehead started to sweat. 'This can't be good,' he thought as he waited for orders to exit the craft.

"Everyone in the shuttle, place your hands over your head and slowly exit." A microphoned voiced ordered.

Lordiah exhaled, then pulled a lever back on the panel by his seat. The walkway under the craft proceeded to open. A cold breeze from outside bathed him as he proceeded to walk down the plank. Eleven armed military soldiers, guns drawn and pointed at his chest greeted him.

"Hands over your head and get down on your knees," one of the soldiers shouted while Lordiah looked down all eleven rifle barrels.

"Okay, no problem, I'm unarmed." Lordiah knelt onto the icy ground. Once his knees touched, soldiers rushed forward, pushing him face down. A firm foot placed on his back pushed the air out of his lungs as they handcuffed his hands behind him. He gasped for air. Several soldiers kept their weapons trained on him while a group entered the shuttle and searched it.

"All clear!" a soldier shouted as he exited.

An armored van pulled up. Lordiah was grabbed by both arms and ripped off the ground. They shuffled him to the vehicle where they threw him in and sped off.

CHAPTER 67:
A SEARCH
FOR THE KING

The guards carried Lordiah to the Royal Throne Room and threw him onto a large wooden chair. They shackled his wrist and ankles to the chair, then exited, leaving him by himself.

His heart pounded. It was icy cold in the once decadent chamber. An eerie quiet rang throughout the space.

This is turning out to be the worst-case scenario, he thought to himself. Once the most prestigious and elegant rooms of the palace, it was now trashed, filthy, and unrecognizable. Antique furniture was now chopped up next to the fireplace. The purple velvet curtains that once hung over the windows had been ripped down. Twenty-nine generations of royal portraits had been stripped from the wall, and pieces of the frames and shreds of canvas laid in the ashes of the fireplace.

He began to shiver. He tried to wrap his body tighter, but the restraints wouldn't allow it. The only sound heard was the tick-tock from the giant grandfather clock built into the wall.

"The climate is drastically cooler since my departure..." Lordiah mumbled to himself. *"The atmospheric decay is much worse than I had predicted."*

Several hours passed before a guard entered and removed his shackles, then stood beside him at attention. Lordiah hugged his body to stay warm.

The door behind him opened. *Finally,* he thought.

More guards arrived, followed by a man wearing a crown and a purple velvet cloak.

Lordiah stood.

"I am King Kanus, King of The Royal City and all of Heofon. And whom may you be?"

King Kanus? Lordiah thought to himself. *I have never heard of anyone called Kanus. Where did he come from?*

He knelt.

"My name is Lordiah, the Chief Scientist, completing a royal mission for King Osilu."

"I am the king, so your mission is with me," Kanus informed him.

"With respect, your lordship, where is King Osilu?"

"With respect, where is Apollyon? Shouldn't I be addressing him instead of a bastard?"

"So, you do know who I am. Sir, King Osilu is my father. Even if he is a prisoner, I would like to see him."

"Bastard, I can have you killed."

Lordiah's heart started to pound. He took a slow breath in, trying to slow it down. *I mustn't show fear*, he thought to himself.

"Yes, you could, sir, but you would kill this entire planet if you do. We completed our mission. I have returned with a ship full of gold."

Lordiah pulled out several bags of gold and laid them on the floor in front of him. The guards in the room started to mumble and whisper amongst themselves.

"Silence!" Kanus demanded. Turning back to Lordiah, *"you are still working for the throne. Your mission is now with me!"*

"My mission is under the orders of King Osilu, sir." He looked around the room, making eye contact one at a time with Kanus's staff and guards. *"If I don't return to my ship within eleven hours from the time I left, they have strict orders to depart and never come back. The cards are in your hands."*

The room was silent as everyone looked over at Kanus. Lordiah addressed the room again. *"If I die, we all die, including your families."*

The room remained silent. Lordiah felt sweat trickle down his back. *I have to change my approach. This guy is a mule head*, Lordiah thought in his head.

"*I know King Osilu is alive. I received a radio transmission from someone in your camp,*" Lordiah boldly lied. "*I will not lift a finger until I speak with him*".

"*If you don't cooperate and do as I say, you will rot the rest of your miserable life in a cold prison cell. Would you like that?*" Kanus bellowed back at him.

Lordiah shrugged his shoulders. "*So, will you.*"

Kanas' face turned red. "*Throw him in the dungeon.*"

Lordiah was cuffed and marched outside. With each step they took, they laid fresh tracks in the newly fallen snow.

"*Pretty snowstorm,*" Lordiah stated to the guards. "*Probably never seen that here before, I bet?*"

A brick building appeared ahead of them. They stopped in front of a secured door. The door clicked and a buzz rang out.

"*You have families?*" Lordiah asked the guards. "*How are they liking this weather?*" The guards proceeded forward in silence.

They approached a large wooden door and opened it. Inside was a dark dank cell with a wood box to sit, a bucket and smelled of stale urine.

He held his hands out for them to remove his shackles. "*If I don't fix things, which I can, every person you know on this planet will freeze to death.*" He stepped backwards into the cell.

They looked at Lordiah for a second, then shut the door and locked it.

Hours passed. Lordiah's cell door creaked open. Several large guards entered, tied his hands behind him and escorted him back to the Royal Throne Room. On his father's throne sat Kanus. The guards grabbed Lordiah, pushed him down onto his knees and forced him to bow.

"*Are you ready to turn over the gold?*" Kanus asked.

"*I haven't spoken to my father, so nothing has changed.*"

"So, are you willing to let everyone on your planet die?" Kanus snorted out.

"Not at all, that is why I have returned. The bigger question is, are you willing to let everyone die? From the time on the clock over there it appears that eleven hours is almost up. The Moonship will leave."

Lordiah turned and addressed the group. "All I ask is to speak with my father."

"Make contact with your ship, then. Tell them everything is okay. You will be handsomely rewarded." Kanus told him smiling.

Lordiah shook his head.

Kanus and Lordiah stared at each other. His anxiety felt like it was driving fast the wrong way down a one-way street. Kanus smirked and broke the silence, "As you wish. Bring him in!"

Lordiah exhaled in relief.

Lead by his shackles, several guards dragged in a half-naked man with a black hood over his head. The stench of foul body odor radiated from him. Kicking the prisoner behind the knees, they forced him to kneel in front of Kanus, next to Lordiah.

King Kanus nodded. A guard yanked the hood off. The gaunt, squinting, unshaven King Osilu was revealed.

"There is your father," Kanus stated as he motioned to a guard. The guard standing behind Osilu grabbed his hair, pulled his head back revealing his throat. The other sentry pulled out his sword and placed it against Osilu's neck.

"It's simple, you work for me, your father lives. If you don't, I remove his head here and now. And yours will follow!"

Lordiah looked over at Osilu, studying the situation. "Hi, Papa. What do I do?"

Osilu glared forward, not taking his eyes off Kanus.

"Silence! You will address me and me only! What is your decision?"

Lordiah's fingers started to tremble. He formed a fist to hide it. 'Do not show fear,' Lordiah pleaded with himself. "If you kill him, then kill me too." He rotated his head and spoke

230

to the room. *"Set my father free, and I promise you I will fix our planet."*

Kanus stood. *"Cut his head off!"* he demanded.

The guard with the blade resting on Osilu's neck made a motion upward with his arm, bringing his sword back. He held this position.

Kanus' face turned red, *"Guard, obey, kill him!"*

As if everything turned to slow motion, a blade swooshed downward. Lordiah turned his head away so he wouldn't have to witness the horrific event.

Blood splattered on his face.

Oh my gosh, he did it, he sliced Papa's head off, raced through Lordiah's mind.

What sounded like a bowling ball rolling across the marble floor toward him, was no ball and Lordiah knew it. It was a head and it stopped when it reached his leg and leaned against it.

"No!" he screamed. He turned his body toward it and kicked his knee out to push it away. The head rolled several feet from him.

From the corner of his eye, he glimpsed to his right. His eyes got large, and his mouth opened. Osilu's was still kneeling, his head still attached, but the guard holding his hair toppled over headless.

Gunshots sounded. More guards raised their weapons and fired. But instead of shooting the guard with the sword, the sentries that protected Kanus took multiple head and chest wounds and dropped to the ground.

Additional guards entered the Royal suite. They apprehended Kanus, his staff, and held them at gunpoint.

The guard with the dripping sword wiped the blood from his blade. He kicked the head out of his path as he circled Lordiah, then stopped behind him.

"Can you truthfully fix this planet?" the Guard asked Lordiah.

"Yes, I can," he replied.

With one stroke of his sword, Lordiah's hands leapt free. He signaled for another guard to unshackle Osilu.

The guard handed his sword over to King Osilu and knelt humbly. *"King Osilu, speaking for all of us that guard this royal room, we humbly turn the kingdom back over to you. We are here to serve and protect under your rule."*

King Osilu stood. He pointed toward Kanus, *"First, demonstrate your loyalty by removing that and throw him in the dungeon."*

"Yes, your highness."

Osilu turned to Lordiah. Lordiah's eyes glazed then he vomited in front of him.

"Welcome home, son!"

CHAPTER 68:
GOLDEN SHOWERS

Planet Heofon

(Lordiah Journal Entry: 03.02.150 Heofon) Having been away so long, it feels strange to be back. King Osilu fully recovered his power and sits back on his throne. Pops demanded our return be celebrated as a New World holiday, so we now have an anniversary in our honor, asking, well more or less telling all the other governments to join in and make it a day to rejoice. Afterward, he pulled me aside and told me it's all a political ploy to remind the entire planet that the Osilu kingdom saved the world. I'm so thankful I'm not a part of the ill political regime it tangles them in.

*　*　*

Before they allowed anyone to leave the moonship, Osilu demanded that he first vet his new special guard unit to make sure they, and the gold, would be safe upon their return.

Osilu placed his arm around Lordiah's shoulder. *"I'm looking forward to seeing everyone, especially those two new grandchildren of mine. What did you say their names were again? Zart and Ramar? And where is Apollyon?"*

"Apollyon is sulking because he was demoted back to a prince again."

"That's nonsense! He should walk proudly amongst us. The mission was an enormous success. He divulged to me he single-handedly destroyed that heinous traitor Aries and his conspirators, took a large role in the mining operations and it was his brilliant idea to bring back the manufactured slave workers to restore this planet."

Lordiah brows frowned, and his mouth gaped open. Then he shook his head and rolled his eyes.

(Lordiah Journal Entry: 03.02.150 Heofon) Project Golden Showers started immediately. Aircrafts by the hundreds flew the skies for the next eleven weeks, leaving behind trails of white exhaust.

The effects transpired quick. The skies became bluer than they have ever been. Within the first few weeks, the planet's climate already responded with a noticeable escalation in temperature. The general population shed their layers of clothes and are now basking in the new warmth. Aromas of flowers emerged, and other plant fragrances we have forgotten about filled the air.

The people celebrated and temperaments transformed throughout the entire planet. And Papa... King Osilu became most popular amongst the people.

As for the 227 manufactured workers, they put them to work right away restoring the palace to its prior magnificence. It disturbs me they are being treated as slaves. In King Osilu's eyes, that is their sole purpose.

The king quoted and made very clear to me, "They exist because we created them. We own them. Even the ones on Earth. I wouldn't mind collecting more of them someday."

King Osilu gathered Zetus and Ramar and showed them all around Heofon. He loved their innocence. Everything was exciting and foreign to them. He brought them to museums, large cities, metropolitan structures, sporting events, government headquarters, and to every country. The concept of restaurants blew Ramar and Zetus away. There was so much food, variety, and waste. Coming from the vast natural openness of the Earth, swimming pools and parks seemed silly to them. There were so many people, strange hairstyles, crazy wardrobe choices, movies, cars, traffic.

After 74 days, the last ounce of gold had been grounded to dust and showered into the atmosphere.

*   *   *

"It's amazing to smell the natural fragrances of spring again. Thank you. Where do we stand now?" Osilu inquired.

"We have replenished about fifty-six percent of the atmosphere. We will need to strategize another operation to collect more gold."

"I did my time. That will have to be an operation without me," Apollyon arrogantly retorted.

Osilu slapped his hand down on the table. *"Hush Apollyon! I will decide who goes and who stays,"* Osilu turned to Lordiah. *"When do you anticipate we should compose another mission?"*

"Relatively soon. We did a Band-Aid repair here. The gold we showered will hold in our core heat for now, but we will start to notice decay in the climate again. The sooner we spray another layer equivalent to what we just did, the better. And that should hold for another five to six hundred thousand years."

"It's actually advantageous to us that the atmosphere is still unstable. That way the people will need my kingdom for their survival. That's power, my sons!" Osilu's voice raged throughout the halls. *"Lordiah, start making plans. Gather the personnel needed and whatever supplies. I would like to see a departure plan before the end of the day."*

"Will do, Sir. I also want to retrofit a few more things on the moonship, if that's possible."

"Anything you need, but I'm keeping all the manufactured workers here, so don't include them in your plan."

CHAPTER 69:
PLAN IT EARTH

Planet Heofon

"Now that we are seasoned astronauts, I would like to retrofit a proton sound wave cannon on the ship and triple the strength of our shields for meteor protection," Lordiah instructed as Major Thomas took notes.

Leilana thumbed through several magazines with her feet up on the table as she listened. *"And since I'm drafted to go without a choice, I need an upgrade to my suite. Some simple modifications transforming it into a getaway from Earth's primitive surface."* She opened a magazine and pushed it to Major Thomas. *"I would like to have my bathroom retrofitted to look like this. I want that bathtub to soak the dirt off of me."*

She pulled out another publication and opened it. *"I also want a bar installed, stocked with brandy, something I think we all missed on our last trip."*

She turned the page to another marked picture, *"And last, a formal living room to hang out in that looks nice and cozy like this."*

Major Thomas took the magazines. *"I will personally make sure you get your wishes Princess Leilana."*

"Thank you," Leilana replied, then stood up and marched out of the room.

Major Thomas pressed his lips together as we watched her leave. Then turned to Lordiah. *"And you sir?"* Major Thomas grabbed his pad. *"What can I do for you?"*

"Sorry, she's not thrilled about being forced into going back."

Once the moonship's retrofit got completed, Lordiah summoned a talk about in The Royal Planning Room.

Only a small group was present. King Osilu, Prince Apollyon, Lordiah, and Leilana. They also invited Ramar to join them.

"Mars was thin of gold, and Earth has an abundance, so the strategy is to return to Earth." Lordiah stated as he started the meeting. *"We won't know if anyone survived the floods until our return. King Osilu has graciously allowed us thirty-eight work convicts to assist so we can mine immediately. I'll bring containers to grow more workers."*

"How much time on Earth will have passed upon our return?" Leilana asked.

"Great question. Several thousand is my calculated estimate," Lordiah shifted in his chair. *"Which is good because if there are survivors, then that would make one-hundred-fifty-five generations to repopulate the planet, and there could be millions of potential workers to hire."*

"Hire?" Apollyon's brows wrinkled. *"We own them. So, no, we don't hire anyone; we tell them what to do."*

"Thousands of years have passed. They more than likely wouldn't know about us as their makers. We may need to form a barter system to get them to do what we want."

Osilu leaned forward. *"Did you plan for this? I recommend you take some military staff with you to establish superiority right away. Use force if needed. They must know we own them."*

"You're rebuilding your guard staff. Can you spare any men?"

"This mission is the utmost of importance. I can lend you eleven men from the royal guards, but no more. Unfortunately, I still have to watch my back."

"Thank you, Sir"

Osilu stood. *"I'm sorry I know you have just returned after being away for so long, but I request that you leave right away."* He looked away to hide the tear that started to form.

Lordiah looked over at Leilana, then back at Osilu. *"Yes, sir. No problem. Everything is actually retrofitted and ready. We will just need to find accommodations for the royal guards you handed us."*

Apollyon chimed in, *"You can house them in my royal suite since I'm not going back to that primitive rock!"*

King Osilu hammered his fist down loudly on the table in front of him as his face reddened. *"Silence, Apollyon! I will say who is going and who is staying! Not you!"*

The room fell silent. *"I would love for you all to stay. I would love spending more time with my new grandchildren, but it's smarter if all of you leave for now. The politics are still unstable. If someone plans to overthrow my power again, they can use any one of you as leverage to get to me. If you aren't here, then they can't. I will not hear another word about it! Are we clear?"*

The group nodded in acknowledgement. What else could they really do.

"In twenty-nine hours, I'm going to have a public beheading of Kanus and his staff in the main square. I want that moonship gone with all of you on it before that happens."

CHAPTER 70:
RETURN OF
THE HEOFONLY BEINGS

Planet Earth – 4,061 years ago

After eleven long weeks of being cooped up, the Heofonly travelers arrived. The moon was luminous in the Earth's sky once again after its absence of 3,080 years.

Major Thomas leaned back in his chair. His brow wrinkled as he studied the screen in front of him. *"Sir, I have hundreds of markers below."*

"Markers?" Ramar asked.

Lordiah walked over and stood behind the Major. *"He's operating a program that locates distinctive temperatures on the planet surface."* Lordiah pointed at some numbers along the top of the screen. *"Well, I'll be...Look at that... In this event, a marker will pop up on the map for anything emitting a temp range between ninety-five to one hundred degrees, the average core temp of living humans."*

Ramar joined them. He pointed to the screen. *"So, all of those red spots could be humans?"*

Lordiah patted Major Thomas on the back. *"Clusters of them actually. Can you pull up the entire planet on the hologram?"*

A large three-dimensional sphere of Earth appeared in front of them.

Lordiah slowly paced around the hologram. *"That's interesting. Looks like the main continent broke up into smaller landmasses. Can you highlight the markers for us on the hologram, Major Thomas?"*

Sixty-five red spots lit up. Most of the hotspots were on the same continent, showing a high populated center point and expanding out. Only a few red spots were glowing on the other landmasses.

"If this is correct," Lordiah exhaled and put his arm around Ramar. *"This could mean that Earth is inhabited with people."* Lordiah smiled.

"Or animal herds," Major Thomas stated, shrugging his shoulders.

"Either way, there are large pockets of something putting out heat that survived the great floods. Let's go find out."

CHAPTER 71:

DOWN TO EARTH

Without wasting a minute, a scout shuttle departed the moonship's docking port. Lordiah led the mission with Ramar in the pilot's seat. Several royal guards joined as a protocol for safety precautions.

(Lordiah Journal Entry: 03.02.24 Earth2) Apollyon and Zetus elected to stay in the moonship until they received confirmation that Earth was safe. Ramar, on the other hand, was the first to volunteer for the mission.

To our surprise, when we flew over the marked hotspots, we discovered cities inhabited by thousands of people. They appeared primitive, with no signs of electricity. Transportation was either by foot or on an animal.

* * *

"Hey Ramar," Lordiah pointed toward the ground. *"Look at that pack of animals."*

Ramar circled the ship back around. Sheep and goat herds grazed below. Lordiah pulled out a hand telescope. *"This is a great sign that Leonardo, rest his soul, survived the floods."*

Excitement filled the cockpit of the shuttle. *"Ramar, what's that over there?"* Lordiah pointed in front of them. *"Fly over so we can get a closer look."*

Ramar hovered over some cattle grazing in a field. *"What on Earth are those?"* Lordiah muttered. *"Look at their size. They're so much larger than the goats, and considerably wider than a sheep."*

The cows started to run away from the airborne craft. *"Ramar, let's pull back and not scare them."* Lordiah nodded his head slowly and a large grin formed across his face. *"Interesting. It's been 3,080 years. There's no way natural evolution could have done that."*

Ramar looked at his father. He noticed a tear started to well up. *"Dad, I miss him too. I'm sure Uncle Leo lived out his life exactly the way he wanted."*

Lordiah put his hand on his son's shoulder and nodded. *"I'm sure he did."*

They continued to explore for another hour cruising over more cities, herds of animals, uninhabited lands and oceans.

The sky darkened as the sun started its journey downward.

"Hey son, night is approaching. Let's land and make contact with some inhabitants on the ground."

Several shepherds were pitching a tent and building a circular pit made of rocks below.

"There," Lordiah pointed to a spot near their camp.

As they hovered downward, the shepherds glanced up. Their eyes grew large. They walked several steps backward, then scattered in different directions.

The ramp lowered under the craft, and several guards exited, weapons loaded and ready. Lordiah got out next, followed by Ramar.

"Please, take a friendly stance," Lordiah ordered the guards. *"Don't scare them any more than we already have. And, don't shoot unless one hundred percent necessary."*

Lordiah took a deep breath through his nose and looked over at Ramar. *"Smells the same. Temperature is nice."*

Ramar grinned and nodded.

They proceeded over to the shepherds' camp. Ramar put his hand on his father's shoulder and whispered in his ear. *"Pops, their house is made from animal hides. Their tools are very primitive."*

Lordiah sauntered over to the tent. *"Hello in there. Please don't be scared. We mean you no harm."*

A few seconds passed. An elderly man popped his head out from the tent door with trembling hands held high.

He immediately threw himself to the ground and bowed with his head at Lordiah's feet. *"Art thou our Lord, the creator from the skies above?"*

Lordiah frowned and looked over to Ramar and the guards to see if he heard correctly. *"Can you please repeat yourself?"*

"Art thou our Lord, the creator from the skies above?" The words trembled out of the elderly man's quivering mouth.

Lordiah looked over at the others, *"That's interesting."*

He exhaled and held his hand out. *"How do you know who I am?"*

"Stories from ancestors passed down. Thou hast created us in thine image and given us commandments by which to live. So, art thou our Lord and hast thou returned to punish the wicked?"

"I am Lordiah, yes."

"Allow me, I beg thee, to fetch some water and wash thy feet," the elderly man said as he shook.

Lordiah looked down at the boots on his feet. He knelt down next to the man and gently put his hand on his shoulder, *"That's not necessary. Please, allow us to join you."*

Something rustled in the brush behind them. Ramar pulled out his flashlight and shined it in the direction of the noise.

"No, please spare them and not strike them down," The elderly man begged as he dropped back down at Lordiah's feet. *"They art my wife and children!"*

"Ramar, turn off your flashlight, you're scaring them," Lordiah barked out.

Ramar shut off his flashlight.

Lordiah helped the elderly man back up. Pointing at Ramar, *"This is my son, my family. We mean you no harm. Please tell your family to come join us."*

The elderly man nodded, *"Thou art truly great gods. I witnessed thou light coming out of the hands of thy son. We will do as our Lord asks."*

The elderly man turned to the wooded area. He put several fingers up to his mouth. A loud whistle blasted out, making Lordiah jump. *"Wife, children, he is our Lord and creator. He commands you to come out."*

A woman in her early twenties, a young boy and girl strolled out of the wooded area. Upon reaching the elderly man, they each knelt down at Lordiah's feet.

Lordiah reached out and helped them up. *"Please, that isn't necessary."*

The elderly man motioned to the young woman. *"Wife, make a fire, kill a lamb from the flock. Let us feast upon it with our guest."*

The young wife, looking down the entire time nodded. She walked over to the fire pit. Her hands quivered as she pulled out several wooden sticks from her pocket. She knelt down and proceeded to rub the sticks together.

She picked up her pace as they started to smoke, then added dried leaves and blew on it. It didn't light.

The trembling in her hands increased. She rubbed the wood together, repeating this process but her shaking hands failed her.

Ramar walked over to her. *"Here, let me help you."*

He reached into his fanny pack and retrieved a lighter and knelt down beside her. He flicked the top and a flame ascended. Alarm crossed her face and her eyes doubled in size. Falling backward, she crab-walked backwards until she reached the elderly man and hid behind him.

"It's OK. Look." Ramar slowly moved the lighter flame to the dry leaves. *"There. See?"* Ramar stepped back. *"The fire is started. There is nothing to fear."*

"We witnessed another miracle. The son of our Lord can make fire from his hands! We are your humble servants," the elderly man cried out. *"We are not like the wicked ones. We are here to serve thee, Lord. Are thou here to punish the wickedness of man as we have been warned?"*

"Warned?" Lordiah looked puzzled.

"The wise one. He brought the animals to life. He warned us, for someday Lord, our creator, will return and strike down all that is wicked like thou did with the great flood."

Lordiah looked over at Ramar. A manic glee appeared in his eyes. *"Leonardo, bless his soul."*

Lordiah put both of his hands on the elderly man's shoulders, *"Thank you. The wise one you speak of was a very dear friend."*

And that evening they feasted on lamb.

CHAPTER 72:
MARKERS
AND HOT SPOTS

Moonship– later

"It's time to strategize restarting the gold mine operations," Lordiah said as he sat down and joined the group. *"With your permission, King Apollyon, I would like to proceed."*

Apollyon nodded, *"Proceed."*

"Before we commence, Major Thomas, will you tell the group what you told me a few hours ago?"

"Yes, sir." Major Thomas tapped on his keyboard. The hologram table came to life and a 3.8-foot diameter image of Earth floated into view. *"Those red markers are pockets of people that inhabit primitive city structures, or in a few instances large populations of domesticated animals."*

Major Thomas typed a few more strokes. Two more areas lit up in yellow. *"The sensors picked up something else though. two places are emitting low level radioactive isotopes."*

"So, what does that mean?" Apollyon asked.

Ramar chimed in. *"We won't know until we investigate, but this is well beyond the current inhabitants' technology range, which makes it peculiar."*

"I believe your king was asking Major Thomas, not you," Zetus snidely remarked.

"Excuse me, Zetus?" Ramar glared.

"It's Prince Zetus. And the King isn't addressing you."

"While you were hiding like a coward in your luxury suite, I scouted several trips to the surface. What have you done?"

Leilana slapped the table several times. *"You two stop it! This is a talk about. Respect the space, please!"*

The young men grew silent. Lordiah continued. *"Major Thomas, please resume."*

"Yes, sir. One of the yellow markers is in a human colonized area, and the other marker isn't. As Ramar mentioned, we don't know what is causing the radioactivity."

Lordiah chimed in. *"So, I propose we form a team and go investigate, starting with the one that isn't in the populated zone. With the permission from our king, of course."*

Zetus folded his arms. *"And who is going to be on this team?"*

"I was thinking myself, Ramar, and several guards," Lordiah answered.

"I demand that I go too!" Zetus insisted.

"Because I'm going, you now feel you must go?" Ramar snapped back.

"I'm going because I'm a prince and I can do whatever I want whenever I want!"

"Stop!" Apollyon interrupted. *"If Zetus wants to go, then he shall go,"*

"No one said he couldn't go." Leilana placed both hands on the table, stood and glared at Zetus and Ramar. *"Boys, if you want to sit at the big boys table, then you are going to have to act like adults. A reminder everyone, we are in the planning stage."*

"And the plans are made. The shuttle is leaving in forty-seven minutes. If you're going, be at the launch pad," Lordiah turned and walked out.

CHAPTER 73:
WMD'S

Earth Surface – Later

Tucked into a shuttle, Lordiah's team of Ramar, Zetus, and several guards set a course down to Earth.

"I don't feel safe with Ramar driving," Zetus challenged when he saw Ramar in the pilot's seat. Lordiah squashed the situation by having Ramar step down and he flew the ship instead.

Minutes after takeoff, Zetus fell sound asleep and remained that way for the entire trip.

"The area should be just over these mountains, Papa." Ramar looked at a handheld monitor. They flew over the peak and came across a valley below. *"Look, over there."*

Below stood a large stone pyramid, overgrown with brush at the base and various twining up the sides. *"I'll be..."* Lordiah's brows raised. *"What's that doing out here?"*

They circled the pyramid several times getting a better look. Ramar pointed, *"Hey, why is there a large opening at the top?"*

"I'm not sure," Lordiah responded with a curious tone in his voice. *"There's only one way to find out."*

They exited the shuttle. With caution, they explored their surroundings.

The stone steps leading up the pyramid were gray with age, peppered with moss and grass, and several bird nests. The edges of the large square rocks were now rounded from erosion and wear and tear from winds and storms for thousands of years.

"It's very quiet here." Lordiah pulled out his electric tablet from his pack. He scanned the area. *"Doesn't have any hot markers aside from our team so it's just us."* He motioned to one of the guards. *"Go and wake up Zetus. The radioactive isotopes seem to be coming from the top tier of the pyramid."*

"Hey, over here." Ramar found the opening on the opposite side. A large boulder blocked its entry. He pushed against it with all of his strength, but it didn't budge *"Bring the anti-gravity dolly too."*

Inside, it was pitch black. An old stale smell wafted towards them.

"Pull out your flashlights, gentlemen," Lordiah reached inside his fanny pack.

Zetus was the only one that didn't have one.

"Rookie mistake," Ramar snidely chuckled as he turned and entered the pyramid first. He walked several meters then stopped. Raising his light, he illuminated something in front of him. *"Hey Papa, come and check this out."*

Lordiah walked over with the others. On the wall was a large diagram carved into the flat rock surface. He placed his fingers on the diagram feeling the letters. *"Interesting... It looks like a directory to this pyramid."*

"It's written in our language," Ramar responded.

"Yes, it is. Which means our ancestors built this during one of their earlier missions here," Lordiah stated, examining it.

Bending down, Zetus picked something up on the ground. It was shiny and round.

"What you got there, cuz?" Ramar asked.

He held it out to Ramar. When he reached for it, Zetus dropped it on the ground. *"It's a cheap peasant's bracelet, so it must be yours,"* Zetus chuckled.

"You found a bracelet, and you think that's nothing?" Ramar shined his light on the object. *"Everything we find right now is something, you idiot."*

Ramar collected the bracelet and studied it. He pulled out his knife and carved into it. *"Nothing, huh? Papa check this out. I think this is made of gold!"*

Lordiah studied the bracelet. *"That's interesting. Keep your eyes open everyone. There may be more."*

Unzipping the pouch on his hip, Lordiah analyzed the bracelet for another second, then stuck it in his fanny pack. *"That's another mystery to add to this place."*

He moved back over to the diagram. *"It looks like there are several passages we need to take to get to the top. Ramar, take a photo in case this is the only directory."*

Lighting the way with their flashlights, they trekked through the darkness. They walked up flights of stairs, down hallways, through tunnels, checking the photo of the directory from time to time for directions.

"Let's stop for a quick second." Lordiah pulled out his tablet and studied it. *"Whatever is emitting the isotopes should be at the top of these stairs."*

Zetus knelt down and picked up something. *"Someone shine a light on me. I found something."*

Ramar turned and illuminated Zetus. *"Whatcha got there? Let me see it?"*

"Nope," Zetus scrapped it up and down the wall next to him. *"This looks like gold to me."*

Lordiah reached his hand out. *"Can I look at it?"*

Zetus put the ring in his pocket. *"Nope, I'm going to keep this one."*

Ramar looked over at his dad and rolled his eyes.

"Let's keep moving, we're almost there."

They walked up the last remaining stairs to the top floor.

Lordiah froze, *"Oh my... What the..."* The others walked in and caught sight of what Lordiah saw.

In front of them were three large, white missiles, and a control panel.

"That explains the radioactive isotopes, but how did they get here?" Ramar asked.

"I heard from General Aries that there may have been missiles left here from the dinosaur extermination."

Lordiah walked over to the panels. He shined his flashlight around the room and stopped at several empty attachments on the wall.

"Are they active?" Ramar asked.

"No. The power accelerators have been removed, so there is no energy to power the panels. Looks like they have been here for thousands of years, so who knows if they work."

"Papa?" Ramar asked.

"Yes?"

"The other area with the isotopes is inhabited by people. They may have access to missiles!"

CHAPTER 74:
THE NEXT BOMB

Earth – five to six hours later

Lordiah paused while he entered data on the screen in front of him. *"My educated guess, the inhabitants are too primitive to operate the missiles, but we still need to exercise extreme caution."*

"Our team will unquestionably stand out," Ramar said.

"I plan to land us 3.8 miles from the city and hike in." Lordiah pulled the thruster control back toward him. The craft started to ascend. *"We'll trade for clothing from the local shepherds. It will help us blend in and cover our weapons."*

"I'm not wearing any smelly old rags from the rats on this planet!"

"Prince Zetus, with no disrespect, either you will wear them, or you'll need to sojourn in the shuttle where it's safe. We don't know enough about the occupants on this planet yet, so we need to blend in and observe."

Zetus sulked and stared out the window. Minutes later, he was asleep snoring loudly.

They flew for another hour. *"Ramar turned to Lordiah, "Hey, can I see that bracelet we found?"*

Lordiah reached into his fanny pack and pulled out the bracelet and handed it to him. *"Ramar, if this is gold, that means there must be rich veins in that area. It could be a great place to set up camp. A pyramid is already built so we can have immediate power. It's big enough for all of us to be housed inside too."*

Ramar handed the bracelet back. *"With only 38 prisoners, Mining will be light."*

"We have to work with what we have until we can enroll some of the inhabitants to help."

Ramar laughed. *"I know a family who thinks you're their god and will do anything, especially keeping your feet clean."*

"Ramar," Lordiah pointed down to a field out the left side of the shuttle windshield. He slowed down the craft and circled left. *"Do you see that?"*

In a green grass field, a huge four-pointed star inside a circle reaching five-hundred-forty-two feet in diameter was mowed out.

"That looks like your symbol, Papa. The one on your journals."

"This day is getting weirder by the minute," Lordiah muttered.

CHAPTER 75:
THE GENESIS
OF A CROP CIRCLE

Earth – 7.4 minutes later

They exited the craft in the field, with the exception of Zetus, who was still snoring, with drool dripping out the corner of his mouth.

Lordiah knelt down. *"The grass is cut with precision, and all at the exact same height. How? It's almost like art."* He bent down and sniffed the end of the cut grass. He shook his head and shrugged his shoulders.

They walked inside the circular grass pattern. *"It's flawless, the edge of the circle, the lines."*

"What do you want to do, Papa?"

Lordiah tapped his finger on the cut grass blade looking at it up-close. He exhaled. *"We park the shuttle here and walk. It's only a few miles from the city."*

Lordiah woke Zetus. The team stuck to the plan and traded food for clothes with some people nearby.

"This cloth is rough and itchy," Ramar stated as he held his breath and put the shepherd's shawl over his head.

Each now had their own outfit that hung to their knees, and a rope belt.

Ramar held up his headdress to the sun and studied it. *"I hope we don't get lice or other critters."*

"Son, please, don't freak us all out." Lordiah frowned and shook his head. *"Just put it on, and if you do get lice, your mom will be able to exterminate them."*

Their headdress hung past their shoulders, also tied with a rope band to hold it on. Last, they removed their boots and replaced them with sandals.

"As I stated, I refuse to wear those foul-smelling garments," Zetus grumbled. *"And you all look stupid."*

"Fine, if they are hostile and attack you, don't come crying to us," Ramar stated.

"Guards, arrest him! I am a prince and that's intolerable."
The guards looked at Lordiah, not knowing what to do.

"Prince Zetus, it's just a precaution." Lordiah held out a sullied shawl and headdress. *"We are walking into unfamiliar territory. They have missiles, and from our encounter with the shepherds, they mentioned there are inhabitants that are wicked. If you refuse to wear the clothing, then stay with the shuttle. Prince, or no prince, I am responsible for your safety."*

Zetus looked at the group. Ramar smiled and laughed under his breath.

"What is it going to be Zetus? Are you staying or coming with us?" Lordiah inquired.

"Fine." Zetus snatched the cloths out of Lordiah's hands.

The sun was blazing bright overhead as they walked down the winding grass dirt path along the low mountain range. Their headdress absorbed their sweat and kept it from trickling down their faces.

"The coordinates say it should be just around the next bend," Lordiah put his tablet away in his shoulder pack and covered it with his shawl.

They stopped when they rounded the corner. There, in front of them was a city with thousands of people, outside shops, storefronts, taverns.

They entered the town. The streets were lined with carts of people selling produce, meat, trinkets, and jewelry. The smell of fish, and meat exposed to the sun for hours lingered. Beggars were on the pathway drunk from wine. The smell of urine hung heavy on their prone bodies.

The town folk stopped and stared. Ramar looked at his father. His lips tightened and he shrugged his shoulders, *"Papa?"*

"Just keep walking, everyone," Lordiah whispered to them. The people parted and moved out of their way.

"Great idea wearing these ass smelling robes. Looks like we fooled them," Zetus joyfully dished out.

Lordiah pointed. *"The isotopes are being emitted this way."*

Several women approached them. *"Hi handsome,"* the older one said. The younger one opened her robe and flashed them with her full nakedness.

"My sister is young and beautiful. How much are you willing to spend for her talents?"

"Hey Zetus, why don't you trade that gold ring you found and make some more freaky red-haired giants," Ramar called out.

Zetus pushed him. *"Shut up, bastard. I should have you killed for that."*

Ramar pushed him back. *"Yeah, right. Get over yourself."*

A crowd started to gather. Lordiah stepped between them. *"What is it with you two? Ever since we have left Heofon, all you do is fight."*

Zetus pointed at Ramar. *"He acts like he's royalty. Thinks he's the boss and all. Well, he's not!"*

"Well, if you weren't stupid and worthless, then I wouldn't have to step up all the time, would I now?"

With a clenched fist, Zetus moved toward Ramar.

Lordiah put his arms up between the two. More people stopped to watch. *"Will you stop acting like children? You both should be more concerned about the missiles. Now come on, not another word!"*

Lordiah shook his head and walked between them.

When they reached the center of town, illuminated from the sun, in all of its glory a large pyramid stood erect.

Off the north wall, a group of slaves were laboring, moving rocks, carving stones with primitive hammers and chisels, building an addition on it. They were guarded by men continuously cracking their whips.

Ramar reached into his fanny pack and pulled out a camera. *"How are we going to get inside with those guards?"* He clicked off a few pictures.

Lordiah studied the pyramid and its surroundings. *"This one is less weathered than the previous and well taken care of. And the guards... That makes things difficult."*

A voice from behind interrupted them. *"Hey, do you think wearing smelly shepherd's clothes will disguise you?"*

Startled, Lordiah and the team whipped around. A man courted by three ladies on his arms stood there. He had his hair pulled back and a beard so long that an owl could nest in it.

The bearded man laughed. *"Try growing a beard to fit in, you idiots."*

"Leonardo?" Lordiah muttered.

He bowed. *"At your service, boss man."*

Lordiah stepped forward to get a closer look. *"It's been thousands of years! How could this be?"*

"At least for me it has. You don't know how happy I was the day I looked up in the sky and saw the moon shining up there. The beautiful, magnificent moonship."

Lordiah stepped forward and hugged him. *"It's so good to see you my friend. I just assumed you died of old age."*

"Yeah, that. Good news, we don't die. Must be the gold injections. I have been knifed, beaten and left for dead multiple times, but I always resurrect to see another day. I don't age either. Look, no gray."

"Nice beard," Ramar stepped forward, hugging him. *"Uncle Leonardo! It's great to see you."*

"If you let go of me and let me breathe, I'll introduce to you a couple of my wives."

"A couple of them?" Lordiah smiled.

"Three of the early risers. My other eight are still in bed. I take it you saw my artwork in the field?"

"That makes sense now. Leo, we have so much to talk about, my good friend, but we are here with purpose. Maybe you can help us. We need to get into that pyramid, but it's guarded."

Leonardo raised one of his eyebrows. *"So, you want to break into my home?"*

"You live there?" Lordiah asked.

"Yeah, it's the only place with power, and comes with a few bonus warheads. If you want to check it out, all you have to do is ask nice. And Zetus, keep your hands off my wives. We don't want any freaky-freak giants running around!"

"Ha, ha, real funny," Zetus snorted back at him. *"In case you have forgotten, I'm your royal prince, and if I want to touch your women, there is nothing you can do."*

Leonardo stepped in front of Zetus, toe to toe. He stood with his face inches from his. He stared at him for a few seconds before he spoke. *"I have been here hundreds of lifetimes. This is my home, not yours, and it never will be. Here, you're nothing but a royal piece of shit to me. You touch my wives, I'll cut your little dick off. So, you can take your royal cockiness and shove it up your royal prince ass. And if you want to survive here, you may want to kiss my peasant Earth cheeks. Now turn around and get the fuck out of my sight."*

Zetus looked like a fish desperately struggling to breathe. He glanced over at Lordiah.

Lordiah nodded telling him he should leave with a simple head movement. Zetus looked down, turned and proceeded to walk the way they came in.

Lordiah signaled for the guard to follow him.

Ramar laughed, putting his arm around Leonardo.

"Great to have you back, Uncle Leo!"

CHAPTER 76:
THE HOUSE
OF LEONARDO

The guards parted to each side of the front door and stood at attention when Leonardo approached, trailed by Lordiah and Ramar.

"Wipe your feet and take off those horrific-stink ass robes. You guys smell like shit."

"Wow, Uncle Leo. This place is finer than Grandpa's home in Heofon."

The interior was lavished with murals, detailed sculptures and candles that scented the room.

The ground floor was open and one large room. Sitting areas and a dining nook were arranged around the perimeter and the center was filled with a bed large enough to sleep several dozen people.

Ramar sauntered in to get a closer look. Handmade furniture was carved out of wood or sculpted of marble. He ran his fingers across an end table and picked up a colorful decorative pillow on one of the many couches and ran his hand across it. *"Where did you get this stuff, Uncle Leo. It's beautiful."*

"I made it. Even the pillows."

"Oh, nice."

Exquisite paintings hung on each wall, with very dynamic details and lifelike human features.

Leonardo and Lordiah followed Ramar while he wondered through as thou in an art gallery.

Positioned every eleven feet between the living room and the bedroom area were sculptures of naked humans, mainly men placed throughout the room. They were true to size and grand in their structure and musculature.

Ramar stopped at a statue of a female holding a baby boy. *"You have some fine artists here Unc. I'm quite impressed."*

"I made that too. I made of all of these, including the murals." Leonardo bowed to them. *"I have been painting and sculpting for the past who knows how many years now. Hundreds."*

On the bed, the other eight spouses of Leonardo were starting to awaken. They stretched and moved out from under their colorful covers. Some were male, and some were female. When they stood, they were naked and moved through the room without embarrassment.

Ramar couldn't take his eyes off the beautiful toned bodies wandering around. Leonardo laughed and winked at Lordiah.

"After we docked that boat, we grew the animals from the DNA codes, planted some seeds, and eventually, we discovered this mysterious pyramid in the middle of nowhere. The mountains must have protected it from the floods."

"Yeah, General Aries said there may be a few present and armed, built when the planet was inhabited with the dinosaurs. They brought the missiles to destroy their project." Lordiah said.

"Yeah, they got tired of getting eaten. Well, lucky for me, it still had the power units in. After I discovered the missiles, I claimed it for myself. Over time, the city formed around it. I have power, running water, and a harem. Life is good."

The trio was breathing heavy when they reached the top floor of his home.

"*Ta da,*" Leonardo sang as the large metal door creaked open. Inside stood multiple missiles, each decaled with colorful Heofon letters down the sides.

Lordiah approached the arsenal. *"It's shocking to find we left weapons of this magnitude here."*

"The power grid for the missiles are functional too." Leonardo placed his hand on the panel. It lit up, turned green and orange then booted up to a screen with icons.

"It looks like everything still works." Leonardo made a fist and knocked on the missile steel casing closest to him. *"Never had a reason to use them, but nice to have just in case."*

Lordiah looked around the room. He recognized the proton laser placed in the corner. *"Well, look over there. That will be helpful when we mine."* Lordiah walked further into the room, peaking around.

Leonardo exhaled and then chimed in. *"Don't worry, I have your precious Adam and Eve trophies. They're still sealed tight, fresh and well-preserved. Just like you left them."*

"Thank you," Lordiah smiled. *"I'm thinking of setting up our operations at the other empty pyramid site. It's already built, and we can move our team in immediately. I'm light on labor though, so next I will need to find some workers for the mines."*

"Fortunately for you, they have discovered slavery here. I'm sure we can persuade some kind of a trade system and get you some workers," Leonardo informed him.

"What are you going to end up doing, Leo?"

Leonardo smiled, *"I'm going wherever you go, boss man. The mental stimulation has been a little lacking since you left. I haven't done any experiments nor inventions for centuries. It's time for me to get back to work. And... I missed you."*

"Are you okay with leaving this plush set up here and starting over with us?" Lordiah asked.

"Very much so. And, I recommend we let Apollyon and his royal dumbass clan move in here. That way they'll be thousands of miles away from us and we don't have to deal with their stupidity."

CHAPTER 77:
BACK TO THE FUTURE

Moonship – Present Time

"Pops, it's kinda whacked that you still had Adam and Eve's dead bods after thousands of years," Luna voiced. *"Do you still have them?"*

"It's not whacked," he put his fingers up in air quotes. *"When it's for the evolution of science. They are one of my greatest accomplishments, still to this day. Look at the simple facts. No one would be here today, including you, if it wasn't for that project."*

"Since you put it that way, maybe it's super cool then. And Leonardo gave up his place just like that?"

"Yep. When Apollyon saw the place and that it had power, water and slaves nearby to serve him, that was all it took too. We were all ecstatic. Kept him and Zetus away from us. Zetus started to think being a prince meant being an asshole."

"So, what did you do?"

"We dropped off Apollyon, Zetus, and Anana, said good riddance, and took everyone else to the other pyramid to set up our new camp."

CHAPTER 78:

HEALER
AND SAVIOR

Carrying only a wooden box of his possessions, Leonardo marched his eleven spouses toward the flying taxi. *"I'm shocked that Apollyon and ding nuts didn't try to keep some of my wives,"* he chuckled, shaking his head.

Ramar removed the wood crate from his hands. *"I think Zetus is still damaged from your threats to remove his dick."* He looked around for more boxes and scowled when he couldn't find any. *"I can't believe you're leaving your art behind. You have some beautiful pieces. That's messed up."*

"It's just art, my boy." He smiled at him and put his hand on his shoulder. *"I can always make more. Living as long as I have, you tend to mellow out about trivial things. I have started over so many times, it's no big deal anymore."*

It wasn't long before they discovered the old mines located close to the other pyramid. In addition, they discovered humanoid like bones inside, but with more ape-like features.

"This is so fascinating," Lordiah beamed while he picked up a skull and looked at it closer. *"This pyramid must have been built hundreds of thousands of Earth years ago. These*

look like the skulls of the first bio-engineered worker from the earlier Heofonly expeditions we studied in school," an enthusiastic Lordiah told Ramar and Leonardo. *"The poor creatures were left behind to survive on their own after they left."*

Leonardo picked up a skull and held it up. He grabbed the jaw, making it mimic as if it was talking. *"We were a lot dumber than the ones you created Lordy."* He gave a slight chuckle. *"Can you imagine if you followed the same recipe and grew these barbaric things? We would have to destroy them like we did the dinosaurs to live here."*

(Lordiah Journal Entry: 03.02.33 Earth2) With the old mines open and the tunnels already bored out, we can start mining immediately. Ramar's role has expanded. He is now in charge of the mining teams and all operations. Leonardo and I got the power system back up in the pyramid. Once we had electricity, the missile grid came to life and went back online. It scared me at first, but Leonardo informed us that it was normal, and we were safe. The missiles have to manually be activated.

With only 38 prisoners, we are short staffed.

*   *   *

The hologram table in the control room flickered. Lordiah stood next to it with a remote in his hand. *"Major Thomas, can you pull up the hotspots in the thickest areas?"*

"Yes, sir." A three-dimensional image of the Earth materialized in front of them. Major Thomas put his hand on the outer portion of the hologram and spun it. He swam his hands out several times, expanding the area to a land area near a body of water with several red markers. *"Here are two populated cities close to each other."*

"Yeah, I know them," Leonardo pointed. *"That's Sodom and that's Gomorrah. Been there, done that. Large population, but a tad risky. They lack the rulebook and have some sacred sexual practices that are even perverse to me."*

"We only need about eleven dozen workers. Do you think we can find them there?" Lordiah asked.

"Why don't we take them from my city, or, I should correct myself, Apollyon's city? Plenty of people there."

Lordiah shook his head. *"Not going to happen. Apollyon clarified that the city and all the people are for his use."*

Leonardo exhaled. *"OK, well, there are plenty of poor people at Sodom and Gomorrah. If we feed them a few meals a day and give them shelter, I think a sufficient number would jump at the opportunity."*

"Then that's the plan." Lordiah clasped both hands together. *"We leave tomorrow."*

Leonardo leaned forward and drummed his fingers on the hologram making it dance. He shook his head and laughed. *"We should land the shuttles several miles out of the city limits and walk in at nighttime then."* Leonardo used his hands to expand the area, then pointed to a spot. *"It will be safer if we keep a low profile. And we should be armed. I could control the people in my city, but things are different there. Who's all going?"*

"Myself, Ramar, you, Major Thomas and Zetus."

"Zetus?" Ramar's eyebrows raised as he looked at his dad.

"Yeah, unfortunately. He's feeling a little insecure and left out."

Ramar shook his head, *"Really? That's ridiculous!"*

"You are the bigger person, so try not to provoke him."

"I'll do my best. Just don't put him on my team. Put him on Uncle Leo's. He knows how to deal with him." Ramar remarked with a grin.

They loaded up and headed out. Lordiah rolled his eyes and shook his head when Zetus radioed back informing them he needed several hours, and that they could wait outside their new royal palace while he got ready.

Dust kicked up from the dirt road near the pyramid before Lordiah shut down the propulsion engines from the shiny black shuttle. The townspeople either ran and hid, or they got down on their knees and bowed to the craft.

"That's so sad. They fear us," Leilana remarked.

More townspeople gathered to watch and bowed down to praise them as the Heofonly crew exited the flying craft.

"Yeah, I'm probably responsible for that. I kept the god angle going. Things got out of hand while you were away, so I had to evoke some fear. I suggest we keep it flowing."

Leilana eyed the crowd. They were all looking back at them as they were the center stage attraction. More were arriving and kneeling. She grabbed her satchel and walked toward them.

"Mom, what are you doing?" Ramar shouted.

"We created them from your father, remember? I want to get a closer look."

A woman with a young boy and an infant baby girl in her arms caught Leilana's attention. The boy was filthy, and the baby girl was wrapped in an old dirty blanket. Leilana walked over to them and knelt down. Ramar and Leonardo followed after her.

"Don't be afraid," Leilana said to the mother. She slowly reached out to the boy and shook his hand.

The baby coughed. Leilana stood. Her lips tightened. She observed the red spots on the baby's face and the mucus that drained and crusted her tiny nose.

"Is your baby sick?" she asked the young mother.

Looking away, the mother nodded her head yes.

"Can I look at her? I want to help."

The woman stared at Leilana, and held her baby close.

Leonardo spoke up, *"It's okay, she has powers to bless your baby."*

Leilana pulled out a silver and black medical scope from the satchel. *"May I?"* she asked as she reached for the baby.

The mother nodded. Leilana slowly unwrapped the soiled stained blanket the baby was wrapped in. She wiped her hand on her pants after.

"Poor girl, she has it all over her. How long has she had this rash?"

The woman shrugged her shoulders. *"Five, maybe six days."*

Leilana gently placed the device on the baby's chest, touching it to different parts of her body.

"I need to get a blood sample. May I?"

The young woman eyed Leonardo.

He nodded, *"Your babe will be fine."*

Leilana placed the device on her chest. A thud sound transpired. Several dials lit up in various colors. The baby started to cry.

Leilana smiled, *"That's all I need."* She pulled out an electric pad and plugged the scope into it. She waited a minute for the results.

"Your baby has the Chicken Pox. I can give her something that will help her."

Leonardo nodded to her again, *"Her hands will bring blessings to your baby."*

Leilana frowned, her brows raised and knotted in the middle as she looked over at Leonardo.

He shrugged his shoulders and gave her small laugh.

Leilana pulled out a syringe and set the dose. She picked up the baby's legs exposing her buttocks and injected the needle. The baby girl started to wail as Leilana administered the medicine. She stroked her chest to comfort her. *"This will make you feel better, honey."*

Leilana turned to her son, *"Ramar, do you have another shirt in the shuttle?"*

"Yeah, I do, why?"

She snapped her fingers several times then held out her hand. *"Good, take the one you're wearing off and give it to me."*

Ramar didn't question his mom and disrobed his shirt and handed it to her. Leilana removed the dirty blanket from under the baby girl and wrapped her up in Ramar's warm shirt.

"Can you bring her back to me tomorrow? Here?" Leilana asked the young mom.

She nodded yes, grabbed ahold of her baby and stepped back.

Another man from the crowd stepped forward. He had a young boy with him who was also covered in red spots. *"Can you bless my son too?"*

For the next few hours while they waited for Zetus, Leilana administered blessings to more children, twenty-nine total.

"I would never think that Zetus could do anything good, but him making us wait saved a lot of children today," an excited Leilana told Ramar. *"I'm not going with you. I need to stay here and help these people."*

(Lordiah Journal Entry: 03.03.14 Earth2) I knew the minute Leilana started to administer medical aid the people, she would stay behind. Her medical attention was much needed here. For them, but also for Leilana.

Zetus finally came out. He was disappointed to find out we weren't impatiently waiting for him.

Myself, Ramar, Leonardo, Major Thomas, and Zetus have now boarded the shuttle. Next stop: The cities of Sodom and Gomorrah.

* * *

CHAPTER 79:
SODOMY & GOMORRAH

(Lordiah Journal Entry: 03.03.14 Earth2) Leonardo filled us in on Sodom and the less than appropriate details of his escapades there. Zetus fell asleep minutes after takeoff and snored through the stories.

Agreeing with Leonardo's advice, we touched down in a meadow several miles outside of Sodom just before sundown. Nearby, 47 yards to be exact, we spotted a large tent. With the probability of having frightened the tent dwellers with our flying craft, Ramar and I walked over to humbly introduce ourselves. A sheepherder named Abraham, his family and their servants were hiding inside. But that's another story for another time. This journal entry is about Sodom and Gomorrah.

*   *   *

"A quick debrief everybody." Lordiah clapped his hands and waved for the group to come together. *"Let's break up into teams. Leonardo, you and Major Thomas be a team. Ramar and I will be the other. Zetus will stay behind and guard the shuttle."*

"If he wakes up. He'll probably still be napping and won't even know we left," Ramar snickered.

Major Thomas reached into his pocket and pulled several black rectangular devices out. He handed them to Ramar and Lordiah. *"Here's a talkie for each of you. It's more than just a communicator though. We can use it for defense, and it's also programmed to track your location."*

The shuttle door opened. Zetus squinted as he exited. He saw the group in a tight circle talking and laughing. His nose flared on one side and his eyes tightened. *"What's going on?"*

"Oh, hey, Prince Zetus, so nice of you to join us," Ramar popped off.

Zetus wrinkled his nose and spit on the ground in front of himself. *"Speak when spoken to, servant."*

Lordiah clapped his hands together several times. He raised his voice up a level. *"Hey team, it will be night soon. Let's finish this debriefing and get moving."* He directed his glare at Ramar. *"Sodom is a few miles out. Prince Zetus, for your royal safety, you stay with the shuttle."*

"Screw you if you think I'm staying here!"

Lordiah exhaled. *"It can be dangerous, Prince Zetus."*

"Yeah, so what? I can handle it. No way am I staying here."

"Easy folks," Leonardo interrupted. *"I can stay and watch the shuttle."*

Leonardo tossed his talkie to Zetus. *"And Major Thomas, you're the one always stuck on the moonship. You should definitely go. Get out, live a little. right?"*

"Yes please," Major Thomas nodded. *"I wouldn't mind going to explore the city if that's okay."*

"That's acceptable," Lordiah answered. He turned to Zetus. *"You and Major Thomas stick together at all times. No wandering off alone."* Lordiah held up his talkie. *"Major Thomas, continue please."*

"On your talkie, there's a button at the bottom. It's the weapons activation." Major Thomas pointed to the button. *"When you hold it down, it will activate."* He held the button down. The face of his talkie lit up bright red. *"When it lights up like this, it means it's armed. Grip it firmly in your hand, and then point it at your target. When you push the button again, it will discharge a bright light wave blast, invisible to*

the eye. It has a scatter pattern of eleven feet and a range of about twenty-nine feet in one direction. It won't kill anyone, but it will knock them down and the light wave will scramble their brains and mess with their vision for several hours."

"Thank you, Major Thomas. Now please don't use the blaster unless it's absolutely necessary. We want to be as invisible as possible. Any questions?"

Everyone shook their heads back and forth. *"No sir."* Ramar responded.

"OK, the sun is setting, so we should move out. Leonardo, we will radio you when we are on our way back."

Leonardo saluted, *"Aye, Aye, boss man."*

The sun had set, and the only light was coming from the stars radiating in the velvet black sky along with the glow from a full moonship.

They didn't walk long on the narrow dirt path before they stopped at the top of a small rise. There ahead of them revealed the outline of Sodom from the glow of the torches and fires placed throughout the city.

"This is where we should split up. Prince Zetus, you and Major Thomas go in first. Ramar and I will pass in behind you. Let's reconvene in about an hour."

Sodom was surrounded by a large rock wall except for the tall wooden gate that was propped open at the entrance. The city echoed with laughter, music, and resonances of celebration. Zetus and Major Thomas proceeded down the path and approached the entrance.

Dozing off on guard duty, an elderly gentleman sat on a wooden stool. He opened his eyes and leaned forward. He stood, reached for his lantern, and squinted in their direction.

They approached closer.

"Who's out there?" The man called out. Both eyebrows on the guard arched and his eyes enlarged. He dropped his lantern and quickly scrambled down to his knees. He bowed to them with his face toward the ground.

"So much for being invisible," Ramar remarked viewing from the distance.

With his face toward the ground, the elderly man spoke. *"Behold now, my lords, I am Lot, your servant. Turn in, I pray to you, into my, ya, y-your servant's house, and tarry all night. Let me wash your feet, and ye shall rise up early, and continue thy journey."*

Zetus leaned to the side to look. Inside the gateway the city was active. People were eating and drinking, buying and selling and even a fight broke out.

Lot stood; his eyes still large. He looked back and forth, at them and at the ruckus going on inside Sodom behind him. Without hesitating, he reached out and grabbed Zetus and Major Thomas by their sleeves. *"Your servant's house is just there, please, follow."*

Zetus ripped his sleeve away from Lot's grip. *"Old man, we have come to see the city, not your stupid shack."*

"The city is wicked. Quick, cover thy smooth face and let it not be shown." Lot removed his head cover and placed it on Zetus, herding him and Major Thomas into the shadows.

Steering them into the dark areas as they moved, Lot pressed them forward. They arrived at a small, wood framed home. Lot opened his door and once inside, shut it quickly behind them. He turned, pushed a board up and looked out a peep hole in the door.

"Good work Major Thomas getting the guard to leave his post," Lordiah murmured as he smiled.

"Yes, good job, Major Thomas," Ramar muttered. *"Because clearly Prince dumbass surly had nothing to do with it."*

Unlike Zetus, they had brought head covers. Lordiah and Ramar pulled them over their heads and wrapped their faces. He grabbed Ramar's arm. *"Let's move."*

With ease, they entered the unguarded gateway of Sodom unnoticed.

When Lot moved away from the door, Major Thomas quickly took the opportunity to peep out the spyhole too. He observed people drinking, eating, several men rolling around on the ground fighting, and even fornication happening just spitting distance outside Lot's porch. His lips tightened, and he shook his head. *This is a terrible, terrible place,* Major Thomas thought. *It's much worse than what Leonardo described.*

His eye was still glued to the peephole. *"Thank you for..."* Major Thomas turned and faced the main room. Several feet in front of him stood three women and Lot looking at him, hands behind their backs with large smiles on their faces. *"Oh, um, hi."*

Lot motioned to the women with a single hand gesture, and they got down on their knees and bowed their heads. *"This is my wife and daughters. Behold now, I have daughters that have not known any man. I pray you, do ye to them freely as is good in your eyes. There is one for each of you."*

"Oh... Ummm, ahhhh," stuttered Major Thomas. His cheeks turned red and he looked away. *"That's very kind of you sir, but uh, that's not necessary."*

"Speak for yourself, Major T." Zetus' eyebrows bounced up and down several times. *"I'll take him up on it!"*

Zetus walked over to get a closer look at the daughters. He helped them stand and looked them up and down as he bit his lower lip. The girls giggled. *"Damn,"* he said to Major Thomas. *"If you aren't taking the old man up on his offer, then that's more for me. I'll take both then."*

Zetus grabbed each daughter by the hand, *"Guard the room, Major Thomas. That's an order."*

The daughters giggled as Zetus led them into the back room. He turned, smacked one of the girls on her buttock, and winked at Major Thomas before he shut the door.

Major Thomas' throat felt dry as his face turned red. He looked dumbfounded at Lot and his wife. His forehead wrinkled as he nodded and stood there quiet.

Lot smiled at Major Thomas. *"Please, sit. Let us eat."* He clapped his hands several times. *"Wife, gather a meal for this, um, traveler from the sky."*

But before any food was served, the men of Sodom surrounded the house of Lot, both young and old.

And the men of the city called unto Lot, *"Where are the men who came to thee this night? Bring them out to us, so we may know them."*

Lot's eyes grew large. He ran over to the door and glanced out. Major Thomas followed.

He stood behind him and looked over his shoulder through the peephole. Several dozen men stood in front of his house with torches in their hands.

"What do they want?" Major Thomas asked.

Lot's face was pale, and he shook his head *"Oh, whatever thy do, do not go out there."*

Major Thomas darted to the backroom. He knocked. *"Your eminence, sorry to bother you, but we have a situation out here."*

A noise of fumbling came from the room. *"You better have a rock-solid reason for interrupting me!"* Zetus shouted.

"It is, sir."

A shirtless Zetus exited the room. *"Yeah, what? This better be good because I didn't get any yet."*

What a horrible child, Major Thomas thought. *We are guest in this family's home.* He shook his head and signaled for Zetus to look out the peephole.

And the men called unto Lot again, *"Where are the men which came to thee this night? Bring them out to us, so we may get to know them."*

Sweat started to bead from Lot's forehead. He turned to Major Thomas and Zetus, *"I pray thee brethren, stay in my house, for these men are wicked in their ways."*

Lot went over to the door, took a deep breath and slipped through, pulling the door tight behind him. Major Thomas and Zetus looked at each other, then moved over to the door, eyeing the peephole.

Lot stood in front of the door as he spoke. *"I pray you brethren, do not be so wicked,"* Lot insisted to the men outside. *"Behold now, I have two daughters that have not known man. Let me, I pray you, bring them out unto you, and do ye to them as is good in your eyes."*

Zetus stepped back after hearing Lot. His brows wrinkled and he pointed a finger at the door. *"That asshole just offered his daughters up to them too. Does he offer them to everybody?"*

Major Thomas turned pale. He backed away from the door and bumped into the dinner table. His hand trembled as he pulled out his talkie. *"Lordiah and Ramar, do you copy? Come in please. We have a situation here."*

There was no response. His heart started to pound faster. He repeated the command. Still no response. Slowly, he moved his quivering finger to the button on the talkie and held it down. The red light flashed several times then locked. It now said *"ARMED."*

Lot's voice was clearly heard as he stood on the porch. *"I pray you, brethren, leave, do not do wickedness upon these men."*

And one of the men from Sodom spoke. *"Stand back! These celestial fellows came to sojourn, and they will need to be judged. We will deal worse with thee, if thou stand in our path."*

Major Thomas's palms grew damp and his heart raced in a fit of tachycardia. *"Lordiah, Ramar, Leonardo, do you copy? We have a situation here!"*

From the crowd a rock was hurled. It struck Lot in the forehead, knocking him backwards. His eyes crossed then he fell to the porch.

Major Thomas stepped back and took several rapid breaths. *"Major Thomas, you can do this. You have to help,"* he said out loud to himself. *"Now is the time to act strong."* He quickly heaved the front door open, flung forth his hands, and pulled Lot toward the door.

Several men charged forward. Major Thomas' trembling hand raised with the talkie. He pressed the button.

Whap! Was the sound heard when the wave hit the men.

From the pack, eleven men hurled backward, flying off their feet, tumbling onto the ground.

One of the men got up. He waved his hands in front of his face. *"I have been stricken with blindness!"*

"I am stricken too!" said another.

The crowd stood motionless. They murmured to each other in shock and fear. Major Thomas grabbed Lot and pulled him back into the house. He secured the door by sliding a board across it.

Lot was on the floor wobbling side to side trying to sit up, but his balance was off. Blood trickled down his face and his nose splattered droplets on the front of his shirt and onto his wooden floor. His wife rushed forward and knelt down beside him.

Major Thomas looked around the room. *"Where is Prince Zetus?"* he questioned, panic in his voice.

Both daughters giggled and pointed under the bed. Major Thomas ran into the other room. He saw a quivering foot sticking out the side of the bed. *"Prince Zetus, stay right where you are. I'm calling for help."*

Major Thomas banged the talkie on his hand a few times then raised it to his face, *"S-O-S. Lordiah, anyone, do you copy!"*

No response. Not even a reply from the shuttle.

Leonardo moved to the pilot's seat and sat down. He raised an eyebrow, hands tented, methodically tapping the fingers across from each other. He placed his hand on a lever. *"It's been a long time ol' chap, but if I recall correctly, this is how you do it."*

The shuttle started to rise off the ground. *"Oh yeah."* It rose several meters higher. *"Let's see what you got, girl."* He hit the accelerator and cranked the steering wheel hard to the left. The shuttle started to rapidly spin in circles in the air.

"Woot, woot!"

A loud pounding struck Lot's front door. And the menfolk outside said, *"Lot, where are the men which came unto thee this night? Bring them out to us, so we may know them."*

"They want to get to know us," Major Thomas turned and said to Lot. His voice was shaking. *"What's so bad about that?"*

With wide eyes, Lot trembled and rapidly shook his head no. He stood up and blocked the front door. *"Thou shall not go out there! Thee and thine friend under the bed won't like how the men of Sodom get to know thee."*

Pounding shook the door and echoed throughout the house. Major Thomas jumped back. *"Lot, bring them out to us. We must touch the men that blinded our brethren. We want to absorb the power of the angels."*

The group outside cheered.

A few seconds passed, then Lot's front door was kicked. Major Thomas rearmed the talkie with his shaking hands.

He pushed Lot aside, spied out the peephole, and studied the crowd standing outside.

"Okay, I need to be strong and fearless," he muttered to himself. *"One, two, three."* Major Thomas took a deep breath and held it. He heaved the door open.

Whap! He fired another sound wave, knocking the group backward to the ground, temporarily blinding them.

But Major Thomas didn't see the man standing to the right side of the door until it was too late.

A piece of wood seemed to appear out of nowhere. Sudden pain and blood splattered across his face.

His vision became blurry, then the lights faded to black.

After a short time, his vision returned. He saw double. Muddy feet in sandals surrounded him and he realized he was face down in the dirt. One eye socket started to fill with blood.

"Grab him and tie him to the post so we may get to know him," a man yelled. The group cheered in agreement.

More men gathered amongst the crowd joining the twenty-nine walking around aimlessly, blinded and bumping into each other.

"Stop, I beg thee!" Lot called out, but they just pushed him aside.

Blood was now gushing from Major Thomas's nose from the strike and the large gash down his face left a trail of blood on the ground as they carried him over to the post and tied him to it.

The men pulled out large knives and began to cut off his pants. Major Thomas struggled, kicked a man in the groin, and dropped him.

The man with the large wooden stick stepped forward and struck Major Thomas multiple times upon his legs and knees. He crumpled, folding onto himself, unable to stand.

Major Thomas was half unconscious. The men laughed as they finished cutting off the rest of his clothes. He was now naked, pale, defeated, tied kneeling to the pole.

The crowd grew, and the air crackled with excitement.

"Wherefore art thine brethren from the sky? Go unto the house of Lot and seek him out!"

Several men rushed into the house. Lot's wife and daughters all pointed to the back room. In no time, a trembling Zetus was discovered under the bed. They grabbed him, dragged him outside and threw him next to Major Thomas.

"Tie him to the post so we may get to know him!" the man with the stick commanded.

Zetus looked at the beaten, naked Major Thomas slumped over next to him. His eyes grew large. Alarm crossed his face. A wet spot formed through his pants and trickled down his pant leg.

The men with their large knives pushed him up against the pole and tied him next to Major Thomas. They pulled out their blades and began to cut away his clothing.

His face darkened, worry tightened his cheeks and his head shook back and forth. Zetus whimpered cowardly. *"No, please, be careful there,"* when they slashed away at the clothing near his crotch.

"Please behold, I pray thee, stop," Lot pleaded on his knees several feet away, *"Do not so wickedly violate these men from the skies."* But the men laughed and pushed him away.

Zetus was now naked, bent over and tied next to Major Thomas.

The leader and the man with the stick positioned themselves behind Zetus and Major Thomas.

Lot shook his head frowning as he crawled his way over to Zetus. *"I pray you, my lord,"* he muttered. *"I'm sorry for such wickedness. Please, forgive me and my family for we did all we could."*

Zetus glanced over his shoulder. The leader was now naked except for his headwrap and sandals. Zetus' eyes watered with the full realization of what was about to happen to him.

The murmurs of the crowd were heard as more gathered.

A pair of hands grabbed Zetus's hips from behind and started to pull him closer, decreasing the gap between them.

His face tightened. He winced and sucked in a sharp intake of breath. *"No!"* Zetus pleaded, He squirmed right and left the best he could. *"I am a prince! You cannot do this to me."*

The man behind him laughed and then slapped him hard on his bare buttocks several times, leaving red handprints.

A tear rolled down his cheek. He closed his eyes, expecting the worst.

Whap!

The men in front of him flew several yards and tumbled to the ground.

Whap! Was heard when another wave blast hit the naked man behind Zetus hurled backward. Zetus opened one eye and peeked out.

Whap! Whap! Men flew, landing all around him.

Zetus turned to see what just happened. He saw Lordiah and Ramar, each rearming their talkies. The men that could see scattered and ran away.

Ramar grabbed the knife on the ground and cut Major Thomas free.

Lordiah shouted into his talkie, *"Leo, emergency evac! Emergency evac!"*

"Copy that. I'm on my way."

Several of the stricken men stood, their hands were out in front of them. *"I am blind, I can't see!"*

Ramar pulled his robe up over his head and helped the delirious Major Thomas put it on. Lot came over to help.

"Hey! Someone untie me!" the naked Zetus screamed.

Ramar moved over to Zetus and cut his ropes. *"Looks like we saved your ass, literally,"* Ramar smirked at him.

Zetus pointed his finger in Ramar's face shaking it. His face turned red, but he was unable to form words.

"Come on. Let's go!" Lordiah waved pointing. *"Leonardo is landing outside the gate."*

With Lot's help, they picked up the battered Major Thomas and carried him.

Zetus stopped to kick a few of the blinded men crawling on the ground. *"You are all going to pay for this!"* Zetus screamed at them as he covered his genitals with his hands. *"Someone get me something to wear."*

"Come on Zetus, let's go!" Lordiah yelled to him.

Zetus threw one last kick then ran to the gate. He stopped and turned. *"You are all going to pay!"* he screamed back into the city, jumping up and down in a tantrum.

Leonardo landed the shuttle. He couldn't help but do a double take when he saw a naked Zetus sprint out the gate, followed by Ramar and Lot carrying the bloodied Major Thomas.

The ramp lowered and he ran out. He glanced at Major Thomas, then back at Zetus, giving Lordiah a confused look. *"What the fuck stick happened?"*

Lordiah shook his head and whispered to him, *"I'll fill you in later."*

Leonardo nodded.

Still barely conscious, Ramar and Leonardo helped strap Major Thomas into his flight seat.

Lordiah walked Lot down the ramp and out of the shuttle. *"Lot, thank you for your help. Take my advice and grab your family and loved ones and escape for your life, and don't look back. Leave this city. Escape to the mountains and get as far away as possible."*

Lordiah turned around and entered the shuttle.

Lot stood frozen; his mouth pressed tight as he watched the shuttle take off leaving vapor signatures in the air. He stared up until it vanished out of sight.

CHAPTER 80:
AND THE ROCKET'S RED GLARE

It was mid-day and the sun shone directly above. The shuttle circled the royal pyramid once before it slowed to a hover. This time the people stood and watched and didn't scatter.

Crouched in front of a patient, Leilana looked up. Sweat soaked her collar. She had been working nonstop healing people since the men departed. She stood, wiped the sweat from her forehead and shaded her eyes from the bright sun as she watched the craft land.

The ramp lowered as Lordiah shut down the motors. Zetus popped out of his seat. His lips were pinched so tight that they were almost white. *"Meet me inside!"* he ordered Lordiah then sprinted out the craft.

Leilana brows wrinkled. She shook her head and proceeded over to the shuttle.

"Did I just witness a naked Zetus run out? What the heck was that about?" Leilana stopped in her tracks. She could smell the blood. Her eyes widened when she spotted the blood-stained Major Thomas lying on the shuttle floor.

"Oh my, what on this planet happened?" She pulled out the medical scope from her pocket, plugged it into a handheld screen and scurried over to him. She moved the scope over him as it scanned his body. One brow raised and a wrinkle formed. *"Guys, his knee is shattered, and there are multiple breaks*

below it. I don't have the equipment to fix him on this planet," she told them sadly. *"He also has several mandibular fractures in his jaw."*

Leonardo put his hand on her shoulder. *"Hey, he was injected with the white gold. Trust me, he will heal fine."*

They each grabbed a limb and carried Major Thomas inside the pyramid. Zetus, now dressed in his formal royal robe of purple and red velvet, along with a junior crown on his head was standing tall by the door waiting for them. Apollyon stood beside him, also in royal attire, but with a much larger crown.

"Zetus, would you like to address the room and make the command, or should I?" Apollyon asked.

"I'll do it, and everyone here must support me." He looked over at his father. Apollyon nodded to him. Zetus adjusted his crown then grasped both of his hands in front of him. *"We will obliterate those morons. Does anyone disagree?"*

"It's doesn't matter if any of you do disagree," Apollyon addressed the room. *"The order is ratified. Let's send a firm message to the city that violated my son."*

Zetus smiled and turned. Not wasting a second, he ascended up the stairs.

Lordiah looked over at Ramar and Leonardo. His lips tightened and he shook his head.

Beads of perspiration swelled on their forehead when they reached the top floor of the pyramid. The air in the room was stale. Apollyon, half out of breath pointed to Leonardo and Lordiah. *"You, go over to the missile panel and get that thing running."*

"It's been thousands of years. It's highly unlikely that they will work," Lordiah stated.

Leonardo chimed in, *"They should work fine. I checked the system every year."*

Leonardo proceeded over to the panel and flipped several switches. Buttons lit up, and the monitors danced to life.

"You may as well learn this too." Lordiah motioned to Ramar, signaling for him to join them. *"Zetus, come over here.*

I'm not pushing any launch button. If you want to do this, you're going to launch it yourself, not me."

Zetus strolled over, chin held high with an air of pride. Lordiah and Leonardo stepped aside. Lordiah folded his arms.

"Tell him what to do," Apollyon pointed at the panel.

Lordiah looked at Leonardo, his lips tightened.

Leonardo pointed at the screen. "Pull up the map, so you can pinpoint the exact location, click twice on the screen and then enter the coordinates that appear."

Zetus stepped up to the computerized panels. With a smug look on his face, he opened and closed his hands several times

Leonardo pointed to several groups of numbers. "Those are your coordinates to Sodom. Punch in each sequence one at a time."

Using his index finger, Zetus methodically typed in the coordinates one number at a time. A second map popped up with a red circle that outlined the area of Sodom.

"Your location is chosen. The area in the red circle is where the missile will hit and annihilate. Press the orange light below," Leonardo instructed.

Zetus laughed and pressed the orange button. An orange circle expanded around the red circle.

"That orange circle will be radioactive fallout. Everything and everyone will be affected and die in that orange circle too. If this is truly what you want to do, hit the green switch. That will launch the missile to the target."

Zetus reached for the green switch.

"Launch what? What is going on here?" Leilana said terse as she entered the room.

"This is men's work, my sister." Apollyon moved forward and raised his hand. "You should be down attending to the injured Major Thomas while we do our business."

Lordiah stepped forward and unfolded his arms. "Zetus, there are two cities within the melting zone. You will destroy both, killing a lot of innocent people if you pull that switch. Am I correct Leonardo?"

"Yep. Not only will Sodom be melted, but also the neighboring city of Gomorrah. And there are three other cities *in the orange circle that will be pelted from the radioactive fallout as well."*

"I don't know what happened in that Sodom city, but am I witnessing this correctly?" Leilana took several steps forward. Apollyon held his hand out to stop her, but she just brushed it aside. *"Are you men really going to launch a missile into that city?"*

The room fell silent. Zetus stared at the switch in front of him as the room watched. He reached up and put his hand on the lever.

"Are you sure you want to do that?" Lordiah asked.

"Let the word go forth to all. Do not mess with Prince Zetus or you suffer the consequences!"

And with a large smile, Zetus pulled the switch.

CHAPTER 81:
NOT MY
SHIT NUGGET!

Moonship – Present time

"Man, that nephew of yours is one big shit nugget!" Luna replied.

Lordiah discarded his cordial tone and summoned authority to his voice. He leaned forward towards her. *"I will never claim that kid as my family. Honestly, I had serious thoughts at the time to leave him to be raped in Sodom. Should have at least waited another hour before we rescued him. I know this sounds harsh, but if I could do that one over again, I would."*

"Wow, Pops has a mean streak in him."

Lordiah stared into space for the next minute. *"I'm sorry."*

"No worries, Papa, he sounds like a real dingleberry."

Luna observed the quietness of her father who seemed to have drifted millions of miles away. *"So, what happened to everyone? You're here. Where's Leilana? Ramar? Leonardo? Apollyon and douchie dew nephew?"*

"Well, after Zetus blissfully demolished Sodom and Gomorrah, I made an oath to part ways with the royal idiot family and leave them at that pyramid for good. We left and set up our home and operations at the other one.

Apollyon, Anana and Zetus were happy to be left there. They didn't have to do any work and had slaves to serve them. Major Thomas, whom you met earlier in the control room has never left the moonship since that incident. He has been here for the past 4061 years. He healed up, but Leilana never had the equipment to set his shattered bones correctly. That crushed my poor girl's heart."

"You have never gone back to your planet since your second tour here?"

He shook his head, *"No, we have not. Remember, if that moon leaves... I don't want to destroy the planet again.*

CHAPTER 82:
OH, ZETUS...

Earth – A week and four days later

Over the last week and four days Lordiah, Leonardo and Ramar had labored nonstop and installed the power generator unit into the pyramids top floor. Now that it was war functional again, the lights came on and fresh air pushed out the old stale smell.

Leonardo took a broom and swept the centuries of dust collected off the missile control station. He held a button down on the panel board and red and green lights flashed across the screens.

"Now that's some serious quality shit. Still works like new. Looks like you're armed and dangerous." Leonardo used his sleeve to wipe the sweat from his brow. He turned to Ramar and beckoned him closer. *"Get over here Ramar. Since you're the big man on campus in charge now, let's school you on some missile board basics."*

(Lordiah Journal Entry: 03.03.23 Earth2) The new mining headquarters is in full operation and running very efficient. We produce our own food, raise animals, and have grown a colony of 254 people.

The mines in the area are rich with gold. We have promoted Ramar to run the operations and he is proving to be a great manager.

I received some remarkable news today. Leilana is pregnant again! We are overjoyed and ready to bring our second child into our world.

*   *   *

"A brother! yes!" Ramar bellowed when his parents told him the news. A huge smile from ear to ear grew on his face as he pumped his fists in the air several times. *"I have fathered how many children now that have grown old and passed? I finally get to have a sibling that will stick around for a while! Ha! A little brother. This calls for a celebration."*

The crackling of the radio on the other side of the room disrupted his excitement. Major Thomas' voice interrupted the space. *"Lordiah, King Osilu has radioed and wants a dialogue immediately with you and King Apollyon."*

Lordiah shook his head and marched over to the table with the radio centered on it. *"Copy that Major Thomas, but I refuse to go to the city where Apollyon resides. He will need to figure out a way to come here, and then I will fly us both up to the moonship for the call with the King."*

Late afternoon the following day, a shuttle arrived. King Apollyon, pressed and outfitted in full royal dress, including a large crown almost the same size as his head covered in jewels, stepped out. Zetus also came along, dressed in the same outfit, but a much smaller crown. He was still strapped in his seat sound asleep, snoring, oblivious to the drops of drool that trickled down his chin.

Lordiah had his shuttle charged and ready for departure. He gave Apollyon eleven minutes, threatening to depart without him if he isn't on board. Apollyon didn't waste any time transferring over to the other shuttle, leaving Zetus asleep in the other ship.

Ramar put his foot on Zetus' seat and shook it. *"Hey, wake up Z."*

Zetus jumped, falling halfway out of his chair. His seat strap caught him as he twisted facing down.

Ramar tried to hold back his laughter, but some trickled out. He unhooked the strap. Zetus wiggled free and fell to the floor face first.

Ramar couldn't contain himself and busted out laughing.

"How dare you do such a heinous deed to me!" Zetus shouted as he turned over and sat, red in the face.

Ramar put his hands up. *"Zetus, sorry, I didn't mean to startle you. Everyone left you in here. I did you a favor and came to get you. I come in peace. My true intention was to wake you and show you our set up here."*

Ramar held his hand out, *"Are we cool?"*

Zetus' exhaled as his face lightened to a pink. *"My dad left me here?"*

Ramar nodded and pulled him up. *"Yeah, sorry."*

"Well, he must've done that because he wants me to check out your operation to see if it's running proper."

"It will be my honor to show you around." Ramar stepped aside and motioned for him to lead the way out of the shuttle.

"OK, but I will need to be fed first."

As Zetus sailed past, he didn't notice Ramar roll his eyes.

There was new construction pounding away around the pyramid, and the gardens were being tilled and tended. Ramar kept his word and took him on a tour, stopping at the mines first.

Zetus walked with his arms folded and his hands buried inside each opposite furry cuff of his sleeves. *"Do they know that a prince is present and amongst them? We should make that clear to your workers."* Zetus probed Ramar walking through the mines.

Several workers approached Ramar and handed him a clipboard. They bowed to Zetus.

"I'm sure they do, and the royal clothing and crown helps," Ramar told him as he signed off on whatever was on the clipboard.

They toured the area for another hour. *"Have you seen enough?"* Ramar asked. *"Let's go inside and check in with mom."*

"Yes, lets," Zetus nodded, then put his hand up. *"You are too soft on your workers. You need to instill more fear into them like we do with ours at the royal city. They can never speak unless spoken to, nor look at us. I demand you do the same here."*

Ramar's lips tightened, and he shook his head. *"Zetus, things are different here. We have a society, and production is running smooth. We are mining more gold now than we ever have, even higher than our first trip here."*

"It's Prince Zetus, and you will respect me by calling me by my proper title when speaking to me."

A frown wrinkled across Ramar's forehead. *"Zetus. Umm."* He put both hands up. *"Excuse me, Prince Zetus. We've had such a great day so far. Please, let's keep it that way."*

"Everything is fine, but remember, I'm in charge, and if I tell you to jump, you need to jump! If I tell you anything, you must do it." Zetus looked at him. His eyebrows raised, and a pleased look molded on his face.

Ramar stared at him then shook his head. *"I'm serving Heofon, and you're serving nothing but yourself. You're such a useless waste, Zetus. Go back to your royal anthill and rule whatever you want there. But here, you're nothing."* Ramar picked up his pack, turned and headed back toward the pyramid.

Zetus removed the black glove from his left hand. *"You will apologize for your insults and disrespect, or I will have you severely chastised. Now get on your knees, kiss my feet and apologize, and I just may forgive you."*

Ramar stopped, turned, rolled his eyes, and chuckled.

"Kneel to me, I said!" Zetus shouted.

"No, I won't, so get over yourself."

Zetus's face turned red with anger as he stared back. His mouth tightened as his lower lip covered his upper.

Ramar looked back at him, staring him in his eyes.

Zetus slapped his glove several times against his palm as he approached Ramar, stopping inches in front of him.

Ramar smiled in his face. *"So, what are you going to do, cuz? Slap me with your royal glove?"*

Zetus's eyes got large and his face turned several shades darker.

Ramar stared back.

Zetus spat on the ground between them, then stepped around him and huffed away toward the pyramid.

CHAPTER 83:

THE CALM BEFORE THE STORM

Lordiah and Apollyon spoke only a handful of words during their 2.18-hour flight to the moonship. Apollyon tried to make conversation, but Lordiah just stared out the windshield in front of him. Apollyon even demanded he speak, but Lordiah blocked him out.

When the two large doors opened in the smaller crater, Lordiah was relieved the trip was over. The doors echoed as they slammed shut solidly behind them, removing any trace that an opening ever existed.

Major Thomas limped over to greet them. *"I received word from Heofon a few minutes ago. They scheduled the call in two hours twenty-seven minutes on King Osilu's request. You may as well make yourselves comfortable."*

CHAPTER 84:

THE WAR
OF THE GODS

Earth

Ramar needed to get away from Zetus for a few hours. He
returned to the mines to finish his daily reports, checked up
on the newer workers, and collected all the gold that had been
gathered for the day. He was quiet, reflecting on what his
father might say about his altercation with Zetus earlier.

I will be the mature one and apologize, he said to himself.
*But screw him if he thinks I'm kneeling or kissing his dumbass
boots.*

Hours passed. Ramar patted the dust off his clothes before
entering the pyramid. He removed his shoes, then stopped to
listen.

Ramar heard his pregnant mother shout from the other
room. *"You can go back to your royal city and do whatever you
want there, Zetus, but not here. You will be respectful."*

"What's going on?" Ramar asked entering the kitchen area.

"Zetus grabbed the female help inappropriately, trying to force his way with her, and I won't let him!" Leilana responded.

"I'm a Prince Zentus." The words slurred out of his drunken mouth. *"And I ill do ass I pleeze with er."*

Zetus walked over to a young, scared girl curled up and trembling against the wall. He clutched her arm. *"You'racominwit me."*

Leilana stood in Zetus' way. Her face turned a darker shade and tightened. *"Zetus, let her go. Now!"*

"You'ra not my boss!" Zetus told her as he pushed her out of his way.

Leilana slapped Zetus across the face. *"Zetus!"*

His eyes widened with surprise. Zetus saw red, and with both hands, he pushed her. Leilana stumbled back a few steps, backing over a chair behind her. She tumbled and landed with a thud on her back.

Gasping for air, she laid on the floor. Her eyes watered. She reached up and held her pregnant belly.

Ramar's eyes opened wide, and he made a beeline over to her. *"Mom, are you all right?"*

Leilana coughed several times. A tear rolled down her cheek. She nodded. *"Help me sit up."*

Ramar assisted her to her feet and helped her to a chair.

"Are you sure you're okay, mom?"

She wiped tears from her eyes and nodded.

Ramar squatted down at eye level to her and put his hand on her arm. *"And the baby?"*

"Yes, I think we're fine." She noticed Ramar's hand was shaking.

His nostrils started to flair.

"Ramar, don't," she whispered.

Zetus went over to the counter and refreshed his brandy. He shot it down in a single gulp.

Ramar's brows narrowed, and his fist clenched. He turned and glared at Zetus.

"You inbred prick," Ramar yelled when he charged him. Connecting at a full run, Ramar and Zetus' bodies flew onto a

table behind Zetus, shattering it before they crashed to the ground.

Ramar sat on Zetus's chest and pinned his arms down under his knees. With years of built up anger, Ramar's fist lashed out on Zetus's face, over and over.

A tooth flew out and landed on the floor near Leilana. Ramar's lips were paper thin tight, his eyes wicked with fury as blood droplets freckled around them.

Leilana's legs were drawn and curled up into her chest. *"Ramar, stop! Please stop!"* she cried as she watched the violence rage from her son explode out of him.

Ramar's fist kept hammering down on Zetus's bloodied face.

An arm grabbed him from behind and yanked him off.

"Ramar, enough," Leonardo said in a calm voice. He spun Ramar around to face him. *"That's enough."*

Everyone turned and looked at Zetus lying on the floor, not moving. His eye was purple and swollen shut. His nose was dripping blood and was flattened and crooked.

"Shit," Leonardo muttered.

Zetus coughed. He slowly turned over to his belly and got up on his hands and knees. He spit out another tooth.

Eyeing his bloody tooth on the floor, Zetus screamed, *"I will behead you for this!"*

Ramar broke away from Leonardo and beelined his way back to Zetus.

Zetus curled up into a tight ball protecting his face. He screamed for help.

Ramar reached down and grabbed Zetus by the hair. He dragged him toward the door and flung him out. *"Get out of here! And never come back!"*

He wiped his bloody hands on his pants. *"Uncle Leo, can you please get that piece of trash out of here?"*

Leonardo nodded. He walked over to Zetus and helped him up. *"Come on Prince Zetus, let's get you home."*

Zetus turned back. His words whistled through his broken teeth. *"This isn't over, Ramar!"*

CHAPTER 85:
THE BIG
BANG THEORY

Moonship– Later

The Control Room was quiet. It was empty except for Lordiah, Apollyon and Major Thomas. They sat waiting, silent, each looking in different directions.

Major Thomas moved over to his station and squinted at his screen. The others watched him. *"Lordiah, sir, you have a communication coming in from Ramar. Would you like to receive it?"*

"Yes, please." Lordiah stood. *"Can you get me a handheld?"*

Major Thomas handed Lordiah a talkie. He walked over to the far end of the Control Room to talk in private.

Apollyon's forehead wrinkled as he watched Lordiah pace back and forth out of earshot.

Lordiah nodded and listened. *"Is Leilana and the baby okay?"*

Lordiah's pace picked up. He glanced up at Apollyon and saw he was watching. He turned his back to him. *"You know we will have some repercussions to deal with. What I'm going to do is bring it up during our call today with King Osilu and settle this through him. He will likely side with you since Zetus showed force against Leilana and you were defending her. Tell me every detail."*

Major Thomas sat up in his chair. His brows creased, and he leaned forward and focused closely on the screen. He typed on the keyboard in front of him. His screen changed. *"King Apollyon, Lordiah, I need your immediate attention."*

"Hey Ramar, can you hold that thought for a second?" Lordiah observed the pale look on Major Thomas face. *"What is it, Major Thomas?"*

"Sirs, a missile has been launched from the Royal Pyramid."

Lordiah and Apollyon looked over at each other.

"What?" Lordiah responded. He ran over to Major Thomas's station. He put the talkie back up to his ear. *"Ramar, a missile has been launched. Do you know anything about this?"*

Worry tightened his cheeks. Lordiah looked over at Major Thomas. His brows raised and his eyes enlarged as they locked onto the screen in front of him. His heart started to beat double time. *"In what direction is the missile heading?"*

"Sir, it appears to be heading due east, in the direction of your pyramid."

"Ramar, a missile is coming your way!" Lordiah turned to Major Thomas. *"How long until the impact?"*

"One-hundred-eighty-two seconds, sir."

"Ramar, evacuate now!" Lordiah put both hands on his head and grabbed his hair in a fist. *"Ramar, do you hear me? Grab your mother and evacuate now!"*

"Major Thomas, open up a com to the Royal Pyramid. Put all communications on speaker."

"Yes, sir. You have an open channel to the Royal Pyramid."

Lordiah yelled out, *"This is Lordiah, along with Apollyon here on the moonship. Do you copy?"* There was silence on the other end.

Lordiah and Apollyon called out several more times.

"Ramar, are you there?" Lordiah shrieked.

"Major Thomas, how much longer until impact?"

"Eighty-three seconds, sirs.

"Ramar!" Lordiah called out several more times.

A visual of Earth popped up on the screens. A yellow circle appeared on the location where Leilana and Ramar were, and a red triangle moved across the screen toward it. A red countdown timer appeared up at the top of the screen. The timer was at forty-seven seconds.

"Ramar! Do you hear me? Please tell me you have evacuated!" Lordiah cried out.

Ramar's voice came over the talkie. *"Papa, I'm sorry, I love you."*

"Ramar, where are you?" Lordiah cried out. The timer ticked down to 29 seconds.

"Papa, we can't evac. Leonardo has the shuttle. He returned Zetus back to his place. There's only one thing to do now. I'm sorry."

"Sirs," Major Thomas interrupted, *"a missile has been launched from your pyramid, Lordiah. It's heading due west."*

On the monitor it showed a red triangle moving west. *"The missile appears to be heading towards your pyramid, King Apollyon, sir,"* Major Thomas spilled out.

Apollyon shouted, *"Zetus! Get out! Ramar has launched a missile. Get out!"*

The red triangle that was heading east hit its mark. A flash of flames appeared where the yellow marker was, followed by a large mushroom cloud, clearly seen on the screen in front of them.

Lordiah's jaw dropped as he stared at the screen. Not a muscle moved in his body except his mouth. *"Leilana... Ramar..."*

Silence pierced the control room while they all watched the second missile head toward its target.

"Zetus, please, anybody! Do you hear me?" Apollyon cried out one last time.

The second missile struck its mark. A circular wave of destruction moved outward devouring everything in its path.

CHAPTER 86:
THE BEGINNING
OF THE END

Earth – 2.36 hours later

The ground was smoldering. An eleven-mile radius was boiling, absent of life while embers filled the air.

Lordiah's mouth twisted in a troubled scowl as he and Apollyon circled the shuttle around the ruins. Zero evidence remained of the pyramid where his loved ones took their final breath. Nothing but a large crater existed now.

"They're gone," Lordiah mumbled over and over again as he landed the shuttle. He was trancelike and numb.

"What are we going to do now?" Apollyon asked.

"We? There is no we! Never was. I'm done with you, with everything!"

Lordiah stood up. His legs trembled; his hands shook, and he fought the urge to hyperventilate. He stared forward; his face robotic with no expression. He lowered the ramp and trudged toward the exit.

The air was warm and vengeful. Thick bands of dark red clouds partially obscured the sun in an eerie shadow.

Apollyon stayed seated and watched him. *"You can't go out there. Won't the radiation kill you?"*

Lordiah ignored him as if he was never there. His feet dragged as he walked forward, leaving long tracks in the sand. Finally, he buckled to his knees, and wept, his wet tears on his cheeks catching whatever ash was floating in the air.

Several minutes passed before Lordiah realized another shuttle was landing.

"Leilana?" He screamed in a high-pitched tone, hyperventilating. *"Ramar?"* He jumped to his feet and sprinted over to it.

The ramp lowered, and Leonardo stepped out.

"Leilana? Where is Leilana? Ramar?"

Leonardo shook his head. *"I'm truly sorry, brother."*

"Are you sure? How are you alive?"

"I flew Zetus back and was in transit when the missiles hit. I have been flying around searching for survivors. I'm so sorry."

Lordiah crumbled and dropped to his knees. He folded into himself, arms around his shins, holding himself together. He tried to scream but only silence emerged.

Apollyon joined them. *"What now?"* he asked again.

Lordiah looked up at him. He bit his lip hard enough to almost draw blood. *"This is your fault!"* He jumped to his feet and charged him. Apollyon turned, hit the ground and curled up into a ball tighter than a roly-poly bug.

Lordiah landed on him and released furious punches anywhere he could find a spot to hit. *"I told you, there is no we! Everything is dead! Destroyed! And it's your fucking fault."*

"I lost my kid, too!" Apollyon whimpered out.

"Your piece of shit child did this!" With both fists together he rained down more furious punches. Apollyon covered his face and squeezed tighter into his ball.

Leonardo exhaled and shook his head. *"Damn, twice in the same day I'm stopping something I'm quite enjoying."* He caught Lordiah's hand on a downward swing and pulled him off, away from the screaming Apollyon.

Lordiah stood, gasping, his heart beating out of his chest. He pointed at Apollyon. *"I never want to see you again!"*

Lordiah turned and walked off toward the burning crater.

Leonardo helped Apollyon stand and loaded him into the shuttle he arrived in. He looked out the front windshield.

Lordiah staggered forward until he collapsed onto his knees. He doubled retching. Nothing came up. He dry heaved a rope of stringy saliva onto the dirt below him.

Leonardo slowly walked toward him.

"Lordiah, brother, we need to leave." Leonardo put his hand on his shoulder. *"Come on, the radiation levels are high here."*

Lordiah rose to his knees, then to his feet. Instead of walking back to the ship, he continued into the crater.

"Lordiah, come on. What are you doing?"

"Go. Leave me. I have no reason to live." Lordiah marched forward.

Leonardo exhaled. He watched him for a few more minutes. His forehead crinkled, and his mouth pressed tight. *"I love you brother,"* he muttered to himself and wiped a tear.

Leonardo turned and walked back to the shuttle. He stopped on the ramp to look one last time back at Lordiah. He shook his head sadly, then stepped inside.

The heat was agonizing on his body, but he persevered onward. Blisters and burns formed on Lordiah's face and arms until his body couldn't take anymore. He collapsed.

Part 4:

BACK TO
THE FUTURE

CHAPTER 87:
PRESENT TIME

Moonship – Present Time

The silence made the room stale throughout Leilana's suite as they both sat. Luna absorbed what she had just heard. She propped herself up on the couch, her lips tightened. *"Shit papa, that's really messed up. Sorry I asked."*

Lordiah got up and moved to the reclining chair. He picked up the round purple pillow sitting on it. He put it up to his face, closed his eyes, and smelled it before he carefully laid it back on the chair.

He sauntered over to a side table and ran his finger across it. It was dustless.

Luna looked around the suite with more awareness. Everything was perfect. The room spotless, clean.

He wandered over to the sink area outside the bathroom. Leilana's medical tools were lined up on the dresser and shelves. In the drawer by the bathroom sink was her hairbrush. Rubbing his thumb against his index finger, he caressed the hair still caught in the bristles.

She folded her arms and turned her body to him and watched him. *"Have you kept it this way for thousands of years?"*

"You may think I'm crazy but this room... It's all I have left of her."

Luna glanced back at Lordiah as he sat quietly staring forward. She smiled at him. *"Papa, I actually find it adorable that you made her room into a shrine."*

His face was frozen as he stared forward. *"The day she passed was the worst pain I have felt in my entire life. I wanted to die a painful death to dull my misery, but unfortunately, thanks to that stupid white gold we injected I wouldn't die. I kept getting blisters and sores but always managed to heal."*

He ran his fingers across the counter, drawing an L over and over. *"Eventually I had to accept the fact that I wasn't going to die. So, I walked back, and flew away as far as I could. I found an island and spent some years there alone. I had no idea where Leonardo or Apollyon went until I saw them again several centuries later. They had separated, gathered and grown their own societies, built pyramids, cities..."*

He ran his fingers over several bottles on the countertop before picking up a glass. It had a lipstick mouth smudge still on the glass. He stared at the red lip marks.

Luna slowly stepped back away from him.

"Luna, don't worry, I assure you I'm not fully crazy. I just had no reason to change the room. And, it comforts me to come in here. I feel her presence when I touch her things."

Luna walked over to the bed. It was made perfectly. She pushed down on it to feel the firmness of it before sitting on it. *"Anything else cool that happened in the following few thousand years, besides me?"*

Lordiah smiled. *"I wish I had my journals, because yes, there is so much more to tell you. Stories that are the truth, and not the lies taught. Thousands of years gone forever."*

Luna thought for a second. *"Like what?"*

"Well, like Apollyon's involvement in shaping Julius Caesar, Hitler, wars. He totally messed with Moses from the bible, using holograms pretending he was God and giving him false hope. I had to clean that up. He was off causing wars with his secret societies, trying to gain power so he could take back

the moon. I also formed a secret society of my own, but we helped people."

"How?" Luna asked.

"With technology. I helped guide the world with the first motor, the microwave, computer technology, even the internet. Aliens from other planets sought out and visited this planet, all with bad intentions, so I helped the governments deflect them. I scrambled the controls of the UFO crafts and caused them to crash in the 1940s and 1950s, and orchestrated what you all know as Area 51. Apollyon formed NASA because I hid all of our shuttles from him so he couldn't get to the moonship. It was a ploy to take the moon. I convinced the top officials to stop all trips there. If Apollyon had gotten control over the moonship, he would take it. Leaving the orbit would destroy the planet again. I have records, names, and pictures documenting all of this in my journals. Photos of Noah, Adam, Eve, E-Den, construction of the pyramids, Sodom before we destroyed it. Even photos of a naked Zetus tied up to the post."

Luna thought for a second. "Papa, what would you say if I told you I have your books?"

"I would hug you so hard your head might pop off!"

Luna shrugged. "I may have taken them if they are the leather books you had stashed under your desk."

Lordiah stood. "Luna, where are they?"

"They're at my apartment."

"Luna, your fingerprints, your DNA could be in my study. These people, Apollyon, they are very resourceful. Have you ever been fingerprinted before?"

"I may have acted up a few times, so yeah, it's safe to say I'm in the system."

"That's not good." Lordiah started to pace. "Anyone at your home?"

"You mean my shithole. Yeah, my boyfriend Rob is there probably sacked out on the couch. He lives there too."

"Luna, we need to go, now. Hopefully we're not too late."

CHAPTER 88:
LOOKING FOR
A FEW GOOD BOOKS

Earth – Present Time

Bathed by the blue light of the moon, Lordiah, and Luna hovered over the secret warehouse in the desert. He was quiet, his mouth twisted in a troubled scowl.

"Why the silent treatment?" Luna asked.

"I'm just thinking."

"Okeydokey... It's just that I opened up to you. The silence is freaking me out a bit."

"Hey, sorry, hun." He tapped a knuckle to his lips. *"Please, give me a second to think this out."* He shook his head and sighed. *"These people... Apollyon... It's crucial that I retrieve those journals."*

The doors to the roof opened. Howls from a pack of coyotes bled in the distant night air as they savaged their fresh caught prey, oblivious to the presence of the shuttle as it silently descended. Halfway down, the lights were automatically triggered by the motion sensors.

They didn't waste a second after they docked and jumped into Lordiah's Tesla and sped off.

"Type your address into the GPS." He pointed to the screen on his dash.

I need to prepare her for the worst. Apollyon was too close last time here, Lordiah said to himself.

He handed her his phone. *"There are apps on here you should know about. Emergency and Electro Mace."*

Luna scrolled through his apps. *"Electro mace... Yeah, I learnt about that one the fucked-up way. I def want that on my phone."*

"In due time. If you press the app, it will light up red and tell you it's armed. Point and press on the word armed, and you know the rest."

"Yep, a blast that makes you shit yourself."

Lordiah pointed at an app below Electo Mace. *"See the one that says Emergency? That will send out a distress signal to Major Thomas. He will be able to track the phone.*

She leaned back and looked at him with one eyebrow raised. *"You look worried, papa. Are we in that much danger?"*

"I hope not but we need to get in, grab the journals and get out. You understand?"

"Aye-aye, sir." She saluted him. *"What a great father-daughter bonding experience. You're the best f-ing papa ever. Totally."*

"Luna, Apollyon is ruthless. He will do anything to take the moon back. Please take me serious."

"I am papa." She rubbed her palms together. *"And I want you to know you got yourself a badass sidekick. Sneaking in and out of places is my specialty."*

They pulled up to an older apartment building in the heart of Koreatown. Trash lined the streets, an old worn out couch was on the sidewalk in front and half of a bike was chained to a tree.

"I'm up on the top floor. I hope you don't mind the mess," Luna told him.

They exited the car. Lordiah looked up and down the street. He halted and raised his hand when he heard a helicopter overhead.

Luna stopped.

He looked around, then gripped her arm and pressed forward. *"Let's get inside."*

Luna put the key into the deadbolt of her building. She jiggled it aggressively and kicked the door several times before the latch turned.

The lobby smelled old and stale with a faint urine scent. Several bicycles were chained to some rusted pipes and stacks of phone books were thrown on the ground. Luna headed over to the stairwell. *"The elevator is broken. Has been for months."*

Beads of sweat bubbled up on her forehead and she was winded when they reached the eleventh floor. *"This is a big step taking my dad to the homestead and meeting the ol' BF."*

Luna didn't lie. The apartment was a mess, and Rob was sacked out on the couch, shirtless, drinking a beer watching Cops reruns.

"Where the fuck have you been?" Rob asked Luna, followed by a burp.

Lordiah walked in behind her. Rob sat up. *"Who in the fuck is this?"*

"Hi Rob, nice first impression for my dad. I'm just grabbing a few things then we're out of here."

Rob stood up. He walked over to Lordiah, pushing out his chest and sizing him up. *"I thought your dad was dead?"*

"I did too, but apparently not."

The forty-seven-year-old Rob kept eyeballing Lordiah. He snorted. *"This dude doesn't look old enough to be your dad. You think I'm stupid?"*

Lordiah folded his arms and stared back at Rob.

Luna walked over to the desk. She grabbed a box on the ground, turned it over and dumped the empty cartons of Chinese food and other trash out on the floor. *"You really don't want me to answer that, Rob."* She collected Lordiah's journals and packed them in it.

Lordiah exhaled and put his hands into his pockets. *"There's no funny business going on here, Rob. Those books she's packing, they're mine. We're just going to grab them and leave."*

Rob's face turned red and his eyes grew large. He heaved his half empty beer, hitting the wall above Luna's head. *"No one is taking shit unless I fuckin' say so!"*

"You ass!" Luna shouted back. *"He's my dad, dipshit."*

"Dipshit, huh? What if I kick his ass and find out?"

"Brilliant statement, Rob. And that will prove what? Huh?" Lordiah pulled his phone out.

The shirtless Rob walked toward him, puffing his chest out, even more than the last time. With a clenched fist, he stopped several feet in front of Lordiah. *"What, you going to call the pigs?"*

Lordiah put both hands up. *"Rob, we're just going to grab the books, and leave."*

Luna placed the last book into the box and turned. *"I would listen to him Rob, if I were you."*

"Fuck you both!" Rob responded, moving towards Lordiah.

Whap!

Rob flew back, flipped over the couch and landed by Luna's feet.

"Sorry, Luna. I put the setting on low. He'll be fine." Rob grabbed his ears. His eyes were crossed, and mucus seeped from his nose.

"Dumbass deserved it." Luna grabbed the box and stepped over the dazed Rob. *"I got everything, let's bail."*

Lordiah looked at her, then back at Rob. He nodded and stepped out of the apartment.

"I told you not to mess with my dad, dumbass. By the way, we're over." She turned and slammed the door behind her.

The sun lit the stairway as Lordiah and Luna ran down the eleven flights of carpet stained stairs. *"I am sorry about your boyfriend."*

"No worries," she snorted. *"It was a messed-up relationship anyways. A girl with daddy issues hooked up with an older asshole. Go figure."* Luna grinned and raised her eyebrows. *"I heart your blaster. Glad it wasn't me this time. Totally want one!"*

Once on the ground floor, Lordiah extended his hand. She stopped. He cracked the front door open and looked up and down the street, then up in the sky. *"It's clear."*
The trunk popped open. Luna set the books inside.
I feel so much better now, a thankful Lordiah thought.
"Mission accomplished!" he smiled big and gave Luna a high-five. *"I hope you enjoyed that as much as I didn't. Let's get back to the moon where it's safe."*

Lordiah placed his keys in the ignition and turned it. The doors locked, but the engine didn't turn over. He cranked the key again. Nothing.

A greenish smoke crept out the air vents on the dashboard.

"What the.." Lordiah's eyes got big and his lips tightened. He recognized the rotten apple smell.

Luna saw the panic on his face.

He grabbed the door handle and pushed. It was locked tight.

Lordiah coughed. His eyes watered. He banged his elbow hard against the window several times, but it was his own fault that the bulletproof glass he installed wouldn't break.

Luna froze as she watched her father panic. Her eyes began to tear, and she coughed.

"Can you open your door?" he shouted at her.

Luna tried, but it wouldn't budge.

Outside, a figure walked toward the car. The greenish gas continued to pour out of the vents. The figure in a black pinstripe suit stopped in front of Lordiah's car. He smiled and slowly waved. It was Apollyon.

"No, no, no!" Lordiah banged his shoulder against the door. He could taste the gas. His eyes became heavy, and the view of the smiling Apollyon was getting fuzzy.

He gazed over at Luna. Her body was slumped, her eyes shut.

He fought to stay awake, but his eyes got heavier. Using the last bit of strength, Lordiah pulled out his phone. He leaned towards Luna, and with every ounce of strength he had left, he shoved his phone down the back of her pants.

Then everything faded to black...

CHAPTER 89:
BROTHERLY
LOVE

Earth – Present Time

"Papa, wake up." Luna's voice was faint and felt miles away.

Eyes are heavy, hard to open…

"Papa!" Lordiah heard her voice again, this time louder. His eyes fluttered. Everything was blurry. He rubbed them. Objects slowly came into focus.

"Hey, you OK?"

Lordiah sat up. His bare feet felt the cold cement below them. His head throbbed.

The metal cot he was lying on was also cold. An old stale odor lingered. Near to the cot was a metal toilet and a rusted bucket.

The cloudiness of his vision dissipated. In front of him were metal prison bars surrounded by a dirty brick wall. He looked around. His eyes got large. It was a familiar setting. He knew the smell. He stood and staggered over to the bars and reached out for Luna who was in the cell next to him.

"No!" Lordiah shouted. *"No, no, no!"* he screamed again as he grabbed his head. *"This can't be happening!"*

"Papa, what is it?"

Lordiah dropped to the ground and sat cross-legged. *"This is where they kept me for all of those years. Now they have you."*

Several hours passed. A door creaked down the hall, and then slammed shut. Footsteps drew closer and several men in dark business suits appeared outside their cells. Apollyon stood in the center.

Lordiah looked away. *I can't believe this is happening. How could I have been so stupid*, he said to himself.

Apollyon reached up and gripped the metal bars on Luna's cell door. He looked at her in silence as he studied her. His nose wrinkled. *"You bitch! To let me think you have been dead all this time."*

Luna looked over to Lordiah, perplexed. Lordiah glanced down. *"What's he talking about?"*

Apollyon kicked the cell door. He yelled, *"You are my family, my flesh! How dare you make me think you were dead all these years! Make me believe my own son killed you!"*

Luna jumped back and pressed herself to the farthest corner of the cell away from him. Her brow wrinkled, and a confused expression appeared on her face. She turned toward Lordiah. *"Papa, who the hell is this, and what the fuck crawled in his ass?"*

"I'm speaking to you, not him! Cut the games out Leilana!" Apollyon screamed at her.

Her head cocked to the side. She looked back and forth at her dad, and the man that just yelled at her. *"Huh?"*

Lordiah stood and approached the bars. *"Apollyon! She doesn't know."*

"Apollyon?" Luna answered, looking at him. *"That explains things. I've heard so many shitty things about you. Not really nice to meet you."*

"Silence!" Apollyon shouted, walking over to Lordiah's cell. *"Apollyon, it's not Leilana."*

Apollyon's brows raised. He walked back to Luna's cell. He grabbed the bars again, staring at her. *"Lordie, you filthy, perverted, sick fuck. I don't know if I should be proud of you or disgusted."*

Luna pressed back into the wall hoping that would make more distance between them. *"Papa, what's he talking about?"*

"Papa!" Apollyon laughed, clapping his hands. *"Not God, huh? Or honey bunch? Little girl, the mighty Lordiah fucking grew you! And from my poor dead sister's DNA. I'll be damned. You look exactly like Leilana!"*

Luna looked over at Lordiah. She slid down the wall until she was sitting on the floor with her knees pressed against her chest. *"Papa?"*

Apollyon laughed and shook his head. *"And she doesn't know? Oh, my, dear brother, this is priceless! Guess this is as good a time as any to tell her."*

"Luna, I was going to tell you. I'm sorry you had to find out this way."

Luna's stare was frozen, and her jaw dropped. For the first time in her life, she didn't know what to say.

"You outdid yourself on this one, brother," Apollyon applauded. *"Impressive. How did you do that? Is she pure or one of your worthless washed down slave versions?"*

"She's an exact copy," Lordiah answered. *"Pure, one hundred percent Leilana."*

"Well, doesn't matter. Since you're factory made, and I'm the king, looks like I own you. Guards, grab her."

"Papa?!" Luna screamed.

"Apollyon, please stop!" Lordiah pleaded. *"What are you going to do with her?"*

Apollyon grinned from ear to ear. He stopped, gripping the cell door bars to Lordiah's cell.

"Guards, stop. And bitch, shut up! I want you to hear this." Everyone stared at Apollyon. He looked toward Luna then Lordiah. *"You know what I want. I will set the girl free if you surrender the moon to me. If not... It will be a very, very slow, painful death to her useless artificial life. Your choice, brother."*

CHAPTER 90:
THE PRICE
FOR THE MOON

Earth – Present Time

Once again, I've been betrayed. My guts are aching. Fuck my life. Why does it need to explode into a shit show all the time? Luna thought to herself.

They marched her across the complex to a section labeled solitary confinement. Every noise they made echoed off the concrete walls. They stopped at a solid metal door. A faded number eleven was painted above it.

When the door screeched open, a stale smell drifted out. They entered a small windowless cell with a light dangling down from the ceiling. A dirty sink and steel toilet empty of water was in the corner. The thugs flung her across the room. She crashed onto the toilet falling over it.

Apollyon stood at the door. He tapped a knuckle to his lips, shook his head, and sighed. *"It's going to be rough on me to kill you. I keep seeing my poor dear sister every time I look at you."*

The door closed behind him with a loud click. A jangle of keys and a lock turning sealed the deal.

Luna studied the room. From her assessment, no cameras. *Well, this is a new low for me. And to top it off, I'm a fuckin lab rat too,* she thought to herself.

The cool temperature raised goosebumps on her arms and her ears throbbed in the ghostly silence. The light flickered. She sat down in the corner. A cockroach scuttled across the floor in front of her. With the back of her thumbs, she wiped the tears from her eyes.

Her head cocked to the side, and one of her brows raised. She stood and reached down the back of her pants and pulled Lordiah's phone out. *"Well, lookie what this lab rat shit out,"* she muttered to herself.

She scrolled through the icons until she found the app labeled Emergency.

I'm pretty sure this would qualify, right? Wish there was a bullshit button here too. Definitely would hit that.

She pressed her thumb against the Emergency icon. A Batman symbol appeared on the screen, then the phone returned to the normal wallpaper.

Luna tried calling 911, but the phone display read No Service. She raised her hand, stood on the toilet for a better reach, but failed to find any signal.

She crumbled into the corner, then slid down to the floor, folding her knees to chest and arms around her shins. Her head thudded dully against the beige wall behind her. Despite her determination to stay strong, tears rolled down her cheek.

It was so quiet that she could hear the scuttle of another cockroach run across the floor. Her fingers scrolled down the apps again and stopped at Electro Mace. She tapped the icon. A red box appeared across the screen with the word *"Armed"* in it. Luna grinned and put the phone back in her pocket.

For several hours Luna sat in the cold cell, shivering. She replayed in her head over and over remembering what Apollyon said, *"I have no problem killing her, and a very slow, painful death."*

The door lock clicked. Luna jumped. The hairs on the back of Luna's neck stood up. She scrambled for Lordiah's phone and checked the screen. She smiled when it still said *"Armed."*

The door slowly screeched open, and a man looked in. Without hesitation, Luna pointed the phone at him.

"Oh Shit!" the man said when he saw the phone.

Whap! The sound rang out.

The man ducked down and did a forward shoulder roll dodging the electro blast.

With minor effort he rolled to his feet, inches from her.

Luna scrambled to arm the phone again, but with lightening hands, the man ripped it from her grasp.

She jumped back, put her hands up and got into a defensive stance.

The man brought both hands up. *"Easy, your highness! I'm the cavalry here to help. Did someone press the emergency button?"*

Luna stepped back, keeping her hands up, ready for anything.

"From your looks, except for the purple hair, you must be Luna. I haven't seen you since you were in diapers."

"I have been hearing that a lot lately. Bigfoot and now you," Luna replied.

The man stepped forward. She hopped back and put her hands up ready to fight. He reached his hand forward and handed the phone back to Luna. She snatched it away from him.

"So, tell me what's going on and why the emergency signal? You're Luna, correct?"

"Yeah, or so I thought. From what I just found out I'm just his experiment thingie."

"With all due respect you are more than a thingie," the man bowed to her. *"I'm Leonardo, at your service, your highness. Now, how may I help you?"*

"Leonardo? Wow. Okay..."

Luna told Leonardo how Apollyon held Lordiah captive and threatened to kill her if he didn't surrender the moon.

"Well, that's not good. Just an F-Y-I, Lordiah would do anything to stop anyone from harming you. But if that moon leaves, it will be catastrophic."

"Why? I'm nothing but test tube XYZ," Luna answered with an edge in her voice.

"Oh, my dear Luna, you do not understand how wrong you are. You are perfection from pure stock, the very best he knew of. So what if you weren't conceived in the back seat of a car? You're here and he loves you, my dear. Let's stop this pouting and go find your pops."

Luna nodded and wiped a tear with the back of her fingers. *"Okay, but I'm still freaking out about all of this."*

Leonardo smiled, *"Fair enough."*

It was eerie with silence as they tiptoed with caution across the abandoned penal facility. Their heads were on a swivel-looking left, right and back.

A gray solid metal door matching the walls and doorframe stood in their path. They stopped. Leonardo raised a hand and motioned for her to be silent.

He reached for the handle, slowly turning it, but it was locked. From his back pocket he pulled out a black leather kit.

Luna glanced around for cameras. Within seconds the lock clicked. *"That was quick."*

Leonardo smiled. *"The perks of being thousands of years old. You obtain a lot of skills."*

He stuck his nose by the door seam and smelled the air coming through. He frowned. Cautiously, he grabbed the handle and pushed. The door creaked.

Luna grabbed his arm to stop him. She pulled out Lordiah's phone and turned on the camera. She stuck the top part of the phone through the crack of the door and scanned the hallway using the camera.

Satisfied with her surveillance, she gave him a thumbs up. *"The perks of being a foster kid. You obtain a lot of skills too."*

Leonardo grinned. *"Impressive. Do you by chance know where Lordiah is being kept?"*

Luna shrugged her shoulders. *"I thought you did."*

"Nope. I came following an emergency distress beacon. Past that, not a clue."

She pointed down the hallway *"I think it might be this way. It's my first time to this sweet AirBnB. Hey, I woke up here, then they said something about killing me and things sorta got jumbled in my little brain after that."*

Leonardo grinned and shook his head. *"I think you and I are going to be BFF's."*

They tiptoed down several more hallways and pick a few more locks along the way. Luna grabbed his arm. Her lips tightened. She whispered, *"Hey, I remember that door. The cell with... Papa, or whatever, is through here."*

Leonardo stepped in front of her and grabbed the door handle. He slowly turned it.

Click!

"Well that couldn't have been any louder." Leonardo turned to Luna, *"Okay, let's live on the edge, sweetheart. Stay behind me."*

He pushed the door open.

"Come on in and join the party. The more the merrier. Keep your hands up though," Apollyon said while he stood behind his men who had their guns aimed at them.

"Well, well, hello Leonardo. Long time no see." Apollyon's enormous smile molded across his face. *"This is such a pleasant family reunion, isn't it? Men, please, let's check for weapons and then escort my good friend into the cell next to our guest Lordiah and make him feel at home too."*

The metal doors clanked when the guards grabbed Leonardo and slammed his body into it. One of them hard-pressed his shoulder into Leonardo's back, squeezing him against the cell bars.

It's game over if they ever trapped me in a cell. Leonardo said to himself. It's now or never.

From what happened next, it appeared Leonardo somewhere in his past 4,052 years has added the fighting arts to his skill list. Within the next few seconds, with elegance and grace, and a few strikes with his hands and feet, both thugs are on the ground, bleeding and knocked out cold.

Leonardo straightened his suit jacket and tie. He leaned over one of the thugs and rummaged through his pockets.

"*Ah ha!*" Leonardo said, and removed a set of keys from of his pocket.

"*Apollyon, sir, sorry about your help. I'm just here to grab Lordiah. We will be out of your hair soon enough,*" Leonardo told him as he fumbled through the keys.

Apollyon pulled a gun out from his waist and raised it at him. "*I'm sorry, I can't let you do that, Leonardo.*"

Bang! Bang! Bang!

Luna and Lordiah looked over at Leonardo. The holes in his shirt began to leak blood. He slumped to one knee. Apollyon fired another round into his chest. Leonardo fell backwards choking on his blood. He became silent and his eyes rolled shut.

Luna and Lordiah were frozen in shock. "*Noooo!*" Luna cried out.

Apollyon smiled. He walked over to Leonardo's limp body and kicked him, checking his work. He raised a brow satisfied. "*Lordiah, it's your fault that your friend just got killed. I hope you feel superb about yourself.*" He pointed the gun over at Luna. "*Now about that moonship. I'm hoping the golden ticket is your test tube trophy here. Let's stop the games. It's simple, turn over the moonship and I will let the girl live.*"

Whap!

Apollyon went flying across the room, slamming against Lordiah's barred prison door.

Luna was holding up his cell phone. She pressed her fingers across the face, and armed the app on his phone again.

Whap! She blasted the dazed Apollyon a second time. This time he slammed into a cement cinderblock wall.

Apollyon laid lifeless, unconscious.

Luna pressed the app. The phone blinked red again. She took a step closer, standing only a few feet from Apollyon. She placed her finger on the screen.

"*Luna, that's enough!*" Lordiah said. "*You don't need to know what it feels like to kill somebody, and the next blast will do that!*"

Luna lowered the phone.

A coughing sound muttered behind her. *"If you aren't going to blast that asshole, give me the phone, I will,"* Leonardo said as he sat up.

Luna sprinted over to him and knelt beside him.

Leonardo spit blood from his mouth. *"Help me up, please. Damn, this dying shit hurts."*

"You've been shot, you need help!"

"Dear, I have been in much worse situations than this. I don't die, at least not today. Last time I got shot, the damn bullets worked their way out of my fingertips. Now THAT hurt. Can't wait to see where those will eventually work out of my body. And I hope it's not my you know what."

Lordiah looked around the room." *We're taking him with us. I'm so tired of running. And he knows about Luna now. I'm going to end this once and for all."*

CHAPTER 91:
YOU'RE FIRED!

Earth – Present Time

Inside Lordiah's desert warehouse, the black shuttle sat vacant. The room was enclosed in gray cinderblock walls, dusty worktables, various tools and safety posters tacked on the walls.

The lights switched on. A low humming noise of fluorescent tubes buzzed above them. On an orange dolly Lordiah, Leonardo, and Luna wheeled Apollyon into the hangar area. He was shackled and duct taped tight to a metal chair, with a gag shoved in his mouth.

The roof slid apart, revealing stars that twinkled on the black velvet open night sky. Above them, another black shuttle emerged. It wings folded upward before it descended between the open doors, landing several yards in front of them.

Major Thomas limped out. He did a double take when he saw Apollyon. His brow wrinkled. He stared back to Lordiah.

"I got tired of his threats, so I gagged him." Lordiah picked up the box with his green leather journals packed inside. He nodded his chin and pointed with his gaze. *"This way everyone. Bring him too!"*

He led them over to one of the brick walls and stopped in front of it. He pulled out his phone and tapped his finger on it a few times. The cinder block wall creaked and moved upward, revealing an elevator behind it.

"Get in everyone," Lordiah motioned.

Once inside, there were no buttons to push. It was just an empty red metal box. Lordiah scrolled through his phone and pressed another app. A beep rang out. He held his hand out in front of him and a red laser body scan pulsated up and down his body.

"Thank you, Lordiah," the phone answered. After a few seconds, the elevator door closed and proceeded to move downward.

The elevator chimed each time it passed a floor. After eleven beeps it opened to an enormous room, much larger than the warehouse space from above.

Luna exited first and looked around. A grin formed across her face. One of the photon lasers was sitting there, and several paintings were leaning up against the wall. She touched the frame of a Van Gogh, then walked over to a large chunk of a plaster wall. Painted on it was Da Vinci's 'The Last Supper.'

"Hey, is this the real McCoy?" Luna asked.

Lordiah nodded his head toward Leonardo. *"He can tell you better than me."*

Leonardo came and stood next to her with his hands behind his back. Then he pointed, *"See that second toe is much longer than his big toe on my friend's foot. It was truly like that on him. No conspiracy theory, just making fun of a pal. He nodded." "It sure looks like the original. But... I favor this one."* He interlocked her arm with his and walked her over to a 'Vitruvian Man' wall sculpture.'

Her brows raised, and eyes got large. She looked at him, back at the sculpture, back at him then to Lordiah.

Lordiah nodded to her and smiled.

She pulled away from Leonardo. *"Leonardo, as in you're the Leonardo?"*

He bowed to her. *"That Leonardo was a long time ago. But he still pokes his head out from time to time."*

She squealed and wrapped her arms around him. *"Oh my god. This is the coolest thing ever. Did I die and go to heaven?"*

Luna continued her stroll and inspected the contents of the room. She wandered past a spacecraft on a platform resembling a flying saucer barely noticing it before she stopped at eleven pallets of gold bars, stacked 5-6 feet high.

She picked up a bar. *"Holy shit these are heavy."*

She ran her fingers across the lettering. *"Federal Reserve? For reals?"*

"You would be amazed what your government will do for a little technology. President Roosevelt actually created the Federal Reserve to help gather gold for me. In exchange I gave him free energy, space travel technology, wireless communications, the internet and other things. Most of the gold that is theoretically locked in the Federal Reserve is actually sitting in front of you."

Luna curled the gold bar like a bicep exercise with both hands.

"President Ford had to lock the doors to the Federal Reserve in 1976 so no one would find out that it was empty." Lordiah let out a chuckle. *"Someday, there's going to be a bunch of pissed off people when they open the doors."*

Luna put the gold brick back and walked over to several glass containers sitting on the floor. *"Is this the famous Adam and Eve Exhibit?"*

"I personally wouldn't call them an exhibit, but yes, they are the last living Adam and Eve samples," Lordiah replied.

Luna bent down and studied the containers. She tilted her head to the side and squinted when she spotted the numbers tattooed on their arms. *"Adam 11 and Eve 38, huh?"*

Lordiah nodded a yes. Luna looked over their naked torsos. She frowned and tapped her fingertips to the surface of the glass. She leaned in so she could get a closer look. Her brows drew together. *"That's weird not seeing a belly button on them."*

Luna continued her exploration. She made her way over to several empty incubation containers and stopped in front of them. She reached out to touch one, but changed her mind, afraid to touch it. She didn't know she was holding her breath. She stared at the one in front of her not blinking.

"Is this my mom?"

Lordiah shook his head and let out a laugh. His face relaxed and he exhaled. *"No, sweetheart. You were grown in vitro, like every other child, within a female host and inside a uterus. That's why you have a belly button."*

"And, technically, I'm royalty by blood? Grown or not, it's the genes that count, right?"

"Yes, you're royalty," Lordiah laughed. *"You most certainly are."*

"So, what are we going to do with him?" she said, pointing to Apollyon.

He stared at Apollyon and tapped his foot a few times. *"We need to get rid of him."*

The room turned quiet.

"So, what are you thinking, boss?" Leonardo broke the silence.

Lordiah pointed at the flying saucer, *"That my friends, is the answer."*

Luna walked over and looked at the upside-down bowl-shaped craft inquisitively. She looked back at Lordiah.

"Area 51 anyone? Long story short, they weren't here for the better of mankind, trust me. I downed the alien crafts by jamming their circuit boards. So, by giving the government the jamming mechanism, they gave me a spaceship as a thank you gift."

"Wow, I had such a simple fucked up life being a thief a week ago, and now look at me, being trusted with the super secrets of the world," Luna smiled and let out a slight laugh. *"What does the flying saucer have to do with him?"*

"If I may, my dear princess and Professor Lord?" Leonardo stepped forward and interlaced his fingers in front of him. *"My educated guess is that we are shipping back the gold to Heofon and throwing in King A-hole as a bonus, flown by Major Thomas in that UFO."*

Lordiah gave him 2 thumbs up. *"That is 100 percent correct."*

"And..." Lordiah put his hand on Leonardo's shoulder, *"Apollyon can get as mad as he wants, and try to seek revenge, but Papa won't let him. Not after the size of this gold shipment.*

And by the time he could gather an army and come back here to wreak havoc, thousands of years will have passed on Earth."

Luna got a sad look on her face. She looked away when a tear formed. She wiped her eyes. "So...Are you leaving too?" Luna asked.

Lordiah shook his head. "Not at all. My home is here now. I'm not going anywhere."

"Neither am I." Leonardo butted in.

Major Thomas raises his hand. "Sir, what about the King Osili's requests for us to ship him a million humans?"

"Yeah, that... Papa will be mad about that one. I just can't do that one."

"Would you like me to say anything when I get there?" Major Thomas asked.

"No. Just get home safe. It's good to see you out and off the moonship for a change. And with you gone no one has the skill or knowledge to fly it anywhere, which is the only vehicle that can transport that many people. And if you come back, then thousands of years will have passed with thousands of years of technology here on Earth."

"With thousands of years of technology, the Earthlings will probably go to Heofon and make them slaves!" Leonardo chuckled.

The final pallet of gold was loaded into the flying saucer. Lordiah drew his phone out, tapped his fingers on the screen a few times and the roof doors opened.

Cuffed to a chair, Apollyon sat with his mouth drooped open. "I sedated him. He won't be giving you any problems. Lordiah chuckled, talking to Major Thomas. "It's kinda freaky that his eyes are still open looking at us."

The craft levitated above the hangar floor, upward towards the open roof and the black night sky. Within seconds Lordiah and Luna watched the flying object jettison out of sight.

Lordiah put his arm around Luna. "So, what are you going to do with yourself now?"

"God, I really don't know. The last few days sorta changed my outlook on life a ton. Oh, I broke up with Rob, so I may need to crash on the moonship until I find a place, if that's cool?"

"Sure. I'll be staying there myself," he grinned. "My place got robbed and partially burnt down."

They stood there for a few more seconds. Luna pointed at the crescent moon in the sky. "I don't even know what to call that thing anymore. The moon? The Starship Enterprise?"

"How about your second home?"

"Ooh, I like that."

Lordiah picked up the box with his journals and walked to the black space craft. Luna followed. "FYI, Henry is technically your brother. I made him out of my DNA too. Obviously, I tweaked a few things."

"Would make for an interesting family portrait," Luna chuckled. "So, what are you going to do with yourself now?"

"I'm hoping to get to know this really cool Luna girl better. And...continue to keep an eye on this world, my children, and help sculpt this world into a better place."

CHAPTER 92:
THE
NEXT CHAPTER

Earth – Several Months Later

In a sterile room with white walls, test tubes and beakers, Lordiah was punching numbers and characters into a computer pad. Standing beside him, wearing white lab coats were Luna and Henry, checking gauges, making notes and assisting him. Surrounding them were rows of incubators. Lordiah and Luna were working side by side like old times when Lordiah and Leilana grew the first batch of humans.

There were 111 active incubators, each one growing a child. Their chests rising as they took in each breath. A new batch. A better, stronger batch...

Made in the USA
Coppell, TX
10 June 2021